Rise

A Novel

By

John McCormick

Prologue

April 1990

The city slumbered in the pre-dawn, unaware of the cautious approach of spring.

There was no fond anticipation for this renewal of old acquaintance. No sense of warm familiarity in spring's playful heart as the dark brute loomed through the mist. Just weary acceptance of the inevitable.

The feeling was mutual.

The brooding metropolis, mistrustful of giddy frivolity, much preferred to huddle beneath the murky mantle of winter than to frolic in the gauzy threads of spring.

The stabbing cold was a cleansing penance, and the city cherished the frost and the gloom and the rain. The drenching, piercing rain.

Proper rain.

Not the anaemic drizzle of an April shower, nor the oxymoronic monstrosity of a sun-shower, speckling the warm, dusty pavements with cheery black spots of paradox.

Proper rain.

Rain birthed by the gods of thunder and rage as they thrashed and flexed in the full-throated roar of a winter storm to punish and to pound, with fearsome deluge, the grim, granite-faced stoicism of the city below.

Belfast just didn't suit Springtime.

Also approaching the city in the misty dawn – and making more of a fuss about it – was the overnight ferry from Liverpool.

With lights smearing the fog and propellers churning the water, it made a boisterous entry into Belfast Lough just as the eastern sky brightened enough to pull the veil from the timorous creep of spring.

In the ferry's tiny cafeteria, a woman in her late middle-age picked up a cup of tea from the counter and turned to look around her. She had friendly eyes, a long, pointed nose and greying hair that was pulled back into a bun. As she gazed around the small room for a place to sit, she regarded her fellow passengers with some dismay.

Most of the people gathered around the few tables in the cramped space were long-distance lorry drivers, who were eating noisily and communicating with each other using a complicated system of grunts, burps, farts and whistles. The woman was considering taking her tea out to the cold deck when she spotted a man sitting at a table on his own, idly stirring his tea and gazing through a porthole at the silent dawn.

'He seems nice enough,' she thought as she made for his table.

"Do you mind if I sit here?" she asked. The man looked up, startled.

"What?" he stammered. "Oh, I'm sorry, of course I don't mind. Please sit down."

The woman took a seat and gave the man a warm smile. He smiled back then looked down at his tea.

"Did you sleep all right?" she asked after taking a sip from her cup.

"I'm sorry?" he asked, startled again.

"On the crossing," she said. "I sometimes have

trouble sleeping if the sea's a wee bit rough. Although, I have to say, it felt very smooth last night. I slept right through."

"Oh right," the man said. "Um, yeah, it was okay, I think. To be honest, though, I don't sleep great at the best of times."

"Really? That's something I've never had a problem with. Except in the middle of a rough sea of course." She gave another smile.

"Do you make this crossing a lot?" The man forced himself to make conversation, hoping to make the time pass more quickly. The ferry seemed to be taking forever to reach the dock and he was beginning to feel the blank, soulless fog close around him, clouding his mind and his shivering nerves.

"A couple of times a year, I suppose," the woman replied. "I go to see my daughter and her family. They live in Birmingham, you see. I've tried Larne-Stranraer before, but I just hate that long coach journey. I'd rather sleep on the ferry than the coach." The woman's chatter was incessant and the man was grateful for it, calmed by it. "Of course," she went on, "I keep telling Sally – Sally, that's my daughter – to come and visit me but her husband says no. He's English, you see, so he thinks everybody in Belfast is a mad bomber. He thinks he's going to get shot or blown up or something if he comes over."

The man shuddered and turned away. He looked through the porthole at the patches of mist and felt suddenly terrified that his demons were crawling towards him through the fog. Instinctively he closed his eyes and placed the fingertips of his right hand on the inside of his left wrist. The feel of the steady pulse was reassuring and he let his breathing slow to the gentle rhythm until his consciousness was able to embrace the peace he had learned, the peace he had been shown, the peace of the universe pulsing in time to the beat of his own heart. He opened his eyes.

The woman was watching him thoughtfully, compassion and understanding in her eyes. She slipped a hand across the table to lightly touch his arm.

"Are you okay?" she asked.

"Um, yeah," he said shakily, "yeah, I'm fine."

"Sure?"

"Yeah, really, I'm okay," he said, smiling now. "I'm fine, thanks."

"Do you live in Belfast?" she asked, her voice soft and sympathetic. "Are you heading home?"

"I don't know," he replied, then laughed at her puzzled expression. "I'm sorry, it's just that I've been away a long time…I mean, I used to have a home here but whether I still do or not…" he shrugged. "I suppose that's where I'm going," he said. "I'm going to find out."

The woman nodded pensively as the ferry's engines changed pitch and the ship slowed and turned in the water. The lorry drivers all stood and stretched before they grunted, burped and farted their way to the vehicle deck. The woman grimaced and grinned and then made a quick decision. She reached into her handbag and pulled out a pen and a piece of paper.

"Look," she said, "I'm going to give you my phone number. If you need a hand with anything, or even if you just fancy a moan, then give me a shout."

She scribbled down her number and handed him the slip of paper. The man took it, genuinely touched by the gesture.

"Thank you," he said. "Thank you very much."

She stood and held out her hand. "I'm Stephanie," she said.

The man got up from the table to shake her hand.

"Martin," he said. "Martin McCann."

One

Several weeks earlier.

Joseph Anderson, known to his friends as Joker, was fantasising about punching the old woman in the back of the head.

He had been standing behind her in the queue for what felt like a million years and now watched with exasperation as she slowly picked up her change and dropped it, one coin at a time, into her purse.

Of course, Joker knew, she was perfectly entitled to take all the time she needed – her slow, deliberate movements hinted at painful arthritis – and he was well aware that she did not deserve to be harried by an impatient wanker like himself. But still.

The old woman finally snapped her purse shut and placed it into her bag. She turned and gave Joker an apologetic smile.

"Sorry for holding you up there, son," she said.

"No trouble at all," Joker told her. "You just take your time."

She made her way to the door and Joker, with a sigh of relief, stepped forward and placed the card he had chosen on the counter. The young shop-assistant seemed nervous as the tall skinhead approached and glowered down at him.

"All right there mate?" said Joker. "Just this card. Oh, and twenty Regal as well."

The nervous young man, no older than sixteen, picked up the card and entered the price into the till. He then turned and scanned the rows of cigarette packs behind him, making it obvious that he wasn't at all sure just what he was looking for. Joker rolled his eyes.

"There, mate," he said, pointing. "Just there."

The shop-assistant followed the invisible line from Joker's outstretched finger but, for some reason, seemed incapable of spotting the little blue and white pack, upon which the word *Regal* was emblazoned in gold. He put a tentative hand on a red pack and gave Joker a hopeful glance.

"No," Joker said, exasperated. "To your left. No, down a bit. Now go right, bit more, bit more."

The shop-assistant seemed to touch every single pack before finally alighting on Joker's preferred brand.

"Aye, there you go," Joker exclaimed. "You're really getting the hang of this, aren't you, mate?"

Joker paid for the card and the cigarettes and left the shop. As he walked across the car park he could see his father impatiently drumming his fingers on top of the car's steering wheel. Pulling open the rear door, Joker clambered onto the back seat.

"Took your bloody time, didn't you, Joseph?" Joker's father grunted as he started the car.

"Oh, leave him alone, Davy," said Katherine, Joker's mother, who sat in the front passenger seat. "Don't be such a grump." Joker felt grateful for her maternal support.

"I mean," Katherine went on, "you know how buying a sympathy card can really take it out of you, don't you? Is that what it was, Joseph? Did you get worn out? Did you have to have a wee lie-down? A wee nap?"

Joker, too much of a dutiful son to rebuke his mother with profanity, remained silent as he pulled the cellophane wrapping from the card he had bought. Katherine held out her hand.

"Let's see it, Joseph," she said.

Joker passed it to her and Katherine ran her fingers over the embossed lilies and the silver, foil-blocked lettering.

"Aye, that's lovely," she said, holding it up for Davy to see. She then handed it back to Joker.

"Would you see if there's a pen there," Joker asked his mother. "In the glove box."

Rummaging through the little compartment, Katherine found a pen and handed it to Joker. She then sat back in her seat and looked through the window at the unfamiliar surroundings passing by outside. They were only a few miles from their own home but Katherine felt they might as well be on the other side of the world. The kerbstones here were painted a hostile green, white and orange instead of the reassuring red, white and blue of her own patch of Belfast. She saw the Irish tricolours and the yellow and white papal flags hanging limply from lampposts and from the upper windows of some of the terraced houses and she gave a shiver of trepidation.

The colours here were too garish, she thought, too bright and gaudy compared to the comforting warmth of the purples and blues and the reds and blacks of protestant Ulster. Stripped of all the colours, though, the little streets became recognisable, reminding Katherine of the streets in which she had grown up, the streets of her city and her home, and she felt a touch of sad regret.

"It's not that different from Sandy Row, is it?" she said.

"Aye, but you still have to be careful," Joker told her. "Remember, if you see any priests then you have to keep really still. Their vision is based on movement."

"Joseph!" said Davy, suppressing a grin. "Stop trying to scare your mother."

Katherine sighed and turned round to face Joker.

"Have you written that card yet?" she asked.

"Yeah, here you go." Joker placed the card inside its envelope and gave it to his mother. He then sat back in his seat, content to spend the rest of the short journey up the Falls Road lost in his own thoughts.

He was aware of how much more pensive he had been lately and felt that it was something he needed to have a think about. He didn't see himself as someone who thought too much; someone who dithered and examined and analysed, someone trapped in the pointless exploration of his own mind, considering options, probing and poking at feelings and emotions that were best left undisturbed.

As far as Joker was concerned, he was a man of action. The image he held of himself was a dashing, gung-ho figure. Carefree, rakish and handsome, decisive and unbound by the cloying grasp of overthinking. A free spirit. A swashbuckling cavalier, dynamic and debonair.

This was not the image, however, that formed in the minds of most people on first encountering Joker.

Immediate impressions of the six-foot-four skinhead cast rather a different picture in the eyes of those who lacked a familiarity with Joker's nuanced personality.

The word 'oaf' has largely fallen from common usage, but if it were still to enjoy the popularity of its heyday then it would likely feature prominently in the uninformed opinions of new acquaintances. There were many who, on first meeting Joker, would instantly judge his shaven head and intimidating muscularity as belonging to a knuckle-dragging moron who would only feel at home in the company of like-minded morons in an environment of unfocused anger and potential violence.

But this image would be wide of the mark.

"What does that say, Joseph?" asked Katherine. She was pointing at some graffiti daubed in white paint on a wall beside the main road.

Náisiún arís
Tiochfiadh ár lá

"I think it's meant to say," said Joker, "*A nation once again. Our day will come*, but, for one thing, it's spelt wrong."

"It's so different from English, isn't it?"

"Yeah," said Joker, "it is." At this point, Joker could have explained to his mother that Irish Gaelic, although sharing a language root with English, had arrived in the British Isles having travelled along the southern coasts of Europe with the Celtic tribes of the east, while English had taken a different route via the

Germanic tribes of the north.

However, he had surmised – correctly – that his mother would not have appreciated a lecture on linguistics at this point in her life, and so he said no more.

Joker's peculiar knowledge and natural intelligence were, for those who knew him well, a source of wonder, but also a cause for some dismay at his blank refusal to use his talents to achieve anything tangible in the world. Language, for Joker, was a hobby and nothing more.

None of this, however, was what was bothering him. Joker cared not at all for the preconceptions of strangers, nor for the despair of his friends at the apparent waste of his abilities, but there was something lurking in the depths of his mind that he was finding increasingly difficult to ignore.

Joker had seen a lot of changes over the past few months that had impacted on his normally unruffled ramble through life. His best friend and flatmate, Ding-a-Ling, had suddenly acquired a pregnant fiancée and was now calling himself 'Gary' for some reason. Another friend, Snatter, was now using the name 'Seamus' and had decided to become a homosexual, while yet another friend, the once reliable Jamesy, had discovered girls and could now be seen walking around with one as if it were the most natural thing in the world.

Perplexing though all of these events were, they were not what was keeping Joker awake at night. Something else was doing that.

It was there and it was not there. A slippery little

irritant that shimmered just below his consciousness, whispering, giggling and teasing. Playing with his memories and stroking his emotions and ultimately forcing Joker to take action. He would have to consult his brain on the matter.

Joker's brain had a mind of its own. There were those who said that Joker's brain didn't work properly and, in a sense, this was true. His brain, on tackling any particular issue, preferred to adopt an approach that would never have been considered by more conventional brains, but would, invariably, turn out to be the more efficient choice. It was this kink in his thought process that allowed him to catch many unawares by his insight and also gave him such a clear perception into the structure of language.

Joker felt, however, that getting his brain involved would probably be unnecessary because, deep down, he knew what was troubling him. Or he had guessed. Or suspected. He just wasn't sure what he was going to do about it.

"Do you think you should write something on the envelope?" Katherine turned round to address her son.

"Oh yeah," said Joker, and leaned forward. Katherine passed the card back to him and he placed it in his lap and wrote neatly on the blank envelope.

To the Maguire Family.

Two

Rosie McCann's self-imposed withdrawal from nicotine, combined with her increasingly obvious pregnancy, was making her a little irritable.

"For the last time, Gary," she told her fiancé, "I'm not walking down the aisle in a bloody tent."

Gary, in Rosie's opinion, had lately been the source of most of her irritation. His constantly cheerful attentiveness was beginning to grate on her nerves as she grew more bloated and miserable. Rosie liked being miserable. It suited her moods at this moment in time. It made her happy.

But Gary had no time for any glum introspection or self-pity. The world he preferred to inhabit was filled with upbeat optimism, with no room for wavering doubts or negativity. Gary wore the same smile today as the one he had worn as a child when the world seemed to bask in the sun and blue skies of an endless summer. The same smile that had dazzled a little girl as her own world crumbled around her, the smile that had cheered her breaking heart and warmed her childhood dreams. The smile that had made her fall in love.

But now it was just getting on her tits. Gary's irrepressible chirpiness rubbed hard against her own moody grumblings but, she told herself, she possessed enough grace and serenity to rise above the persistent aggravation. She prided herself on her restraint in the face of Gary's provocation and her ability to remain steady and calm, composed and tranquil and sedate.

Rosie had lately become an unpredictable psycho-bitch, thought Gary, but he had to concede she did have a point.

"Yeah, all right," he said. "I can see how that would look in the photographs but I just thought that it may be better to get it all over with."

"Get it over with?" Rosie shrieked. "That's bloody lovely, that is! Did you hear that, Ellie? Gary's really laying on the charm over here, I'm not sure I can resist." Rosie glanced over to where her sister sat, but Ellie was poring over some letters that lay on the coffee table in front of her and was oblivious to all around her.

They were in the front room of Ellie's house in the Ardoyne area of North Belfast, with Gary standing by the window and Rosie sitting by herself on the sofa. Ellie was more than happy to share the house with her little sister but there were times when she would have liked some time to herself. Ellie had always been the quiet one and was usually to be found engrossed in her work, either in her occupation as a nurse or in the more personal project on which her attention was now focused.

"Oh, you know what I mean," said Gary. "But I suppose you're right. There's no harm in waiting till after the baby's born."

"Well thank you, Gary," said Rosie. "I don't understand what the rush is anyway. If you had it your way my waters would be breaking when we're standing at the altar. That's really classy, Gary." Rosie grinned and turned to her sister, expecting Ellie to be similarly amused by the notion. Ellie, however, did not even look up.

"So yeah, Gary," Rosie went on, "what's the big bloody rush all about?"

"No rush," said Gary hurriedly. "There's no rush at all, it's just that me and the lads were talking about maybe having a bit of a stag do and we thought that-"

"A stag do?" Rosie exclaimed. "A fucking stag do?"

"Well yeah," Gary explained, "I mean, you have to think about these things, don't you?"

"Yeah, because we don't have anything else to think about, do we?"

"You know what I mean."

"Okay, Gary," said Rosie, her suspicions aroused. "What exactly did you have in mind then?"

"Don't know really." Gary shrugged. "Oh," he said, as if a thought had just struck him, "I think somebody might have said something about Italy. Not really sure though. Sometime in June I think it was, maybe, or something like that, I don't know but I thought that-"

"Italy?" Rosie asked, her suspicions now fully erect. "Why Italy?"

"What?" said Gary defensively. "Why Italy? Well, why not Italy? It's as good a place as any, isn't it? I mean when you think about-"

"Isn't the World Cup in Italy this year?" Ellie asked as she looked up from the papers on the table. Gary felt that Ellie had really picked her moment to take an interest in the conversation.

"Is it?" he asked in all innocence. "Is it really?" He knew he wasn't fooling anyone but he decided his best plan would be to forge ahead.

"The World Cup?" Rosie said as she looked from Ellie to Gary. "The bloody World Cup? I wonder when that would be then? No, no wait...let me guess! It wouldn't be June by any chance, now would it?"

Gary dumbly shook his head as if the looming occasion of the world's biggest football tournament had somehow slipped his mind. Rosie gave him a look that would have withered a smarter man.

"Oh, Gary," she suddenly sighed, "I'd be only too happy for you to go to the World Cup, but you know what money's like at the minute. We'd struggle to get to Ballycastle, never mind Italy."

Gary nodded. He had actually been having similar concerns. It had taken a few informal enquiries to let him know that attending even just one game at the tournament would be much more than he could afford. In fact, out of all of his friends, he was sure that only Seamus Green, his oldest friend, would be able to raise the necessary finances for such a trip. Everybody else, he reckoned, was just fantasising. He was about to make a comment when the squeal of the garden gate being pushed open caused him to glance out the window.

"Here comes Sna...um, Seamus," he said. "Are you sure you don't want to come?"

"No, you two go ahead," said Rosie as she pushed herself up from the sofa. "I just wouldn't feel right."

The main front door to the house was already open, exposing a little square of hall at the foot of the stairs, so there was just a quick knock on the lounge door before Seamus pushed it open and stepped inside.

"All right there?" he said as he closed the door behind him. "Hiya, Ellie. Rosie, how's it going?"

"Yeah, okay, Seamus," said Rosie, arching her

back, "but I'm crawling the bloody walls gasping for a smoke."

"Oh, I'm sure you are," said Seamus, "but you know it's for the best, don't you? You okay there, Ellie?"

Ellie looked up as if taken by surprise. "What?" she exclaimed. "Oh sorry, Seamus, I'm just trying to sort through all these letters from places in England to see if there's anything useful about daddy."

Rosie, Seamus noted, looked at Gary and rolled her eyes while shaking her head.

"Well, is there?" Seamus asked. "Anything useful, I mean?"

Ellie sat back with a sigh. "Not really," she said. "You'd think there would be something, you know? Some trace, or some sort of lead or something."

Ellie and Rosie's father had been torn from his family almost two decades before and had been missing for over fifteen years. He had been caught up, through no fault of his own, in the turmoil of internment at the beginning of the 1970s.

The British had introduced internment – imprisonment without trial – in a desperate attempt to quell the eruption of militant Irish republicanism that had been largely dormant since the partition of Ireland in the 1920s.

Martin McCann, like many others, was an innocent victim of circumstance and his experiences in custody had contributed directly to a complete emotional breakdown, which led to him passing through a variety of mental health institutions until the trail went cold during the turbulence of the seventies.

Ellie, Rosie and their younger brother, Jack – now living in Derry – had been brought up by their mother, Shauna, who had eventually succumbed to the effort and had died when Rosie was a teenager. Jack had no memories of his father and any memories that Rosie may have had were either discarded or suppressed, which meant the legacy of Martin McCann lived on only in the heart of his eldest child. And Ellie preserved that legacy with a firm resolve.

"Well, I'm sure something will turn up," said Seamus.

"I know," Ellie said, "but hopefully it'll be soon. I just wish that-"

"Oh, for God's sake, Ellie," Rosie snapped, "just let it go, will you?"

"What do you mean let it go?" Ellie was shocked by Rosie's outburst. "How can you say that about your own father?"

Rosie, standing by the window, turned on her sister. "My own father?" she shouted. "My own bloody father? Then where was he, Ellie? Where was he when we had to leave home? Where was he when ma died? Where was he when…?" Rosie stopped as she tried to control her anger. Seamus and Gary began to shuffle towards the door.

"You can hardly blame him for any of that," Ellie insisted. "How can you-"

"I don't care!" Rosie cried. "I don't care whose fault it was! He left us!"

"But-"

"He left *me*!" Rosie banged a fist against her chest. "I was only fucking six!"

Seamus had a hand on the door handle but, despite Gary's silent urgings for him to turn it, he felt frozen; helplessly caught up in the moment. Tears had begun to well in Rosie's eyes, but she forced them back. She wouldn't cry over this, she thought. Never over this.

"Just move on with your life, Ellie," Rosie said grimly. "I have. And as far as I'm concerned, he's already dead. In fact, I hope he is."

"Rosie!" Ellie cried. "God forgive you!"

Rosie shrugged and sat down in the chair by the window, her face hard and dark.

"Right then," said Gary, clapping his hands together. "We should make a move here. You ready there, Seamus?"

"What? Oh, right, yeah." Seamus was still getting used to Ding-a-Ling, or rather Gary, calling him by his name. There was a lot to get used to this year, he thought, so an unstable pregnant woman was just par for the course. He opened the door and turned to address the chilly silence in the room.

"Well, all the best," he said. "See you later."

"Yeah, see you," Gary added as he and Seamus hurried outside and pulled the door closed behind them.

"Jesus!" Seamus exclaimed as they walked down the path towards his car. "What the hell was that all about?"

"Don't know," Gary replied. "And I'm not sure I want to know." They got into the car and pulled on their seatbelts. "Did you get the Mass Cards?"

"Yeah," said Seamus. "They're on the back seat there. Have you heard from Tone lately?"

"Yeah, he seems okay."

Seamus simply nodded as he drove out of Ardoyne and crossed to the Woodvale, heading for the west of the city and the Falls Road.

Three

Tone was standing, in the midst of a small crowd, in the front garden of his parents' house in a housing estate just off the Falls Road when Joker's father's car pulled into the street. Tone waved in acknowledgement as Davy parked in the nearest available space and he, Katherine and Joker got out and walked towards the house.

Davy and Joker took turns to shake Tone's hand while Katherine gave him a quick hug.

"So sorry to hear about your daddy, Tony," she said.

"Thanks," said Tone.

"We got a wee sympathy card," Katherine told him, holding up her handbag. She then stepped closer and lowered her voice, "but I'm not really sure what to do with it, you know? Is there somewhere I'm supposed to leave it?"

The system of political and religious segregation in many parts of Northern Ireland meant that Katherine, a Protestant, would be unfamiliar with the customs and procedures that Catholics would normally adopt in situations like this. Removed from her own environment, her own little patch of the same city, she was self-conscious and fearful of standing out from the crowd.

"No problem," Tone assured her. "My da's laid out in the front room, so you can just put it in the coffin with the rest of the cards. You don't want to go in just yet though, there's a priest in there saying a decade of the rosary."

"A decade of the rosary?" Katherine whispered

conspiratorially. "What's that?" Katherine was fascinated by all forms of spirituality, searching, as she was, for her own personal enlightenment.

"Oh," said Tone, "it's nothing, really – just mumbling the same words over and over again."

Davy passed some cigarettes to Tone and Joker and proceeded to light them up, while Katherine wanted to learn more about the whole rosary business.

"So, what's it for?" she asked. "Is it supposed to do anything? Or serve some purpose, or something?"

"Yeah," said Tone mischievously, "I think if you do it right then it's supposed to bring the corpse back to life."

"Tony!" cried Katherine. "That's terrible! You're as bad as Davy, so you are!"

"Yeah, you're right," Tone smiled. "Sorry, Katherine."

"So what does it do then?" she persisted.

"I have no idea," Tone told her. He shrugged. "Unless it's to give the priest something to do." Tone looked over Katherine's head to see a small, portly figure emerge from the house. "Here's somebody who can answer your question, Katherine," he said. "All right there, Hugh?"

Father Hugh was the type of priest who gave the priesthood a good name. He served his parish with self-effacing humility and good humour. He was widely loved by his parishioners and even Tone held a grudging respect for him.

"What's that, Anthony?" Father Hugh asked as he approached. "A question, you say? Something furrowed your brow, has it? Well, I'm always one to enlighten the bewildered." He gave Katherine a friendly wink. "Anthony here is a Godless heathen," he told her, the lilting brogue of his native Galway had been bludgeoned over the years by the staccato snarl of West Belfast. "A shocking man, he is. Just shocking."

Katherine grinned, she had warmed instantly to this jocular priest.

"So tell me, Anthony," he went on, "what is it that's troubling you? Has something cast some doubt in your sceptical mind? Something punctured your certainties and scattered a few clouds across your sunny sky?"

"As you can see, Katherine," Tone said, "Father Hugh here suffers from an affliction that ails many a priest. He's addicted to the sound of his own voice."

"And sadly," Father Hugh observed, "I'm one of the few people who will actually listen. So what was your question, Anthony? I'm all ears."

While Tone, Katherine and Father Hugh discussed the finer points of catholic protocol, Joker ambled through the front gate and let his attention wander. It strolled across the street and became transfixed by an empty crisp packet that was tumbling along the pavement. It then got distracted by a scruffy cat wandering past and was finally aroused by the sudden appearance of a sleek, black Mercedes that pulled up just behind Joker's father's car.

'Damn!' thought Joker as a young man emerged from the driver's side and walked towards him. Joker had met Johnny Gee on only a few occasions but had still managed to form a less than favourable opinion of him. Though harmless enough, he thought, it was

Joker's firmly held belief that Johnny Gee was a cloying and eager-to-please little prick whose ingratiating manner was intensely irritating.

"Johnny Gee," said Joker. "How's it going?"

"Joker?" Johnny Gee replied, a little surprised. "Yeah, I'm not too bad really. What about yourself?" Johnny Gee, Joker felt, seemed more subdued than normal, not quite as annoying, which, given the circumstances, was understandable.

"Yeah, I'm doing okay," Joker told him. "Not as well as you, obviously," he said, nodding to the shiny black car with the three-pointed star on the bonnet.

"What?" Johnny Gee followed Joker's gaze. "Oh right, well it's not mine, of course."

"Doing a bit of joyriding, are you?"

"It's my da's car," said Johnny Gee. "My folks are away in Spain at the minute, so I thought I could-"

"Spain?" Joker interrupted. "Bit early in the year for a holiday, isn't it?"

"Well it's not that," Johnny Gee explained. "They're looking for some places to buy over there. They've already got a beach-house there, you see, and they're looking to-"

"Your folks have a beach-house?"

"Yeah, it's sort of a-"

"In Spain?"

"Yeah, it's-"

"A beach-house?"

"Yeah."

"On a beach?"

"Yeah."

"In Spain?"

"Yeah."

"So let me see if I've got this right. Your parents have a-"

"Look, Joker," Johnny Gee said hastily, "I just noticed Tone there, so I should really go and pay my respects."

"Oh yeah, no probs," said Joker. "You go ahead there." As Joker watched Johnny Gee enter the garden he began to think.

'Yeah, I know,' he told his excited brain. 'He's a great lad, that Johnny Gee. I've always said so.' Joker's firmly held beliefs were, of course, infinitely flexible.

At that moment Seamus drove past and parked a little way down the street. Joker watched as he and Gary got out of the car and walked towards the growing crowd outside the Maguire home. They each punched Joker on the arm and then went into the garden to shake hands with Tone and to say a few words of condolence. They then, along with Katherine and Davy, stepped into the house to place their cards and to take a final look at the shell that had been abruptly emptied of a lifetime's worth of ideas and tears and laughter and memories and hopes, joys and dreams.

"Not going in then?" asked Tone as he stepped to one side of Joker.

"Don't fancy it myself," Joker told him. "If that's okay?"

"Can't say I blame you," Tone replied. "There's something a bit morbid about death really." He offered Joker a cigarette.

"No, I'm all right, Tone. I've just put one out."

"Yeah, so have I," Tone said as he lit his cigarette. "Just seem to be chain-smoking at the minute."

"It's to be expected, I suppose," said Joker. "The funeral's the day after tomorrow, isn't it?"

"Yeah, ten in the morning."

"Have you heard from your brother?" Tone's elder brother had moved to Australia when Tone was only twelve years old and they hadn't seen each other since then. "Is he planning to get back for the funeral?"

"Yeah," said Tone, "he's already on his way. He's due to get to Heathrow early tomorrow, so he should be here tomorrow afternoon. I'll pick him up from the airport."

"That's going to be weird, isn't it? After all these years?"

Tone shrugged. "Don't know," he said. "Just have to wait and see."

Katherine and Davy reappeared to let Tone know they were going to head on.

"You staying then, Joseph?" Davy asked Joker.

"Aye, I'll get a lift with Seamus," said Joker. "I'll see you later." He watched his parents walk off towards their car then turned to see Johnny Gee emerge from the crowd.

"I'm going to shoot on here, Tone," Johnny Gee said as he shook Tone's hand again. "If there's anything I can do for you, then just let me know, okay?"

"Yeah okay, thanks Kevin," said Tone.

"Oh, it's not Kev..." Johnny Gee began, but then stopped and simply nodded. As he stepped onto the road to walk to his car, Joker chased after him.

"Hang on there, Johnny Gee!"

"They seem very pally," said Gary as he and Seamus appeared beside Tone. The three of them watched, bemused, as Joker and Johnny Gee stood in the middle of the street, deep in conversation. After a few moments, Joker gave Johnny Gee a pat on the arm and turned back towards Tone's house. Johnny Gee got into his car and drove off.

"What the fuck was that all about?" asked Gary when Joker stopped in front of him.

"You'll just have to wait and see," said Joker, before changing the subject. "Bobby said he was going to call over at some point," he said to Tone. "Have you seen him?"

"Yeah, you just missed him. He drove over with Sean and Jamesy."

"Jamesy?" said Seamus. "I haven't seen him in ages."

"Aye," Joker agreed, "he's been lying low, hasn't he? Horny wee bugger."

"Oh, I don't think there's anything like that going on," Tone said. "Can't really imagine it with those two, can you? Jamesy and Hannah?"

They all fell silent as they began to imagine it.

"Okay, okay," said Tone, "maybe we *can* imagine it, but I think that says more about us than about them. I mean, I don't think Hannah's the type that would even think about sex before marriage, and Jamesy's hardly a wild stallion, is he?"

"Oh, you never know, Tone," said Gary. "Still waters run deep and all that."

"Yeah right," Tone grunted. "How's Rosie doing these days anyway?"

"Dead on," replied Gary. "Does my head in a wee bit like, but you know how it is, hormones and all."

They quietly nodded. They had all heard of that word. Dusk began to creep over the rooftops so Seamus, Gary and Joker took their leave and drove off towards Gary and Joker's flat near the city centre, leaving Tone to chain-smoke in the encroaching gloom.

The number of people who came to the house to pay their respects eventually dwindled until it was just Tone and his mother sitting together in the front room, with the open coffin by the window. They sat quietly with their own memories of the man that once was until Tone persuaded his mother to go on to bed.

"Are you sure, Son?" his mother asked, breaking Tone's heart with the sadness in her voice. "You'll be okay on your own?"

"Yeah, you go on," Tone told her. Convention dictated that he would stay up to keep vigil throughout the night and he thought he would prefer to do so alone. "You could do with trying to get some sleep," he said. He watched his mother head off to bed then he got up and went into the kitchen. He took a beer from the fridge, set it on the kitchen table and sat down. He lit a cigarette and opened the beer and then, to his astonishment, he quietly and uncontrollably wept.

Four

Africa, 1963

Dr Maher locked up the surgery for the day and made his way across the road, weaving through the noisy, static traffic of rush hour. He had still not got used to the heat, despite being in the city for more than a month, and he could feel the sweat begin to prickle the skin on his back.

He thought back to a cold, wet morning in February when, on a visit to the library near his home in South London, he had searched for Kano in an atlas and had been shocked by the city's proximity to the southern edge of the Sahara Desert. Even on the flat, lifeless map, the desert seemed to be on a relentless march to engulf the city, nudging ever closer to the bustling outpost in the far north of Nigeria's Northern Region. Dr Maher realised then that, even for Africa, Kano would be hot, but still he was unprepared for the furnace that greeted him as he disembarked from his flight from the capital, Lagos, down on the south coast.

He was not entirely sure what had made him volunteer for this Pan-African initiative. He had been perfectly comfortable working as a general practitioner in London, but there was something about the new initiative, when he first heard of it, that fired his imagination. The idea was to spread modern medical practices throughout Africa, paying particular attention to the former colonies that were beginning to emerge as new independent states, and it had come along at just the right time.

He had been thinking about becoming involved in some teaching role and was considering looking into the possibility of taking up a position at a university or a teaching hospital, when Dr Henry Rafferty, his old friend from college, had shown him the article in a medical journal.

The idea of spending several years in Africa helping to educate and train a new generation of medical students had a sudden appeal for him. Africa especially, for it was his continent after all.

Benjamin Maher, despite training and working in England for much of the last ten years, had been born in Cairo and had witnessed, as a child, the ebb and flow of a world war that would come to devastate his life and leave him orphaned and alone.

He took a quick glance at his watch as he jostled through the crowds on the busy pavement. The heat of an early evening in April discouraged rapid movement but he walked briskly, keen to reach the café in time.

"Benjamin!" Dr Maher's friend, Odi, was already seated at a table outside the café and called to him as he approached. "Don't worry," said Odi as he stood to embrace his little Egyptian friend. "You have plenty of time."

"What?" Benjamin exclaimed, taking a seat at the table. "What do mean by that? Plenty of time for what?"

Odi roared with laughter. "You are so obvious, my friend," he said. "A blind man would be able to see it."

"I don't know what you mean," Benjamin said primly. He pushed his glasses up the bridge of his nose and sat back in his chair dismissively.

"Of course you don't," mocked Odi, laughing all the more. "Anyway, what would you like to drink, my friend? I will go and order."

"Just a glass of palm wine, thank you," said Benjamin. Odi got up and, still laughing, went inside. 'Have I really been so transparent?' Benjamin wondered. 'Surely not. Surely Odi is simply having some fun.' He looked along the pavement and saw Adanna, Odi's girlfriend, approaching with a few of her colleagues from work.

"Good evening, Dr Maher," she said formally. "Have you seen Odi?"

"Hello, Adanna. Yes, he's just gone inside."

Adanna embraced two of her workmates and they went off on their way. A third colleague, Zara, stayed behind.

"I will share a drink with you, Adanna," said Zara, glancing at Benjamin. "I'll have a tea, if you're going inside."

Adanna smiled and went to find Odi. Zara took a seat at the table beside Benjamin.

"How are you today, Benjamin?" Zara smiled sweetly.

"I'm well, thank you, Zara," said Benjamin. He liked Zara. Her pretty face was constantly enlivened by a broad smile. "And you?"

"Yes, I am very well," At that moment Odi and Adanna appeared with drinks and they joined Benjamin and Zara at the table.

"So, Dr Maher," said Adanna, "has your Hausa girl passed by yet?"

Benjamin was aghast. "What?" he stammered. "What do you mean?"

Odi shook with laughter. "He thinks that we haven't noticed," he said, slapping his knee. "Oh, Benjamin, do not look so surprised."

Benjamin felt himself flush with embarrassment. Zara smiled sympathetically at his discomfort.

"Do not worry, Benjamin," she told him. "I think she is very beautiful."

"How can she be beautiful?" Adanna snapped. "She is Hausa."

"You must not say that, Danna," Odi gently scolded. "We are all Nigerians."

"So I have been told," Adanna said coldly. Zara laughed at the serious look on her friend's face.

"Yes, Adanna," she said, "do not be like that. It is the weekend. We must make some plans for our days off."

"Very well," said Adanna with a brief smile. "Perhaps we should help Dr Maher pursue his *beautiful* Hausa girl. He is clearly incapable of doing so himself."

Zara clapped with delight. "Yes!" she cried. "That is an excellent idea."

Benjamin would normally have squirmed at being spoken of in this way, but he had spotted the approach of a familiar figure. It was the girl again, and he could no longer hear the teasing of his friends. It was the girl. His girl. His beautiful Hausa girl.

Five

Jamesy had never been one for romantic love in the traditional sense. Love, for Jamesy, was a straightforward, biological process that was responsible for the release of identifiable chemicals in the brain. The whole concept of love was nothing more than a mechanism which slavishly followed natural laws in order to perpetuate the species.

When such clinical scrutiny is brought to bear on a subject then the mystery vanishes but that, Jamesy believed, was no bad thing. No subject had ever been diminished by the truth. In fact, he thought, once the mechanisms for driving the human race forwards were revealed then those mechanisms could only appear to be more wondrous and more inspiring than if they were still veiled in ambiguous mysticism.

Jamesy knew all this. He knew these things and he understood them. And he also understood that the embellishments to this biological urge, symbolised by a hopelessly inaccurate representation of the organ for pumping blood around the body, had given rise to an entire industry. An industry that drove the myth of love's throbbing heart through most of popular culture.

This, of course, was nothing new. Words of love had been around for as long as words had been around, and love had always been seen as an ephemeral, spiritual experience rather than a mundane, physical one. The subtle deceit was, Jamesy understood, probably necessary from an evolutionary standpoint. Those groups of early humans that cherished the notion of love as a heightened state of personal bonding, rather than as a simple, and often aggressive, physical act, would likely have been more successful than those that didn't, and this benign philosophy would then be passed down, becoming more ingrained with each generation. Ideas that benefitted society would naturally thrive.

Necessary and harmless the deceit may have been, but it was deceit nonetheless and that, for Jamesy, was unacceptable. Jamesy needed to peek behind the curtain. He needed to see the structure and the clockwork. His inquisitive nature demanded nothing less. He needed to know. He needed to understand.

But now, it seemed, he could not only accept the lies, he could willingly embrace them.

Meeting Hannah had shaken Jamesy's cool restraint, and his detached, analytical approach was struggling to cope. He could still, of course, cast a cold eye on the reasons for his physical attraction to this particular girl. The components of her face, he understood, were arranged in such a way as to appeal to the part of his brain that dealt with aesthetics. And that part of his brain, Jamesy could imagine, would experience a surge of neurological activity when those same components of Hannah's face were temporarily rearranged when she smiled.

Such a sterile evaluation, however, no longer seemed appropriate. It was no longer an adequate description. And when Hannah smiled, Jamesy felt, it was not even close. What Jamesy was experiencing was unfamiliar and intriguing and had left him unsure about things that had once been firmly established.

His frustration at being unable to neatly interpret his

emotions was leading to unwelcome ambiguity and uncertainty, but there was one thing that Jamesy was sure of. He was certain that at some point in the very near future – at a time convenient to them both – he would very much like to have sex with her.

Hannah walked quickly along Botanic Avenue, propelled by a cold wind and by her eagerness to see James. She had been thinking for a while now about what exactly her feelings were towards him and she had come to the conclusion that a large part of what she felt was gratitude.

Hannah was not so naïve as to believe that James would turn out to be the one great love of her life, but he had undeniably alerted her to the fact that such a thing might be possible.

She had grown up in the small town of Saintfield, just south of Belfast, and had lived her life closely tied to a local branch of Presbyterianism that held firm views on biblical scripture. The path that led to her future had been, up to now, clearly defined. She had, over the years, grown close to a boy named Greg who was in the same youth group of her church and, though never mentioned outright, it was assumed that they would one day join their lives together in a union bonded by their shared love of Jesus Christ. There was no great passion there, but that had never bothered Hannah as she happily accepted the wisdom of such an outcome that would be safe and sensible and would provide a framework for them both to come to a greater understanding of Christ's love.

Then, last Christmas Eve, she met James and

everything changed. She understood her immediate attraction to him, for James was extremely good-looking, but it soon became apparent that her passive acceptance of a future of bland domesticity had, in that very instant, evaporated.

James had aroused feelings in her that she hadn't been aware of before, but she now believed that the fuel for these new feelings had always been within her, just waiting for a spark to drift by and set it alight. And James had come along with a flamethrower.

She was still coming to terms with the strength of her new passions and the unexpected stirrings of – dare she even think it? – *lust*. The thoughts that James had sent spinning through her mind were thrilling and frightening, but it was the actual existence of these thoughts, rather than the cause, that excited her the most. She accepted that James could turn out to be little more than a catalyst, a first step on a new journey of possibilities, but she was also painfully aware that he was the first person she had ever met with whom she was considering committing a wicked and sinful act.

Jamesy occupied the ground floor of a student house in a quiet street that ran directly off Botanic Avenue. He sat at the kitchen table, glancing continually at the clock on the wall. The minutes ticked past nine-o-clock until, finally, the doorbell rang and he jumped to his feet in happy anticipation of a certain smile.

"Not too late, am I?" asked Hannah as Jamesy led her into the small front room.

"No, not at all," said Jamesy. "In fact, we've got

time for a cup of tea, if you fancy it."

"I'd love a cup of tea," she told him, and Jamesy ushered her into the kitchen.

"We can have it at the table," he said. "There's a bit more room in the kitchen."

Jamesy's front room, Hannah had noted before, was filled with books of all sizes and subjects, piled in stacks of various heights, at seemingly haphazard locations all around the room. Outside of a library, Hannah thought, she had never seen so many books. Her family home in Saintfield had only one bookcase, in the hallway, but even that was not completely filled. It contained a Bible, of course, and a few other books concerning theology and scriptural analysis, as well as the writings of John Calvin and the philosophy of Presbyterianism. For anyone to possess so many books not related to Christianity was, for Hannah, something of a revelation.

She sat at the kitchen table and watched as Jamesy filled the kettle.

"Don't tell me you've read all those books," she said, smiling.

"Well, not cover to cover," Jamesy told her. He switched the kettle on and reached for two cups that were hanging on hooks below one of the cupboards. "but I've certainly dipped into to most of them. You know, for reference?"

"But they're not all about history, are they?" As far as Hannah understood things, James was at university to study history, though the truth was a lot more varied than just *history*.

"No," Jamesy admitted, "they're about all sorts of

things."

"Then why have you-?" The kettle came to the boil and Jamesy turned his back to pour the water into a teapot. He then placed the teapot along with the cups on the table and sat down to wait for the tea to brew.

"Why have I got books that aren't about history? Is that what you were going to ask?"

"Well, yes."

"It's just something I do," Jamesy explained. "Like, I'll be reading about something and I'll come across a reference to something completely unrelated that might arouse my curiosity. Especially if it's something that I've vaguely heard of but I don't really know anything about. So then, of course, I have to investigate. I need to find out all I can about it." He poured the tea and got up to get some milk from the fridge.

"You need to?" asked Hannah, bemused.

"Well, maybe not *need* to," Jamesy said as he placed a carton of milk by Hannah's cup. "but it's certainly something that I like to do. You're looking a bit perplexed."

Hannah laughed. "I am a bit perplexed, actually. I can't imagine just going off on a tangent like that. Especially not when I'm studying. I try to stay focused on the subject in hand."

"Yeah, but knowledge is knowledge, isn't it?"

"Mmm," said Hannah. "I'll write that in my next exam. It'll go down well in a programming assignment."

"Okay, fair point," Jamesy conceded, grinning. "Maybe it's just me, but I seem to be curious about just about everything."

"Maybe it is just you," said Hannah, though, to Jamesy, she seemed a little thoughtful. She splashed some milk into her tea and took a sip. "I've got more than enough to keep me occupied," she said, "with my course, and with Scripture too. There can be times when I really struggle with God's message, you know? I can spend a whole day going over the same passage again and again, just trying to work out what the true meaning is." Hannah smiled, assuming that James would be knowingly sympathetic.

Jamesy had a sudden picture of himself grabbing the lapels of Hannah's overcoat, shaking her and screaming, *But there's so much more!* Instead he drank his tea and nodded.

"So what sort of things are you talking about?" asked Hannah.

"Oh, anything and everything," Jamesy said. "For example, the other day I was reading about eels, and that got-"

"Eels?"

"Long story," said Jamesy, laughing, "but it got me thinking about the Sargasso Sea, you know?"

"The Sargasso Sea? That name rings a bell. Is that where all the eels come from?"

"A lot of them yeah, but I suddenly thought that I had no idea where the Sargasso Sea actually is."

"So, where is it then?"

"Well," Jamesy said, "I'd always assumed that Sargasso was a place, you know? An actual geographical location."

"But it isn't?"

"No, not really. The Sargasso Sea is an area in the Atlantic Ocean."

"A sea in the ocean?"

"Yeah, apparently it's full of a weird sort of seaweed called sargassum. And that's where the name comes from."

Hannah looked at Jamesy and laughed. "Well," she exclaimed, "that actually was pretty interesting. And I was expecting to be bored to tears."

"Well, don't be getting too used to that sort of wild entertainment all the time," Jamesy told her. "I mean, I am fairly boring most of the time."

They laughed and chatted as they drank their tea and, after a while, Jamesy stood up. He carried their empty cups over to the sink and glanced at the clock.

"We should make a move," he said. "We'll just walk down and get a taxi in Botanic. You're looking lovely by the way."

"Thank you," said Hannah as she stood up. "And you look very handsome too, James," she added with an accompanying smile. "Black really suits you."

Six

Wee Paulie was a coming man. He could sense it. He could feel it in his water. He had worked his way up with quiet determination, always making sure he was there when needed, always happy to do whatever was asked of him, becoming more and more indispensable, nudging his way ever closer to the top. And it was all starting to pay off.

He liked to think that he was already the right-hand man to the right-hand man; the person who was called on for tasks of the highest importance. This particular job was a perfect example. It was true, he supposed, that one of the reasons he had been selected for the mission was that he was originally from Ardoyne, and so would be able to mingle in some of the drinking clubs without arousing too much suspicion. But that detail, he was sure, was just a minor consideration. He was sure that it was his discretion and cool professionalism that had really swayed his selection and he felt confident that a successful outcome would confirm his position in the upper echelons of the organisation.

He watched his girlfriend, Gemma, rush between the bedroom and the bathroom as she got ready for work. He sat up in bed and stretched, leaving his hands behind his head and leaning back against the headboard.

"You know," he said as Gemma hurriedly assembled the persona she used for work, "I reckon this could be the big one."

"The kettle's on," Gemma told him during a brief

appearance in the bedroom. "Can you finish making the tea. Where the fuck are my shoes?"

"What? Oh yeah, okay." Wee Paulie got out of bed, pulled on a dressing gown and walked to the kitchen. Their one-bedroom flat was on one level so he didn't have far to go. As he dropped some teabags into two large mugs he continued with his observations.

"Yeah," he went on, "I think I'll really be on my way after this one."

"Can you stick some toast on?" Gemma called from the bathroom. "Have you seen my other earring?"

As the kettle came to the boil, Wee Paulie placed some bread in the toaster before filling the two mugs.

"Very important, by all accounts," he said. "In fact, it's even-"

"Got fucking mascara in my eye," moaned Gemma as she burst into the kitchen, holding a tissue to her eye. The toast popped up and she grabbed a slice, spreading some butter as Wee Paulie finished making the tea. "What were you saying?"

"I was just saying that-"

"Shit! Is that the time?" Gemma took a few gulps of tea to wash down a mouthful of toast, then rushed back to the bathroom. A moment later she reappeared, grabbed her bag and keys from the worktop, then paused briefly on her way to the front door to give Wee Paulie a quick kiss. "I'll see you later," she said and, pulling her coat from a hook on the door, she was gone.

Wee Paulie took his tea and went back to the bedroom. He got into bed and sat up sipping the hot drink and thinking about how his mission had been going so far. It was a straightforward job of surveillance and information-gathering and was centred on a monstrous figure by the name of Hegarty in the nationalist enclave of Ardoyne in North Belfast.

Having managed to escape from Ardoyne in his late-teens, Wee Paulie had been loath to return there, but he could see the sense in having a known face in an area where the unfamiliar was viewed with suspicion.

As far as the residents of Ardoyne were concerned, their exuberant sense of freedom and independence was viewed as seditious by the British, and that, coupled with the close proximity of hostile unionist communities, had given them something of a siege mentality. Strangers to the district tended to stand out and were treated with mistrust until they could be vouched for by someone *known*. And this was why Wee Paulie could go and drink in the local clubs without having to face any awkward questions, for, despite no longer living there, his face was still *known*.

Wee Paulie had been working on the group of friends and workmates with whom Hegarty tended to socialise. Hegarty had assembled a gang of tradesmen that worked together in building sites around Northern Ireland and Wee Paulie had been getting to know them as individuals and as a group, slowly building up their trust. Wee Paulie knew how to play the long game. He was assembling a wealth of information to bring to his superiors that, he hoped, would provide what they were looking for.

Hegarty himself, Wee Paulie had learned, was a skilled carpenter who, despite his enormous size, was capable of the most intricate and delicate feats of woodworking. Wee Paulie had managed to have the odd casual word or two with this uncommunicative brute but it was the other members of the gang that were proving to be more open.

There was Plumber Pete, loud, raucous and friendly, Darren, the self-proclaimed God's gift to women, who also did some plastering, the two brickies, Andy and Tom, both surly when sober and Terry the Spark, whip-thin and cool as Elvis. Wee Paulie was on friendly terms with them all by now and was confident that he was working towards a satisfying result to his mission.

What, exactly, that result would be, remained to be seen. Wee Paulie wasn't entirely sure what Mr Jippsen-Phillips was after but he seemed to be happy enough with all of the reports he had received so far. There was a chance, Wee Paulie felt, that this job was in some way connected to Mr McClelland's stay in hospital over Christmas and if that was the case then Wee Paulie was linked to the very head of the firm, and the thought made him giddy.

He finished his tea and lay back in bed, allowing the dreams and the little fantasies of a glorious future play around in his head. Wee Paulie was a coming man.

Seven

Tone watched the motorway traffic hurtle in and out of the city, far enough away to be eerily silent. Probably wouldn't be able to hear it anyway, he thought, over the priest's endless droning. A chill wind brushed a shiver through the crowd and Tone found himself thinking it was always cold at funerals. Maybe it was because Milltown Cemetery was situated on an exposed hillside, but Tone was sure he had always shivered at funerals here, even on the hottest of days. His mother would probably say it had something to do with the spirits of the dead or some other such nonsense that Tone would dismiss. He had no time for paranormal explanations but still, he had to admit, it was always cold at funerals. The priest droned on.

Tone glanced at the mourners gathered around the graveside. They were mostly friends of his parents that he had known from childhood, but he could just make out, lurking at the back, a small group of his own friends. He could see the shaven head of Joker and, further back, standing even taller than Joker, he recognised the huge figure of Harry, Gary's brother-in-law. Tone smiled inwardly. Harry, he assumed, had been dragged along by Karen, Gary's sister, who had, no doubt, been dragged along by Rosie, Gary's fiancée, who, in her present condition, would have needed more support than even a mad rip like Gary could provide. The priest droned on.

Tone's drifting thoughts eventually settled on his father and how, without warning, he was shockingly no longer there. A heart attack, a little defect in a physical muscle, had bridged the gap between existence and oblivion and had turned a normal morning into a maelstrom of grief and loss and uncertainty. Tone looked at his mother standing at the graveside and saw her, for the first time, as an old woman.

He found it impossible to equate this sad, tiny figure, almost fading away before his eyes, with the woman who had shaped his childhood. The woman who could both ease his fears and cause his fears. The woman who could scold and terrify, and praise and hug and reassure. A tyrant, a teacher, a bully and a friend.

There are memories from childhood, Tone thought, that blaze forever through life. Moments that stay with you. He would never forget, for instance, one summer in Donegal when he and his brother had walked with their father across a meadow in search of a river to fish from and had stumbled upon a sun-dappled paradise. A slow, shallow stream trickling over rocks and hidden from the world by broad, leafy trees.

They had all stood and quietly gaped. Guilty, almost, for catching nature with her hair down in tranquil, private repose. Tone could still picture the clear water in the shallow pools between the little rapids of the river with the occasional buzz of an insect that only intensified the silent beauty of the scene.

But there are other memories, Tone mused, that sit quietly between the big moments of walking in the world; memories that come gently to the surface at a sudden sight, or a taste, or a scent. New pyjamas at

Christmas or the welcome oasis of a hot water bottle in a freezing bedroom or the tending of wounds earned in summer escapades, and Tone knew, glancing at the diminishing figure beside him, that all of those unassuming moments were filled with her.

The droning of the priest finally came to an end and the mourners relaxed. A few took their leave of Tone's mother and began to drift away to their cars but most stayed behind to chat and to catch up with old acquaintances. Tone lit up a cigarette while his mother and his brother went over to talk to Father Hugh.

"You flashing the ash there, Tone?" asked Bobby, pushing through the crowd.

Tone handed over his cigarettes and lighter. "Well, did you enjoy that?" he asked.

"He did go on a bit, didn't he?" said Bobby, taking and lighting a cigarette before handing back the pack. "But apart from that it was okay."

Jamesy appeared and shook Tone's hand. "All right there, Tone?" he said. "How are you bearing up?"

"Yeah, not too bad, Jamesy. Thanks."

"Is that your brother over there with the priest?" asked Jamesy.

"Yeah, that's Donal."

"So, how have you been getting on then?"

Tone shrugged. "Don't seem to have much in common, to be honest."

"He seems a bit serious, doesn't he?" said Bobby, glancing over at Donal.

"Well, this is a funeral," Jamesy pointed out.

"I know, but even so…"

"You've got a point, Bobby," said Tone. "I don't

think I've seen him smile since he got here."

"Be fair, Tone," Jamesy said. "The guy's just flown halfway around the world to bury his father. He's hardly going to be in a mood for the giggles, is he?"

Bobby looked at Jamesy. "What have you done with Hannah?" he asked. Hannah was Bobby's cousin and he felt that maybe he should show some concern for her wellbeing.

"I left her talking to Rosie," Jamesy told him.

"I was surprised to see Hannah here today," said Tone. "Fair play to her though. It showed some guts coming here and mixing with a load of priests and rebels."

"Yeah, it was her idea," Jamesy said. "I certainly didn't suggest it."

"Probably curiosity," Bobby suggested. "See what you Taigs get up to."

"We're all heading to the Foresters after," Tone told Jamesy, "if you fancy it."

"Probably not, Tone," said Jamesy. "I was just going to say we're going to be heading on soon."

"Aye, no problem, Jamesy. Tell Hannah I really appreciate her coming today, will you?"

"Yeah, of course. All the best, mate, and I'll see you later."

Back at the flat, Jamesy surveyed the contents of his kitchen cupboard.

"I've got a tin of spaghetti hoops," he told Hannah, "some tuna, a half a jar of marmalade and…some dog food, apparently. I could probably rustle up some sort of casserole from all that."

"I'm not very hungry," said Hannah.

"Or we could go out somewhere."

"Oh yeah, I'm starving."

Jamesy laughed. "It's still a bit early though," he said. "Fancy a cup of tea?"

"Love one."

Jamesy picked up the kettle, went to the sink and, as he turned on the tap, he let his mind wander over to a subject that had lately been attracting a lot of his attention. He wanted to make Hannah aware that he was not averse to the notion of taking their relationship to a more physical level, but he was struggling to think of a way of doing so without coming across as a ravenous sex beast. He just wasn't very good at this sort of thing.

Jamesy had played a fairly passive role in all of his previous sexual encounters, even, on a few occasions, going along with the whole thing only out of politeness. It may have been that he didn't have a particularly strong libido, or maybe it was because he had never had to try too hard, but he had never felt the same overwhelming urge for sexual release that he had observed in all of his peers once puberty had hit.

Now, though, he was beginning to appreciate the sexual frustration that had plagued his friends, as he tried desperately to come up with an appropriate way of broaching the subject with Hannah. It didn't help, of course, that Hannah's religious views would, presumably, make her less amenable to the idea and would make raising the topic so much more delicate than it would normally have been. He certainly would not be able to use the approach of someone like Joker who would just come straight out and ask to have a little rummage around in her underwear. Jamesy smiled to himself at the thought.

"I was talking to your friend, Joseph, at the funeral," said Hannah from her seat at the table.

"Oh, sweet Jesus!" Jamesy muttered.

"What?"

"Oh nothing, nothing." Jamesy placed the kettle on its base and switched it on. He then sat down facing Hannah. "So, um, so, what was he saying?"

"Well, I think he said he was going to be taking somebody to a gay bar," said Hannah. She frowned. "He's not gay, is he?"

"Joker? No, no, he's not gay." Jamesy assured her. He didn't quite know how to proceed. He had a sense that fundamentalist Christian types were not well disposed towards the homosexual community, but as he had so far avoided any deep religious discussions with Hannah, he wasn't sure what her own feelings would be on the matter.

"Then why is he-?"

"You've met Seamus, haven't you?" he asked.

"Seamus? Yes," said Hannah. "I like Seamus. He's nice."

"Well," Jamesy explained, "Seamus has recently come out as being gay and, for reasons best known to himself, Joker has decided help him out."

"Help him out?"

"Yeah, it doesn't bear thinking about, does it?" Jamesy got up to finish making the tea, relieved that Hannah didn't pursue the matter. She leaned back in her chair and stretched lazily.

"You never answered my question, you know," she said as Jamesy sat back down at the table with two cups of tea.

"What question?"

"Why can't dolphins breathe underwater?"

"What?"

"Don't you remember?" Hannah said. "It was something you said when you were having that argument with Greg."

"I wouldn't call it an argument," said Jamesy defensively. "More of a discussion, really."

"Well anyway," Hannah went on, leaning forward to gaze into those mesmerising, milky-blue eyes that were Jamesy's most striking feature, "you came up with that question as some sort of example, I think, as the type of thing we should want to find out about. Remember?"

"Sort of," Jamesy replied. "What's your point?"

"Well, it sort of stuck with me," she told him. "The more I thought about it, the less sense it made."

"What do you mean?" Jamesy was uneasy about the direction this conversation seemed to be taking.

"Well, fish can breathe underwater, right? And that makes sense because they live in water their whole lives. But then so do dolphins." Hannah looked at Jamesy and frowned. "But if dolphins don't keep jumping out of the water every so often then they'll drown. Whales too, for that matter. It doesn't seem fair."

"Doesn't seem to bother the dolphins," said Jamesy.

"I know, but it's the same as us having to stick our heads in a bucket of water every now and then just to stay alive. It's mad! I just don't understand why God would make dolphins that way."

"Yeah, well," Jamesy said as he finished his tea, "we should probably make a move. I reckon we should try that new Italian place in Botanic."

Hannah gave him a curious look. "You're still avoiding the question, aren't you?" she said.

"What makes you think I know the answer?"

"You said it yourself. You need to know everything."

"I thought you said you were starving?"

"Wow!" said Hannah, laughing. "You really don't want to answer the question, do you?"

"Come on." Jamesy stood up. "We can talk about it over lunch."

"Are you going to tell me the answer then?" Hannah got up and they both headed for the front door.

"If you want," Jamesy told her. "Although," he said as he pulled open the door, "it's more of a theory."

Eight

"Father Hugh was telling me you've lost your faith," Donal said as he sat down at the table across from Tone.

"I didn't lose it," said Tone. "I threw it away."

"Why?"

"I just never felt comfortable kneeling in front of a man in a dress."

Donal sighed. "What happened, Tony?" he said. "I can remember when you wanted to be a choirboy at St Peter's."

"Yeah well, they do say youth is wasted on the young."

"You're still young," Donal told him, "but you've got really cynical. So what happened to you? What made you reject your faith?"

"I read the Bible," said Tone. Donal was beginning to irritate him. They were supposed to be celebrating the life of their father with drinks and songs and memories, not going over all this old nonsense again.

Tone had been surprised to learn that Donal had become more religious since moving to Australia. He had assumed the opposite would be true, believing Australia to be a lot more secular and forward-thinking than Northern Ireland.

"Never mind *me*, Donal," he said. "What the hell happened to *you*? I don't remember you going to Mass much when I was a kid."

Donal took a sip of his beer and leaned forward, resting his elbows on the table. "I think the Church really helped me," he said, "when my marriage broke up."

"What? When did this happen?"

"A couple of months ago," Donal explained. "One day Donna just took the kids and left. They're staying with Donna's parents in Melbourne."

"Why though? What happened?"

"A lot of things, really," said Donal with a shrug. "Maybe I should have put in a bit more effort. I don't know. It looks like it's over though."

"Does ma know?"

"Not yet. There hasn't really been the right time, you know? I'll tell her before I head back though."

"Jesus, Donal," said Tone. "You really know how to bring down a funeral."

Seamus and Sean were talking with Tone's mother on the other side of the bar, so Bobby joined Tone and Donal's table.

"All right there, Donal?" he said, sitting down. They had been introduced earlier. "Have you noticed many changes since you've been back?"

"I haven't really been here long enough," said Donal. "Although from what Tony's been telling me, the town seems to have got a lot livelier. When I left, the whole city centre would shut down at five-o-clock every day. Didn't open at all on Sundays."

"Yeah, I know what you mean," Bobby agreed. "It has all opened up a lot in the last couple of years. I can remember a lot of the Bible-Bashers on our side being up in arms about places opening on Sundays."

"Donal!" someone called from the bar. "Come and see your Aunt Jessie."

Donal got up from his chair and melted into the crowd. Tone threw a cigarette across the table to Bobby and lit one for himself.

"Cheers, Tone," Bobby said. "So how's it going with you and Donal then?"

Tone shrugged. "He's got his problems," he said. "Like everybody else."

"Mmm," Bobby muttered. He took a sip of his beer and looked intently across the table at Tone. "Did I ever tell you," he began, "that I was planning to get engaged this year?"

Tone gave him a look. "Uh, yeah," he said with as much nonchalance as he could muster. "I'd heard."

"Well, it didn't work out," said Bobby.

"Really?"

"Yeah, it turns out," Bobby casually replied, "that she met somebody down in Dublin last year."

Tone said nothing. He simply looked at Bobby and took a draw from his cigarette.

"Yeah," Bobby continued, "a bit of an arsehole by all accounts."

Tone remained silent, waiting for Bobby to go on.

"He's actually from Belfast apparently." Bobby paused to take a long drink before continuing. "Some cunt by the name of Tony Maguire. Sounds like a right wanker."

"Look, Bobby," Tone quickly interjected, "I had no idea that-"

"I know, I know," Bobby waved away Tone's protestations, "I'm only messing with you." He seemed amused by Tone's reaction. "So when did you realise?"

Tone looked uncomfortable as he answered. "You were rambling away about her at the pub-crawl," he said miserably, "and it just clicked."

"Really?" said Bobby. "I don't remember that."

"I haven't seen her since." Tone admitted.

"No, you haven't, you dickhead!"

"What?"

Bobby leaned forward. "That's what I want to talk to you about," he said. "Claire's really confused about why you haven't been in touch. She thinks she's done something wrong."

"I know but I just thought that…" Tone stopped and thought for a second. "Did you tell her that you knew me?" he asked.

"No," Bobby told him, "I thought I should see you first. Got to say it was a hell of a shock though, when it all came out."

"I'm sure."

"So, what are you going to do about it, Tone?" Bobby went on. "You can't just leave it like that."

"Well, what about you two? Did you actually propose?"

"Never got a bloody chance, did I?" Bobby leaned back in his chair with a smile. "You managed to fuck up that plan, didn't you? Lucky I never bought a ring."

"Sorry about that."

"Yeah, well," Bobby shrugged, "you know me, Tone. It was just the next step really."

"Even so…"

"Anyway, shit happens, but you still need to talk to Claire."

"Yeah, you're right," Tone said, an unfamiliar

glimmer of hope flickering within him. "I'll do that."

Seamus and Sean arrived at the table with a tray of drinks. They had to shout to be heard above the shouts and laughter of the crowd as old friends met up and hugged and reminisced and drank to a man that used to be.

"It's a pity Joker and Gary had to work this afternoon," Sean said as he and Seamus sat down. "They'd have been in their element here."

"Yeah," Tone agreed. "Gary was saying he doesn't think he can manage the World Cup this year."

"No, I'm not surprised," Sean said, "There's no way I can afford it either."

"I'm out too," Bobby added. "Bloody skint."

"Yeah, it was a nice idea," said Tone, "but it was always going to be a long shot." He looked at Seamus. "I hear you've got a big night coming up," he said with a grin. "You and Joker then?"

Seamus nodded. "Saturday night," he said.

Bobby laughed. "I'd love to be a fly on the wall that night," he said. "Are you looking forward to it?"

"Of course," Seamus replied. "Well, you know, sort of." He wasn't sure how he was feeling about Saturday night. On the one hand, he would be glad of the support, but on the other hand, it was Joker.

Anything could happen.

Nine

The Front Page bar was so-called because of its proximity to two of Belfast's main newspapers; the *Irish News* was across the road and the *Belfast Telegraph* around the corner. It was an upstairs bar, elegantly furnished with seating areas off to the right of the entrance and another, raised area across the way from the bar. There was also a small stage in the left-hand corner that looked to be set up for some live music later in the evening, with microphones and instruments already in place.

Joker sat at the bar by himself. It was still early, so the place was quiet with just a few people dotted here and there. An elderly couple sat in silence at the far end on the right, while a gang of women, with bags of shopping at their feet, gossiped around a table a little closer to the bar.

Joker glanced in the large, ornate mirror behind the bar and saw a couple of cool, young dudes sitting at a table in the middle of the raised section. They were huddled in deep conversation.

As Joker watched, one of the cool dudes got up and walked furtively to the left of the bar. He then leapt onto the stage and, grabbing a microphone in its stand, made a request of the smattering of disinterested punters around the room.

"Ladies and gentlemen," he said with enthusiasm, "could you please put your hands together for 'Blues Boy' Morrison!"

Then, to no applause, the other cool dude – presumably 'Blues Boy' Morrison – bounded onstage, picked up a guitar, and launched into a hurried version of *Drink That Bottle Down,* before a red-faced bouncer came through the door and began remonstrating with 'Blues Boy' and his mate. After a heated exchange, the dudes were bundled out the door and down the stairs to the street below.

Under normal circumstances, Joker would have been highly amused by such shenanigans but his current, reflective state of mind had curbed his fondness for mischief and so he simply gestured to the barman to refill his glass.

As a fresh pint was placed in front of him, Joker lit a cigarette and pondered this strange new contemplative condition. It was clear that his attempts to suppress his feelings – to bury them in the darkest of depths – had not been entirely successful by the fact that his brain revelled in nagging him about it. There were times when Joker wished his brain would just fuck off and leave him alone. Especially when it was being, he believed, largely unreasonable.

It was all very well, Joker felt, to constantly highlight the issue, but if his brain had nothing constructive to offer then what was the point? Just what did his brain expect him to do about it?

"Right there, Joker? Been here long?"

"Hiya, Seamus," Joker replied as Seamus arrived beside him. "Nah, not long. Just a couple of pints."

"You okay there?" Seamus asked, nodding to Joker's pint.

"Yeah, you go ahead."

Seamus ordered a drink and sat up on the barstool next to Joker.

"Still up for it then?" he asked Joker as his pint arrived.

"Aye, no problem." Joker grinned. "What's the worst that can happen?"

Seamus winced. "For fuck's sake, Joker," he said. "Don't say things like that."

"So what time do you want to head round at?"

"Well," said Seamus as he took a drink from his pint and held it up, "not till I've had several more of these."

"Good plan."

As the evening wore on, Seamus could not help noticing that Joker was a lot more enthusiastic about his drinking than normal. He had never been much of a slouch in that regard but tonight he seemed to be attacking each beer with an almost solemn intent.

"Take it easy, Joker. We've got all night," he said as Joker downed another pint.

"Just thirsty, Seamus, that's all," Joker told him. "Besides, you can't expect me to walk into a gay bar sober, now can you?"

"God forbid."

The Parliament was Belfast's first openly gay venue and so, being a new thing, people were naturally against it. The problem for the people who disliked new things though, was that, over the last few years, Belfast had been trying to catch up with the rest of the United Kingdom and so new things were happening at an increasing rate. It was hard for the protesters to keep up.

It also meant that the protesters were having to spread themselves ever more thinly to ensure that they covered every new thing that appeared. But the protests, the protesters believed, were necessary because if groups of people who were not the same as them were to be given the same rights as them, then other groups of people who were not the same as them would want to be given those rights too. All sorts of groups. Even women. And then where would we be?

So as Seamus and Joker headed towards the Parliament, they were confronted by a sign-waving mob of three people who tried to explain to them that they were both abominations in the eyes of God and if they did not repent then, after they had died, things would start to get very unpleasant indeed.

Seamus had to restrain Joker from voicing his opinion so Joker contented himself with putting his fingertips to the tip of his thumb and showing the protesters the universal sign of the wanker.

Once inside, they found a booth close to the bar and Seamus sat down while Joker went off to get the drinks. When he returned he sat down and looked around him.

"I'm a wee bit disappointed," he told Seamus.

"Why?"

"Well, I don't know what I was expecting," said Joker, "but these people are all just sitting around being dead boring."

"What else would they be doing?" Seamus asked with some amusement, though, in truth, he hadn't known what to expect either.

"I don't know," said Joker thoughtfully. "Maybe I was expecting a wee bit more flamboyance, you know? A bit more pizzazz, a bit more *joie de vivre*."

"You thought they'd all be in drag, didn't you?"

"No, no, it's not that," Joker insisted as he passed a cigarette to Seamus. "Well… you know, maybe a bit."

Seamus rolled his eyes as he lit his cigarette. He looked around. Everything did indeed appear to be perfectly ordinary and he wondered if he too felt disappointed. When he looked a little closer though, he could spot a few obvious differences. On the dancefloor men were dancing with other men, and then it suddenly hit him. These men were gay. They were gay men. And *he* was a gay man. He felt almost sick with nerves. He was a gay man in a room with other gay men and he had no idea what he was supposed to do.

"See anybody you fancy?" asked Joker.

"What?"

"You're sussing out the talent, aren't you? What about your man over there? He looks like a bit of a ride."

"Jesus Christ, Joker," said Seamus, gulping down his pint. "Stop fucking pointing."

"Fuck, I think I might be in there," Joker exclaimed. "That would be funny, wouldn't it?"

Seamus was squirming as the reality of the situation began to sink in. He stared at the table, thankful that, apart from the odd curious glance, no one seemed to be paying him much attention.

"These bloody pints don't last as long as they used to," Joker moaned, holding up an empty glass. "Do you want another one, Seamus?"

"No, Joker, I'm okay. You go ahead." Seamus was beginning to regret the whole thing. He felt out of his depth. He felt like an imposter, an intruder. He had no right to be here, in this place where everyone was smiling and confident and self-assured.

"The barman likes my shirt," said Joker on his return from the bar. "*Very sexy*, he said. And some other fella called me *Darling*. I must say, they seem like a friendly bunch."

Seamus felt a sudden surge of gratitude that Joker had come along with him tonight. It could be just a normal night out, he thought. No pressure. He could simply spend the rest of the evening drinking and chatting with his friend, and feel under no obligation to do anything else. He began to relax. It could turn out to be a good night, he reckoned. Just a couple of old mates, out on the beer on a Saturday night. You could always rely on your mates. He turned to Joker who was resting the back of his head on the plush upholstery of the seating. He was snoring loudly.

Seamus stared in disbelief. This had never happened before. He could not recall a single occasion when Joker had passed out in a bar while the bar had still been open.

"Is your boyfriend okay there?"

"What?" Seamus turned to see a concerned young man with wispy red hair gesturing at Joker. "Um, yeah, he's just…oh, he's not my boyfriend," Seamus said hurriedly, "He's my…" 'My *what*?' he thought. 'My *chaperone*?' "He's just a friend," he said finally.

The red-haired guy smiled. "Bit of moral support?"

"What?"

"Well, I haven't seen you here before and you were looking a wee bit nervous."

"Um, yeah," Seamus stammered, "I suppose so, yeah."

"I'm Alan, by the way," Alan leaned over to shake hands.

"Um, Seamus," said Seamus.

"Do you mind if I join you?"

Joker was leaning heavily on Seamus as they both stumbled along the Dunbar Link on their way to Joker's flat. Gary had arranged to stay with Rosie for the night so Seamus was going to stay in Gary's room to save having to get a taxi back to Ardoyne.

"We showed them, didn't we Seamus?" Joker slurred. Alan had gone by the time Joker had woken up and Seamus had decided not to mention him. On waking, Joker had picked up his pint and had simply carried on as if nothing had happened. "We showed them gays, didn't we? They won't mess with us again in a hurry."

"Isn't that missing the point?" asked Seamus, trying to keep Joker walking in a straight line.

"You're right, you're just fucking right, me old mucker," said Joker, patting Seamus on the chest. "I've missed more points than you've had hot dinners."

"I don't doubt it."

Joker then lifted his face to the sky and, to the dismay of Seamus, began to sing.

"*Ooh…ooh… Carol, I am but a foo…ooo…oool.*" It was sung with passion and heart, but with no discernible ability. Joker then seemed to forget the song as he stared at the night sky.

"Fuck me!" he exclaimed in wonder. "Look at the size of the moon!"

Seamus followed Joker's gaze. "That's the Albert Clock," he said.

"What? Oh fuck, so it is," said Joker, and then he giggled. "I'm fucking hammered."

"I hadn't noticed," said Seamus untruthfully.

"*Daaarling, I love youuu, though you treat meee cruuueeeel…*" Joker sang with obvious feeling, but soon the cacophony petered out and he fell silent, becoming almost morose. "Do you remember Carol, Snatter?" he asked. "Do you remember? She was class, wasn't she?"

"Of course I remember Carol," said Seamus. "How could anybody forget Carol?" When Seamus had first met Carol, his cautiously emerging sexuality had almost been sent scuttling back to the closet, slamming the door closed behind it. "How is she these days? Have you heard at all?"

"Oh, she's gone," Joker told him. "Gone far, far away." He drunkenly waved his arm in the direction of far, far away.

Seamus remained silent, lost in his own thoughts. Joker was enigmatic enough at the best of times, but when he was this inebriated it was wise not to get too involved. They stumbled on through the night.

When Seamus finally managed to pour Joker into bed, he went into Gary's room and lay down. He reached into his pocket and pulled out the little scrap of paper that had Alan's phone number written on it.

Staring at it, as he played it around between his

fingers, he could feel his heart beating with anticipation. And exhilaration. And fear.

Ten

His companions were getting up to go, but Michael McClelland remained seated. He watched his associates shuffle out with the rest of the Kitchen Bar's lunchtime crowd and then sat back and rubbed his eyes. He had a few moments to himself before his next appointment and he took the time to dwell on his growing sense of unease.

It seemed to him that there would always be one more score to settle. There would always be someone who needed to be put in their place, taught a lesson, forced to show respect. It would never end, he realised and he sighed as he sipped his wine.

The macho posturing and endless retributions were beginning to wear him down and, as he thought more about the future, he was learning to despise the life he led. He had started to hate the secretive dealings and the single-minded thugs with whom he was forced to mix. He hated the snobbish condescension of his neighbours, the constant police harassment, the hypocrisy of the paramilitaries. He hated the need to keep to the shadows, knowing he would never be accepted by the 'legitimate' business community. He hated telling his wife to be more discreet with their wealth and – perhaps more than anything – he hated his bloody nickname.

Throughout Belfast, especially among certain elements of society, he was known simply as Sticky Mickey, and he cringed every time he heard it. Still, he soberly reflected, in his line of work it was best to keep a low profile. Better to remain anonymous behind an embarrassing nickname than to have your own name bandied around the streets.

Thinking of it, led his thoughts to what his line of work actually was and how he had ended up in such a profession.

He preferred to think of himself as a businessman, but how did others see him? As a thief? He was more than that. A dealer in stolen goods? He was more than that too. A gang boss? A criminal? A hood? He supposed he was all of these things, but wasn't there something more to him – more to his life – than all of that?

And how was it, he wondered, that he had ended up like this? As a child his small stature had prompted some people to suggest he could be a jockey, but he was not a great lover of horses. In fact, one time, during a school visit to riding stables in North Down, he had been bitten on the arm by a horse and had since developed a passionate hatred for the vicious, four-legged bastards that would likely be frowned upon at the Jockey Club.

Not that Michael would dream of trying to link one traumatic event in childhood to his drifting into a life of crime as a teenager, though he could imagine some psychologist, or psychiatrist somewhere drawing all sorts of excited conclusions, while trying to shoehorn in abandonment issues or issues with his father or his mother or some other such nonsense.

There were no dark, complex reasons for his involvement in crime, he decided. He was simply good at it.

At first it was easy money, selling goods that had

mysteriously filtered through from the docks, but Michael had been shrewd enough to spot opportunities where others had seen only a quick profit. He had been shrewd enough to see that the real money could lie a little further down the line if you were prepared to make investments. He had been smart enough to stay below the radar and smart enough to keep one step ahead of the authorities.

Bit by bit he had built his empire but, he was now asking himself, to what end? The wealth and the power had always been enough for him. He had never craved social acceptance. Even his dopey wife had understood the wisdom of discretion and had curbed her natural instinct for showing off. Money had a tendency to compensate for a life on the shadowy fringe of society.

Now though, Michael realised, everything had changed, and it had come from an unexpected quarter. It was his son, Peter.

When Peter had been born, a little under ten years ago, Michael had given him little thought. He was not planning on having much to do with a child who, he assumed, would grow up to be a typical brat, spoilt by a rich, soft-headed mother who would lavish upon him everything he demanded. Michael had seen it all before, and he knew that he couldn't, and wouldn't, be bothered to make any effort to prevent it. It was inevitable anyway, he believed.

Maddy, his wife, would now have something to focus on. The long dull days married to Michael would now have meaning, and Maddy would now be able to watch her own life spread out beyond the restrictive household. She could develop and grow as the child grew, and the child, Michael knew, would feel the burden of the extra life and would grow to resent it. He was wrong though.

Peter was a joy. Michael would find himself rushing home as often as he could just to spend time in his son's company. Despite the heavy-handed soppiness of his mother and the initial disinterest of his father, Peter flourished.

To Michael's great surprise the boy was selfless, clever, funny and polite. He charmed all who met him, and Michael's cynical old heart warmed with every smile and softened with every unselfish gesture from a child who seemed to give nothing but happiness.

And that was why Michael was feeling compelled to question his life. The thought of Peter, as he moved into secondary education, being teased, bullied or ostracised simply because of his father's 'business' dealings caused Michael genuine pain. Would he be the cause of his son's journey into adolescence being a nightmare of mockery and rejection? The idea that the light that Peter brought to everything in life could be dimmed because of him was agony for Michael and he had lately begun to explore his options.

Michael had a passion for cinema and he saw his life echoed in the struggles of Michael Corleone in the Godfather movies. His namesake wanted to distance himself from the criminality at the heart of his empire and to make the Corleone family business entirely legal and legitimate, and Michael McClelland harboured similar ambitions. Breaking free from the myriad of complicated, interwoven little ties, however, would not be easy.

Jippo, Michael's right hand man, entered the bar and sat down facing Michael. He didn't order a drink – Jippo rarely drank, and never during the day – but got straight down to business. They discussed a variety of pressing topics and upcoming dealings until Jippo finally brought up the current status of the ongoing Hegarty situation.

"Not a great deal to report from the Ardoyne side of things," Jippo told Michael. "I've still got a close eye on things though. But I do have something you should be aware of."

"Oh?" said Michael, trying to generate some interest. He would rather not have to deal with this matter, but Jippo had been pushing it and he reluctantly could see the sense of it. He, Jippo and several of his men had been completely humiliated by Hegarty, and a guy called Anderson, at Christmas, leaving Michael with a fractured skull and Jippo with a broken nose, and in this business, Michael knew, reputation was everything. There would need to be some payback.

"Yes," Jippo replied, "Anderson was seen going into the Parliament, on the Dunbar Link, on Saturday night."

"The Parliament?" Michael asked, surprised. "That new gay place?"

"Exactly."

"Is Anderson gay then?"

"Looks like it."

"I have to say I never thought he was the type."

"Well, you can never tell, can you?"

"Suppose not. Who was he with?"

"Seamus Green," said Jippo, "You know? He owns a shop in Bridge Street."

"Yeah, I know who you mean," Michael replied. He thought for a moment. "So, is there any way we can use this?"

"Not sure," Jippo said as he leaned back. "If anything though, it may be something that we want to keep quiet about."

"Oh yeah," said Michael, "I see what you mean." His reputation, he felt, would be tarnished even more if it came out that he had been hospitalised by a gay bloke.

"I'll have a think about it," Jippo told him.

"What about that other gobshite?" Michael asked. "Lingfield, isn't it?"

"Gary Lingfield, yes," said Jippo. Gary Lingfield, along with Anderson, had been the original target when everything had gone wrong at Christmas. "It sounds like he's planning to move back to Ardoyne to be with his girlfriend. She's pregnant, by the way."

"Yeah, I know that," said Michael. He looked at Jippo. "Why? You're not suggesting we use that, are you?"

Jippo said nothing, but gave a tiny shrug.

"Jesus Christ, Jippo!" Michael shook his head. He had complete faith in his right-hand man but he knew that Jippo could be a ruthless bastard. Jippo had even suggested that they should make a move on their targets when they had recently all gathered together for a funeral, but Michael had instantly rejected the idea on the grounds that too many people would be around.

That was the excuse he had given Jippo, but on top of that it was a funeral, for God's sake, and Michael liked to think he still had some shred of decency.

"Anyway," he said, "there's no rush. I'd rather wait for exactly the right moment and do it properly."

"Of course," said Jippo. "You're the boss."

Eleven

Gary had been on the early shift and had arranged to call up, after work, to Ardoyne to see Rosie. She was looking at some brochures when he stepped through the door. Ellie was at work and Rosie was listening to some music on the radio.

"Jesus, Rosie!" Gary shouted. "Turn it down a bit, love. You can hear it at the end of the path."

Rosie turned down the volume on the radio and looked at Gary. "It's supposed to be good for the baby," she told him.

"What is?" Gary asked. "Being born deaf?"

"Music in the womb, Gary," Rosie explained. "It's the latest thing. It's meant to be very soothing. Relaxes the baby."

"I've never heard Motorhead described as soothing before."

"That just happened to be on when you came in," she said. Gary sat down beside her on the sofa.

"What's that you're looking at?" he asked.

"Hannah got me them," she said. "They're all about different computer courses you can do."

"Computers?"

"Yeah, Gary," Rosie sighed as she leaned back on the sofa. "I've been thinking that I'm going to have to do something, you know? We're going to need the money when the baby's born, especially if we're going to be getting some place of our own."

"Why computers though?"

"It was one of the few things in school I was actually interested in," Rosie said. "I got talking to

Hannah about it at the funeral and she said she'd look into some courses that would suit me."

"See anything you fancy?"

"Yeah, there's a couple of things that look really good. I mean, I won't be able to do anything about it till next year, but it's worth getting an idea, isn't it?"

"Yeah, absolutely," said Gary. He stood up and headed for the kitchen. "Fancy a cup of tea?" he asked.

"I'd love a cup of tea," she said. "There's some biscuits in the cupboard there as well."

"KitKats and Penguins!" Gary called from the kitchen. "Now I know how the other half lives. Me and Joker are happy with the odd Jammy Dodger."

"Oh yeah," Rosie shouted back. "how did it go with Joseph and Seamus the other night at that gay bar?"

Gary popped his head through the door. "I haven't seen Seamus," he said, "but Joker reckons it went well."

"Did Seamus meet anybody?"

"Don't think so," Gary answered, "but I would imagine that Joker would have scared anybody off. You know what he's like."

Gary went back to finish the tea. He returned with a plate of chocolate biscuits and then brought in two mugs of tea. He sat down again beside Rosie.

"What are you thinking of doing on Saturday?" he asked, taking a sip of tea and unwrapping a Penguin.

"Well," Rosie began, gesturing at her pregnancy bump, "I'm not going to be going out drinking all day, am I?"

Gary patted her hand in what he assumed was a gesture of sympathy. It was unfortunate, he thought, but it was hardly *his* problem.

"So, I thought," Rosie continued mischievously, "that me and you could go to early Mass together and then go over some of the wedding plans the rest of the day."

She watched with sadistic amusement the look of horrified panic on Gary's face. Her heart went out to him as she saw the confusion and the anguish in his eyes.

"But…but…" he spluttered.

"I don't think Ellie's working that night," Rosie went on, seemingly oblivious to Gary's turmoil, "so the three of us could just have a wee quiet evening in."

"Evening in?" Gary dumbly repeated, the words falling automatically from his mouth as his mind raced in frenzied alarm. "But…but…"

Rosie could hold it in no longer and shrieked with laughter. "The look on your face!" she screamed. "I'm only messing with you, Gary."

Gary gave a weak, uncertain smile as the relief flooded through him.

"I wouldn't do that to you, Gary," Rosie said, wiping the tears from her cheeks, "I just couldn't resist it."

Gary's heart had started beating again after the shock and he turned to stare at his fiancée. He did love this mad bitch, he thought, but there were times…

"No," she assured him, "I'm just going to spend the day with Ellie. Though we might call down the Short Strand to see Sheila. She was saying she's got nothing planned, so the three of us could just sit around slegging off men."

"Um, yeah," Gary put down his tea, as he felt his hands were still shaking, "that's a good idea."

"Because, obviously," Rosie teased, "women have nothing better to do than just sit around slegging off men."

"Um, no…no…of course not."

"Are you okay?"

"Yeah, yeah," Gary said, putting a hand to his chest to check his heart was still going, "just give me a minute, that's all."

Twelve

Hannah was afraid she might be a sex maniac. At first it was just a tiny flicker of an image, a spectre in her mind that was gone before she realised it was there, but now it seemed to be growing in intensity and becoming ever more frequent. It had even happened at the funeral.

At a funeral!

She had been respectfully standing by the graveside, aware of James at her side and thinking of nothing in particular when, from nowhere, a thought flashed vividly in her mind. It was a stark picture of the tips of James' fingers. And they were stroking the top of her inner thigh.

It had come so suddenly and so shockingly that she was terrified she may have gasped aloud. A quick glance around, however, assured her that no one was staring at her. Her mind was still reeling as the service ended, and she was grateful for Rosie coming over to talk to her, giving her a chance to regain her composure.

It had happened again just now. She was in the library of the university's IT Department, supposedly studying, when she felt – physically felt – James' lips on the back of her neck as he unhooked her bra.

She closed her books in exasperation. It was impossible to study when you were a sex maniac.

She decided she had done the right thing when she'd told James that, for a while at least, they should stop seeing each other.

It had not been an easy decision for her to make

because James was becoming an obsession. But then that, Hannah told herself, was exactly the point. It would be impossible for her to go any further into a relationship with someone who could not see the truth.

Hannah may still have been struggling with many points of Scripture, but she knew that all of the things she'd been told to believe were true. It followed, therefore, that those things that others had been told to believe, if different, were clearly untrue. But there was so much ignorance in the world, so many differing beliefs, that Hannah began to wonder why God would allow it. And that had led her to think that maybe it wasn't God. Maybe it was Satan who was flooding the world with blindness. Which brought her round in a circle. Why would God allow Satan to have such sway over His Creation?

She prayed to God every night to let her understand. To give her just a glimmer of insight. But the continuing silence suggested that God wished her to make the journey using her own abilities, and she accepted the wisdom of such a strategy. It was cheating, after all, to be given the answers.

The casual discussion she had had with James over lunch had shaken Hannah, and had made her see him in a new light.

She had always suspected, she supposed, that James had held beliefs that were antithetical to the true Word of God, but she had suppressed those suspicions because of …because of what? Because of lust? Her selfish desires? Temptation? Sin?

Hannah knew – knew in her heart – that the evil seed that would become the lie of evolution had been planted by Satan in the mind of the unfortunate man, Charles Darwin, but what she couldn't understand was why the idea had so strongly taken root. It seemed that God's Word was receding from the Earth, while Satan's lies were spreading unchecked and unstoppable throughout all the peoples of the world.

Her little church group was doing its best to stem the tide of wilful ignorance, but it seemed an impossible task. Hannah was able to see for herself the insidious rise of secularism, of humanism, of atheism, of sheer disbelief in everything that was true, and she despaired that God was allowing it to happen.

She understood, of course, that she should never question His plan, but the fact she found it difficult to see even the simplest points of Scripture was leaving her deflated. She didn't even feel she could approach anyone in the Church about her concerns because she was embarrassed by them. The elders of the Church, she felt sure, would be appalled by her lack of insight, by her inability to grasp what small children could happily absorb from the outset.

One of the things from Scripture that Hannah struggled to comprehend was God's omniscience. God was perfect. She knew that. That was easy. God was without flaw. And, Hannah also knew, He was all-powerful and everywhere at once. Nothing was beyond God.

So why then did a plan that was conceived and executed by a perfect, all-knowing deity go so catastrophically wrong, right at the very beginning?

It was the fault of the serpent.

But God would have been fully aware of the serpent

and the serpent's intent. God was omniscient.

It was because Adam and Eve had been given free will.

But God would have known exactly what they would do with their free will. God was omniscient.

God got angry by the actions of Adam and Eve. God got angry? But God was omniscient. He would have foreseen these events, so why would He be surprised enough to get angry?

Hannah knew that all of those parts of Scripture that she perceived as contradictions were deliberately shrouded to test her comprehension. Enlightenment required effort, dedication and focus, and that was why she despaired. Because she was failing.

She could feel James' lips in the small of her back and she leaned forwards onto the desk, put her head in her hands, and shuddered.

She had laughed when James had told her how some people explain why dolphins can't breathe underwater. He had said that some people believed that the ancestors of dolphins weren't dolphins at all, but had walked on the land and breathed air. As she was laughing, however, Hannah couldn't help noticing that James wasn't.

"Surely *you* don't believe that, do you?" Hannah asked.

Jamesy shrugged. "Well, it's the theory that's currently accepted by the scientific community."

"Theory!" Hannah declared triumphantly. "It's just one guess after another, isn't it?"

"Well, to be honest," Jamesy explained, "that's sort

of how science works. If you observe something that doesn't have an obvious answer then you make a guess, then you test that guess to see if it's viable. If it is then it might lead to the next step in a process that leads eventually to an answer that's the most likely to be right."

"So," Hannah said dismissively, "just lots of guesses then?"

Jamesy's analytical mind bridled at Hannah's rejection of the scientific method but he suppressed his distaste and tried to carry on as diplomatically as he could.

"That's one way of putting it," he ventured, "but, you have to admit, the process seems to work. We never would have walked on the moon otherwise."

"Yes, okay," Hannah said, smiling. "Don't you think though, that if more people searched for answers in Scripture then the world would be a much better place?"

"But surely Scripture can only provide answers up to a point," Jamesy replied. "Can it give you the square root of two, for example?"

It was Hannah's turn to bridle at Jamesy's attitude. "I was talking about meaningful answers," she said. "Answers to important questions about life and about the real things that matter."

"Of course," Jamesy muttered, "I should have realised."

"Are you being patronising?"

"No, no," he frantically tried to explain, "it's just that there's nothing wrong with broadening your horizons, is there? Seek and ye shall find. Isn't that in the Bible?"

"Yes," Hannah replied, a little uncertainly, "it's a verse in Matthew." The verse haunted her because she *had* been seeking. She'd been seeking for a long time. It was the finding part she was having trouble with.

"And that phrase doesn't restrict you to Scripture," Jamesy continued. "Does it?"

"No, I don't suppose it does," said Hannah. She looked troubled. "Okay then," she exclaimed. "Educate me! Explain your theory."

"What theory?"

"Evolution."

"It's not my theory."

"You know what I mean."

"Really, Hannah?" Jamesy sighed. "You want me to explain the Theory of Evolution over lunch?"

"Why not? We're not in any rush, are we?"

"Okay," he said wearily, "but first you have to open your mind a bit."

"What do you mean?"

"Well, you have to accept the possibility that not every word in the Bible is literally true."

Hannah sat up straight. "It's the Word of God," she said. "How can it not be true?"

Jamesy pointed to her lunch. "You're eating a seafood salad," he said.

"Yes, but what does...? Hannah's words trailed away.

"Look, I've read a fair bit of the Bible," said Jamesy, "and doesn't it say in Leviticus that you can't eat prawns?"

Hannah gave a sigh. It was just one of the many

passages in Scripture that she had problems with. Greg had once pointed to passages in both Matthew and Mark where Jesus dismisses the notion of any food being unclean, but then why would God set down instructions that He knew – God was omniscient – He would later rescind?

Greg also explained to her that certain passages of the Bible belonged primarily to a specific period in history and should not be transferred to modern times with any great significance. But then how was she meant to distinguish which passage to follow and which to reject? What criteria should she use? Leviticus describes both homosexuality and shellfish as abominations, but Greg had insisted that one description could be accepted and the other dismissed. On what had he based his conclusions, though?

Hannah had never felt comfortable with the discrimination of people based on their sexuality. She accepted that homosexuals who acted on their desires were sinners, but then the sexual act outside of marriage was a sin for everyone. If gay people were allowed to marry, she wondered, would homosexuality cease to be a sin?

It was just this type of quandary that was causing Hannah's anxiety over her failure to reconcile the words of Scripture with what she experienced in life. She hesitated to believe it might be Satan who was deliberately clouding her understanding, but then what else could it be?

"All right," she relented. "My mind is open."

"You sure?" Jamesy looked uncertainly at Hannah.

"Yes! Go ahead!"

"Okay then," Jamesy began, "I would imagine you've already heard what the basic idea of evolution is."

"Yes," Hannah told him, "we're all descended from monkeys, isn't that right?"

"Well, not exactly."

"But that doesn't make sense, does it," she went on, "because there are still monkeys around, aren't there?"

"You're talking about the modern species of monkeys, aren't you? Well one modern species can't evolve into another modern species. That doesn't make any sense."

"That's what I'm saying."

"But it's not what evolution is saying."

"Okay then," Hannah said, exasperated. "What is evolution saying?"

"Evolution," said Jamesy, trying to collect his thoughts, "simply gives an explanation for how all living things on Earth have developed over billions of years. The progression can be traced in the fossil record and in the different layers in the ground. In the very simplest of terms, the most basic forms of life are found in the bottom layers, which obviously are the furthest back in time, and as we go up through the layers then the different forms of life become ever more diverse and complex." Jamesy glanced at Hannah. "Like I said, though, that's a very sketchy outline. You'd really need to ask a biologist if you want to get more details."

"So, what were Adam and Eve then?" Hannah asked, testily. "Hamsters?"

Jamesy rubbed his forehead. "You're still thinking

in terms of modern species," he said. "You've seen dinosaur fossils, haven't you?"

"Yes, of course."

"Well, dinosaurs don't exist anymore, and there are thousands of other fossils of creatures that also don't exist anymore and that's because over time they evolved into something else. We know this because we can see the progression of one form, in a lower layer of earth, to a slightly different form in a slightly higher layer of earth. Then the higher up the layers we go, the more different the form becomes. Evolution can be a very, very gradual process."

"But that's just the thing," said Hannah. "Where did all these billions of years come from? The Earth hasn't been around that long, has it?"

"Yes," Jamesy stressed, "it has."

"What are you talking about?"

"We know how old the Earth is," said Jamesy. He had known this discussion would happen at some point and he had not been looking forward to it. How was he supposed to convince someone that their ideas about the universe were not just wrong, but wrong by an unimaginable margin. "And it's a wee bit older than you thought it was."

"What do you mean by a 'wee bit'?" asked Hannah.

"About four thousand million years."

"Oh, come on, James," Hannah scoffed. "Seriously?"

"Look, okay," Jamesy conceded. He felt he'd gone as far as he dared. "I'm just letting you know what the mainstream understanding is, all right?" He knew he was ducking out of the argument but he felt it would be wise to take it slow. One small step at a time.

"So, why would the *mainstream* come to an understanding as mad as that?"

"Well, that's another story," Jamesy said, "for another day. Do you want me to order you a coffee?"

"You're being evasive again," Hannah told him.

"I know," he said, "it's one of my more endearing quirks."

Hannah laughed and Jamesy breathed a sigh of relief. He wondered, though, just what the next step in Hannah's journey would be.

Hannah gathered her books together and stood up. She had decided to give up on studying for today, her thoughts were too jumbled. As she left the library she convinced herself that she had been right to call James to tell him she didn't think they should see each other anymore, for it had become inescapable. The whisper-soft breath she could sense on her skin could only be one thing.

It could only be the breath of Satan.

Thirteen

Africa, 1963

Benjamin arrived at his surgery in the afternoon and sat down with a sigh. He had spent yet another fruitless morning at the university trying to discern the reasons for the latest hold-up.

Everyone had been very polite, very courteous, but had told him exactly nothing, and he had returned to his surgery still no further along than when he had first arrived in Kano.

The task he'd been set seemed simple enough when he and a team made up of various medical professionals and administrators had been briefed by members of the World Health Organisation back in Lagos.

They were required to open up a new medical department at the university in Kano that would eventually serve as a template for similar faculties to be set up all over the North. The people of the North, however, seemed to have other ideas.

What Benjamin had gathered from his discussions with Odi was that this was to be expected. The people of the North, Odi had told him, had a distinct character from the people who inhabited the other regions of Nigeria. The majority of the North was formed by the Hausa-Fulani people who had been drifting southwards for millennia from their origins far to the north of Nigeria's current border, bringing with them their religion of Islam.

Nigeria, Benjamin was coming to understand, was a

country in name only. Like many countries in Africa, Nigeria's borders had been drawn by Europeans with no regard for existing tribal boundaries, and had thrown together a host of different peoples, tribes and traditions. The country had three distinct regions: the North, which had the largest geographical area; the West, which was actually in the south-west and which was where the capital, Lagos, was situated and was home mostly to the Yoruba people; and the East, actually in the south-east, where the majority of people were Igbo. The south coast of Nigeria formed the southern border of both the West and the East and held the country's sea ports; Lagos in the West and Port Harcourt in the East.

"So you see," Odi cheerfully explained, "we have the Hausa in the North, the Yoruba in the West and the Igbo in the East. Simple, you see?"

Adanna snorted loudly from her seat at the kitchen table. They were in her and Odi's small apartment in Sabon Gari. She sat reading at the table while Odi and Benjamin were in the lounge area on the other side of the room.

"Did you say something, my sweet?" Odi called to her. He smiled and winked at Benjamin.

"You are the only thing here that is simple," Adanna said. "Have you forgotten the Ebu, the Ouguri, the Bashiri, the Tiv, the-"

"Yes, yes, yes," Odi waved his hand impatiently and looked at Benjamin. "My beautiful girlfriend is pointing out that, yes, there are many tribes besides the Hausa, the Yoruba and the Igbo, but my point is this, you see," he leaned closer, "my point is that we are all Nigerians, and the-"

"Ha!" exclaimed Adanna.

"I fear my delicate flower may be developing an ailment of some sort," Odi told Benjamin. "Did you cough, my cherub?"

Adanna stood up and walked towards the lounge area. She had an intensity that Benjamin found unnerving.

"We are all Nigerians, do you say?" she asked, not expecting an answer. "Then why must we live in Sabon Gari, eh? If we are Nigerians and the Hausa are Nigerians then why do we live in the strangers' quarter? Why can we not live where the Hausa live? Why are Igbo children not allowed to go to Hausa schools? Are we unclean?"

"Of course not, my beloved," Odi grinned, "but you know that the Hausa have their traditions just as we have ours. They are a proud people and they like to do things their own way." Odi turned again to Benjamin. "It's just what I was telling you," he said. "I think you will find it very difficult to make your changes at the university. The Hausa do not like change, you see. They are very set in their ways. Not like the East now. The East is very different. We Igbo demand to be educated, you see. We must always be learning. You will find more schools in the East than in all of the rest of Nigeria."

"Is that true?" Benjamin asked.

"It is probably true," said Odi with his habitual grin. "There is a distinct possibility that it is true."

Adanna sat on the arm of Odi's chair. "Perhaps,"

she said to Benjamin, "you should have gone to the East to set up your medical school. You would have found it much easier there."

"Maybe," said Benjamin, "but I've been sent to Kano, so I have no choice but to do what I can here, in Kano."

"But didn't you say," Odi interjected, "that other members of your team have already left Nigeria? They have given up, isn't that right?"

"Maybe they aren't as stubborn as I am," said Benjamin, smiling. "But, yes, some of my colleagues have been reassigned to other projects, but I believe it is only until the issues at the university have been resolved."

"*If* those issues are resolved," Adanna said.

"Oh, I'm sure they will be," Benjamin replied, "and in the meantime I have the surgery to keep me busy."

"How are things going at the surgery?" Odi asked him.

"Fine," said Benjamin, "It gets busier every day."

"Do you have many Hausa patients?" asked Adanna.

Benjamin thought about it. "Actually, no," he said. "Now that I think about it, most of my patients are from Sabon Gari."

"You see!" Adanna declared firmly. "It is like I told you. The Hausa do not trust strangers."

Benjamin was feeling nervous as his final patient of the day left the surgery. The receptionist at her desk offered to lock up for him but he told her she should just go on home as he had a few things in his office he needed to see to.

When she had gone he went back to his office and sat at his desk. He felt like a schoolboy waiting to go on a date that his friends had arranged for him.

Odi, a telecommunications engineer, had talked with some of his Hausa workmates and had discovered that the girl Benjamin liked was called Jamilah and that she was the daughter of a Kano haulage contractor.

Zara worked as a secretary and was able to make use of a network of other secretaries in the town to make contact with Jamilah and to see if she would be interested in meeting with a handsome Egyptian admirer. It turned out that Jamilah had already noticed the exotic young doctor who would cast furtive glances in her direction as she walked back from the market every day, and arrangements were made for them to meet at a nearby park.

Benjamin felt embarrassed by all the infantile zeal involved on his behalf but still he could not deny his own childish excitement at the prospect of finally speaking to Jamilah. He changed into the crisp, short-sleeved, white shirt that was hanging in his office and, when the specified time approached, he locked up the surgery and walked along Abuja Road to the little park, where he sat down on a bench and waited.

He was not waiting for very long when he saw Jamilah appear from the other end of the park. She was walking with two friends, which Benjamin had expected. It would not have been seemly for a Muslim woman to approach a strange man unaccompanied.

As they got closer, however, Jamilah's friends held

back, giggling, to allow Jamilah to make the final few steps to the bench on her own. Benjamin stood and gave a polite bow, to which Jamilah gave a coy smile and a nod of her head.

"I'm very pleased to meet you," said Benjamin. "My name is Benjamin."

"Nice to meet you. I am Jamilah."

"Would you like to walk with me for a while, Jamilah?"

Jamilah smiled again and nodded her assent, so they walked side-by-side along the dusty path that meandered around the park.

"Tell me about yourself," Benjamin suggested. He was beginning to feel a nervous exhilaration to be actually walking alongside the beauty that had been distracting him almost since he had arrived in Kano. She was even more beautiful up close, he thought.

"What would you like to know?" she asked shyly, before glancing back to her friends who were following a few steps behind.

"Anything at all," Benjamin happily replied. "What are your interests, for example? Do you have work that you do? Is there anything that you wish to do in the future?"

"My!" Jamilah laughed. "That is a lot of questions."

"Sorry," Benjamin said, smiling.

"I have a stall at the market," Jamilah said after a while. "I don't make a lot of money from it, of course, but it is something that I like to do."

"That sounds very interesting," Benjamin told her seriously. "What sort of things do you have on your stall?"

"I sell jewellery. It is just silly stuff that my friends and I make when we have some spare time."

"You make jewellery? Then you are an artist," said Benjamin.

Jamilah laughed. "Not really. It is just a hobby, but we enjoy it all the same. We like to listen to music as well," she said, "especially the new music that is coming from England. Do you like music?"

"Yes, I like music," he answered, "but I'm afraid my tastes are rather more classical than popular."

"Have you heard of The Beatles? They are a wonderful new group from England."

"Yes," he said, "when I was living in England, everyone was talking about The Beatles." In Benjamin's opinion The Beatles did little more than make a lot of painful noise. "They seemed to be very popular."

"You lived in England?"

"In London, yes."

"I would love to live in England," Jamilah said. "I could go to see all these wonderful bands play whenever I wanted to."

"Well, there are many other things that one could see and do in England."

"Yes, of course," she enthused, "my father has visited London and he has told me of streets that are filled with shops devoted only to clothes, or to jewellery, or even just to hats." Jamilah laughed. "Is this actually true?"

"Um? Oh yes, quite true," said Benjamin, feeling a little distracted. Jamilah carried on discussing her love for popular music, for fashion and jewellery and shoes.

She spoke quickly and without pause, allowing Benjamin little room for reply, and after a while his eyes glazed over. Closely followed by his ears. And then his brain.

After their first date, they went through the motions of several more polite and increasingly awkward meetings until Benjamin began to feel like someone who had been entranced by dancing patterns of sunlight, only to realise that, as a cloud passes overhead, he has been staring all the while at a blank wall.

He soon came to view Jamilah as a decorative wine glass that held no wine. Or a shapely violin that was lacking its strings.

Such comparisons, Benjamin knew, were unfair. He was sure that, in the right company, Jamilah would be a positive delight, but he knew that he was not, nor ever would be, the right company.

It came as a great relief, therefore, when Jamilah eventually fluttered away, distracted by the next shiny object that caught her eye.

Odi found this all highly amusing and illustrated the fact by throwing his head back in riotous laughter. Adanna looked at Benjamin with wry amusement and gave Odi a playful slap.

"Do not be so insensitive," she said. "Can't you see the poor doctor is broken-hearted."

"Yes, I can tell," laughed Odi, "by the huge smile on his face."

Zara was the only one who seemed distraught.

"Are you sure, Benjamin," she asked with a look of

concern in her eyes, "that you are not upset?"

"Oh no, not at all," Benjamin was quick to reassure her. "I think it was good to discover so quickly that Jamilah and I are incompatible. I believe that it has saved me a lot of trouble."

Zara smiled. "In that case," she said, "I am very happy for you. Perhaps we should celebrate."

"This woman," Odi stated, suddenly very serious, "is a woman of great wisdom." He turned to face Adanna. "My beloved," he said, "would you do me the great service of going up to the bar and purchasing many beers so that we can celebrate the liberation of our great friend here?"

"My beloved," Adanna replied softly, lowering her gaze, "it is my humble and respectful opinion that the mighty lion that has captured my unworthy heart should get off his fat, lazy behind and go and do it himself."

Odi looked at Benjamin. "This is also a wise woman," he said. "Perhaps we should listen to the women."

Benjamin laughed. "I will give you a hand at the bar," he told his friend. They had found a little place in the middle of Sabon Gari, well away from Jamilah's normal route home, and as Benjamin followed Odi to the bar, he realised that he did feel liberated. He felt that he could now devote his full attention to his problems with an intransigent university, and his task in Kano could begin in earnest.

At the bar, Benjamin listened to all the voices of the crowd. There were some that spoke English, of course, but there were many conversations in Igbo, in Yoruba, in Fula, in Edo, all spoken in a host of different variations and dialects that was the sound of Sabon Gari, the stranger's quarter in the middle of Kano.

Sabon Gari was home to many of the tribes that were now fellow countrymen in the country of Nigeria that had only recently become independent from Britain.

They were now in control of their own destiny. All together. All Nigerians.

And, here in Sabon Gari, all strangers in their own land.

Fourteen

Sean knelt with his hands clasped together and touching his lips. He then pushed himself up and back to sit once more on the hard, polished wood. After a while he stood and rested his knuckles on the back of the wooden bench in front. His body was automatically going through the familiar routine of the Mass as his mind wandered onto other things. Looking across the aisle, he caught a glimpse of Gary standing beside Rosie and looking uncomfortable in his stiff-collared shirt and tie. Gary turned to see Sean watching him and gave an exaggerated grimace. Sean smiled then turned to the front as the familiar old hymn began and everyone sang along.

After the Mass, the crowd of worshippers, smiling, laughing and looking their best, milled around in the grounds of Holy Cross, the pompous old chapel that gazed down, as if in disapproval, at the little streets of Ardoyne. Sean stood chatting with his parents and his sister, Siobhan, but took his leave as he spotted Gary and Rosie coming down the chapel steps.

"Hiya, Rosie," Sean said as he walked over to greet them. "Right there, Gary?"

"Hiya, Sean," said Rosie. Gary tugged dramatically at his shirt collar, then loosened his tie and undid his top button.

"Jesus!" he said. "How do people wear these things?"

"How's it going with you then?" Sean asked Rosie. "You're looking well."

"Aye, I'm sure I am, Sean," Rosie said as she

pressed her hand to the small of her back, "but thanks for letting on. Those seats are murder on the back," she went on. "I feel stiff as hell."

"Pews," said Gary.

"What?"

"Pews," Gary repeated. "The seats. They're called pews."

"Jesus!" Rosie turned to Sean. "See what I have to put up with, Sean?"

"I'm only saying," Gary protested. "The bloody things are called pews!"

"You really put the 'dick' in dictionary, don't you, Gary?" said Rosie. "You trying to show me up in front of Sean?"

"No! Look, I'm just saying that-"

"All right, all right," Sean interrupted, laughing. "So, what plans have you got for the rest of the day then, Rosie?"

"Quiet day," Rosie told him. "Ellie finishes work at lunchtime so we're just going to spend the day together. I'd rather be going out with you two, though."

"I'm sure you and Ellie will have a nice enough day together," Sean assured her.

"If you two can stop gabbing away there," said Gary, "We need to head on here."

"Yeah okay, Gary," Rosie grumbled, "I know you can't wait to get away from me."

Gary put a comforting hand on her shoulder. "It's good that you can see things from my point of view," he said. "It's why we make such a great wee team."

"Piss off!" Rosie said with a grin.

Sean and Gary walked Rosie round to Ellie's house, then headed off towards the Ardoyne Black Taxi rank.

"Where's Seamus then?" Sean asked as they walked.

"Haven't seen him since the funeral," said Gary, "but he phoned the other night and said he'd see us in Lavery's."

"Is he working this morning?"

"Must be."

They joined the taxi queue and Gary pulled off his tie and stuffed it in his pocket. Sean gave him a glance.

"Everything okay with you and Rosie?" he asked.

"Yeah, dead on," Gary said, puzzled by the question. "Why?"

"Oh, no reason," Sean replied. "Just asking, that's all." He looked thoughtful. "You know," he said, "I've never called the chapel seats pews in my life."

"No, neither have I," said Gary. "It's still their fucking name though, isn't it."

So, what had he been expecting? Fireworks? A sweeping orchestral score? A choir of angels? Seamus walked through the centre of town, thinking about the night he had spent with Alan.

It was always going to be a memorable occasion, he thought, being such a new experience, but was it what he was looking for? And what, exactly, *was* he looking for? Was it love's great adventure he sought? Or was it something of a baser nature?

It had been an enjoyable evening, and Alan had been just what Seamus had needed him to be – relaxed and funny and understanding – but Seamus had always felt it would be nothing more than a brief physical interaction with a like-minded individual. And was that it? Was that enough?

Seamus stopped to light a cigarette and then smiled to himself. If some further research was needed, he decided, then that wouldn't be a problem for if there was one thing that the night had confirmed to him was that he was definitely gay.

Any few remaining doubts regarding his sexuality had been dispelled and because of this he felt a new sense of liberation that was exhilarating in its unfamiliarity. He was now free to experience life on his own terms and to experiment with his own desires.

He felt a spring in his step as he strode along Great Victoria Street heading for Lavery's. There was a new confidence to his manner and he enjoyed the sense of happy anticipation for the day ahead.

"What?" Claire was incredulous. "You know Tony?"

"Known him for years," said Bobby.

"Why didn't you say when I told you about him?"

"I'm not sure," Bobby told her. "Well, I wanted to make sure, for one thing. There's more than one Tony Maguire in Belfast, you know."

"More than one Tony Maguire who occasionally works in Dublin and supplies linen to the catering trade?"

"Yeah okay, fair enough. Maybe I just wanted to see how Tone felt about the whole thing. You said he'd stopped getting in touch."

"Well, now we know why, don't we?"

"Yeah, we do." Bobby had explained to Claire that Tone had backed off once he realised that Claire and Bobby were involved.

"Very noble of him," Claire said bitterly.

"Well, it sort of is, isn't it? And anyway, at least you know it had nothing to do with you."

"What did he say then?"

"He said he'd be in touch."

"Oh great," said Claire, "I can hardly bloody wait." She was trying to feign anger, but her sudden burst of happiness was thwarting her efforts and she knew she could never fool Bobby.

"Are you sure you don't want to come along today?" Bobby asked her. They were in Bobby's flat in Belfast's university area and Bobby was just about to head out for the day.

"No, I can't," Claire said, picking up her bag, "I said I'd call up home today."

Bobby walked her out to her car, gave her a hug, and watched her drive off. He then turned and set off in the opposite direction. Towards Lavery's.

"You'd better behave yourself today," Joker warned his brain. He was looking in the bathroom mirror as he got ready for the day ahead, but he was bothered by his muted sense of excitement. He would normally be hopping eagerly from foot to foot on a morning such as this, but his mood today was sanguine, almost sombre.

Still, he reckoned, he knew of a perfect remedy for such despondency and, besides, there was always the secret idea that he was planning to unveil. That should generate some interest, he decided.

The thought of it seemed to cheer him and, as he checked his pockets for keys, wallet and cigarettes before leaving the flat, he felt his mood begin to brighten and the prospects of the coming day began to assume the significance that he would normally have expected.

If only his brain would stop nagging him, he thought. If only for just one day.

Tone had called round to see his mother, but was surprised to see her getting ready to leave the house.

"Are you going out again?" he asked as she pulled on her coat.

"Yes, I am," she said, annoyed by his attitude. "Why shouldn't I go out? You're going out today too, aren't you?"

"Well yeah, but..." Tone wanted to say that he could go out because he hadn't recently buried a spouse but he stopped himself. Although, if he were being honest, what he really wanted to say was that he could go out because he was young and vibrant and he had his whole life ahead of him, whereas she was...She was what? Just hanging around waiting to die? Was that what he believed? The thought was unworthy of him and it was unfair because his mother was not old. She had not yet turned sixty, so why shouldn't she go out? Why shouldn't she enjoy her life? Her husband's life had stopped but hers was still going on, so why was Tone being so negative?

"Look, Anthony," his mother said, "life is too short. Your daddy dying showed me that. Donal too, for that matter."

"What did Donal say?"

"He told me about Donna. He says he doesn't think they're going to get back together, but you never know, do you? But I told him that even if it is the end of his marriage then it doesn't have to mean it's the end of the world. Life goes on, doesn't it?"

Tone felt that his brother had given up on this life and was pinning all his hopes on there being another one, but he kept the thought to himself.

"So where are you off to?" he asked.

"I'm meeting Jessie and Maureen round the club. There's a wee band on today, so, come on, Anthony, I don't want to be late."

Tone left the house with his mother and accompanied her as far as the Falls Road. He gave her a hug and watched her as she set off for the club. She seemed all of a sudden to be filled with strength and life and purpose, and Tone wondered at his feelings on the matter.

He needed a drink, he thought as he held out a hand to hail a Black Taxi, so it was lucky then that the prospect of such a thing was looming large.

The towering spire of the gloomy old gothic chapel looked incongruous in the little street of shops and showrooms and offices, and the colourful clothes of the worshippers spilling into Donegall Street contrasted with the soot-blackened sandstone of a building that seemed to be sinking under its own weight.

Jamesy had gone back to his childhood parish of the

New Lodge to attend Mass with his family and was now standing on the pavement outside listening to the chattering of his sisters and the gossiping of his mother. He and his father exchanged rueful glances, both keen to get away and to start the day's drinking.

Eventually, after much hugging and well-wishing, he was able to peel himself away and make his way through the town, heading towards the south of the city. Hannah dominated his thoughts.

He supposed that he shouldn't have been too surprised when she had called to essentially break up with him. Break up? Was that the right phrase to use? That would suggest they had been in a relationship and Jamesy wasn't sure if that had been the case. Apart from friendly hugs and the occasional chaste kiss on the cheek, there had been no intimate physicality to their…companionship?

Of course, he accepted, they had not been together for very long but, even so, Jamesy felt that it would have required a considerable amount of effort to penetrate Hannah's sense of religious propriety.

And that was why he shouldn't have been surprised that it had all ended so quickly. Hannah's beliefs.

Jamesy had initially been carried away by the strength of his attraction to Hannah, and had believed, naively perhaps, that love would conquer all. Nothing, he had felt, was insurmountable. There was nothing that couldn't be overcome by the sweeping grandeur of his newly discovered passion, but it had not taken long before he had come to understand the scale of the task confronting him.

He soon came to realise that Hannah's beliefs were

so entrenched, so intractable and so deeply woven into the fabric of who she was, that his tentative attempts at chipping away at them were ineffectual. But then, he asked himself, what right did he have to chip away at Hannah's beliefs at all?

Who was he to judge which beliefs were valid and which weren't? Were his own beliefs, as Tone had once pointed out, just as irrational as Hannah's? Hannah's faith was certainly a lot more robust than his own, but then wouldn't that make her faith more valid than his?

Jamesy had never given his faith much thought. His Catholicism, for him at least, was more of a cultural experience than a firmly held set of opinions. So did that make his faith less offensive? Less harmful? Less real?

He knew that the dry theological discussions tumbling around in his head were only there to distract him from the fact that he was in pain.

Nonsensical, irrational pain. He hated feeling this way. There was no physical reason for the clenching agony in his guts, or the overwhelming sense of despair and torpor that draped over him like a blanket. He had always despised the term 'lovesick' and now found himself desperately trying to rationalise the heaviness he felt when Hannah's face, electrified by her smile, came suddenly to mind.

Was that it then? Was that the one great love of his life? And was it now doomed to come to a clattering halt because of irreconcilable differences over beliefs? It seemed unfair to Jamesy. Stupid and pointless and unfair, but he could see no way around it.

He tried to put the matter out of his mind as he reached Shaftsbury Square. Instead of taking the road to the left which led to his flat, he went to the right which would take him to Lavery's bar.

He forced himself to focus on the day that now beckoned. There was a time, he thought, when a Saturday spent in a bar with his friends would not have been considered unusual. A bar would be nominated, a time agreed and everyone would arrive with the unspoken understanding of being in this together to the bitter end. Which would be, generally speaking, closing time. But no longer.

It seemed to Jamesy that life had managed to slither its insidious way into the little circle of friends, corrupting the group dynamic and pulling everyone in different directions. It was no longer usual to lose an entire day to drinking, carousing, cajoling and laughing. It just didn't happen anymore. Jamesy pulled open the door to Lavery's and was greeted with chaos.

Today was different though, he thought. Today was Saint Patrick's Day.

Fifteen

He had never had any great desire to go to Dartmouth but, he thought bitterly, it was a family tradition. His father had served as a midshipman on escort missions during the Battle of the Atlantic, while his grandfather had fought at Jutland.

If he delved back far enough, he supposed, then he would likely find some ancestor who had taken a three-decker through the French and Spanish lines at Trafalgar, or had sailed with Drake into the Bay of Cadiz. The history of the Royal Navy was irrevocably entwined with the history of his own family so it was only natural that he should continue the tradition.

It had come as a bit of a shock, therefore, when the Britannia Royal Naval College at Dartmouth had quietly but firmly insisted that, halfway into his second year, he should pack his bags and leave. A shock to his parents that is, for as far as Simon Jippsen-Phillips was concerned, it hadn't been a shock at all.

Too many complaints to his superiors, he reflected. Too many little incidents, too many personal items that went missing, too many suspicions and accusing whispers, too many pointless misdemeanours that accumulated to the inescapable conclusion: he was not Royal Navy material.

From the window of his South Belfast apartment he watched the river make its unhurried way to the docks and to the sea beyond, and he remembered how he had looked down, from his parents' back lawn, to another river in another life as he broke the disappointing news. He remembered how he had enjoyed his father's spluttering anger and his mother's speechless disbelief. He had relished their shock. Revelled in it.

He knew that the senseless acts of disobedience that coloured his time in Dartmouth could be put down to youthful rebellion, but he had hated the Royal Navy He hated the idea of it, the stuffiness of it all, the stultifying aura of propriety and protocol. And he hated his parents for their blithe assumption that he would toe the line, that he would simply do what he was told with no questions asked.

He sighed as he sipped his tea and went to sit down. There were many things in his life that he hated, or had hated, or would probably hate at some point in the future, but there was one thing he hated most of all; he hated his bloody nickname.

It was only Michael who called him Jippo – no one else would dare – but it still grated. He knew that he had a lot to be thankful to Michael for, but he didn't feel that that should excuse such disrespect.

Simon had landed in Belfast over five years ago, after a spate of menial jobs on a variety of cargo ships, and had met Michael in a bar by the docks. They had discovered an instant rapport and Michael had taken him under his wing and had introduced him to the city's underworld, where Simon had thrived. He had often wondered if criminality, or malevolence, or whatever you wanted to call it, was something that a person is born with. He certainly could not point to a deprived upbringing, or any of the other standard excuses, for his own tendency to lean towards the less legal side of life, so was it just in his nature? Was it who he was?

There were those who would accuse him of dodging his responsibilities, of taking the easy way out to coast through life. If that were true, though, then he was working awfully hard to avoid working hard. Simon liked the fine things in life. His beautiful apartment was furnished with impeccable taste, he had his eye on a new Porsche, even the tea he was drinking was a special blend that was sent over from Fortnum and Mason in London, but, he understood, he could have acquired all of these things and more if he had simply followed the road his family had laid out for him. So why all the crime? He shrugged. Maybe it was just something he enjoyed.

He was now second only to Michael in the organisation, helped, he believed by the respect afforded by his English Home Counties accent and by his natural officer-class bearing – a family tradition and all that – but he could never feel satisfied; there were always things that needed to be done. He gingerly put a finger to the bridge of his nose. It still felt tender and misshapen, even though the attack which had shattered it had taken place months ago, at Christmastime.

That was something that would have to be addressed at some point, but he believed that he had that matter well in hand and was simply waiting for a suitable opportunity to present itself.

A few other tasks shuffled for priority in his mind, though there was one idea in particular that kept coming to the fore. He had given only brief consideration to this idea in the past but, just lately, he had been looking upon it with a cooler eye.

Plans began to form in his mind. Possibilities and consequences were played out and addressed, and a coherent strategy took shape.

He would need to involve someone from the organisation, he thought. No one significant, of course. No one important. In fact, it would be preferable if it were someone who was almost invisible. A nonentity. Someone completely pliable and easily coerced.

A halfwit, in other words.

He already had someone in mind.

Sixteen

Wee Paulie knew that wearing anything green today would mark him out as a Catholic, so he felt that the dark green socks he wore would be a concession to his heritage while still being subtle enough to go unnoticed in loyalist Tate's Avenue.

Mr Jippsen-Phillips had told him he could have the night off, so he told Gemma to get herself dolled up because she was about to get wined and dined.

"You *have* to go out on Saint Patrick's Day," he told her. "I think it's actually the law."

"Where did you have in mind?" Gemma asked.

"We could go to that new French place on the Lisburn Road."

"Oh, very fancy," said Gemma. "It'll probably be expensive, though."

"Doesn't matter," Wee Paulie declared grandly. "Like I said, I'm becoming a bit of a big deal these days. Mr Jippsen-Phillips talks to me all the time, you know, and not just about work stuff either. He asks me about all sorts of things."

"As long as you're not getting involved in anything too dangerous," said Gemma. She had long ago accepted the fact that her boyfriend was a hood but she felt that as long as Wee Paulie confined himself to those areas where the distinction between what was and wasn't legal remained a little hazy, then there shouldn't be a problem. And, besides, everyone had to make a living in some way, didn't they?

"Nah, me and Mr Jippsen-Phillips are above all that sort of stuff," he explained. "We leave all the dirty work to the goons."

"Well, in that case, I'd better start getting ready. I'm not sure I've got anything classy enough to wear to that French place though."

"You'd look classy in anything," Wee Paulie said sincerely. He really knew how to turn on the charm, he told himself. Gemma laughed dismissively, though she was pleased, and she went off to get ready.

"I can't believe all the different places that are opening up these days," Gemma said as they walked, arms linked, along the Lisburn Road. "I can remember when I was a kid there'd just be a chippy, and that would be about it."

"Aye," Wee Paulie agreed, "I know what you mean. Belfast has really taken off the last couple of years, hasn't it? It's starting to look like a proper city all of a sudden, instead of the ghost town it used to be."

"Why do you think that is though?"

"Money!" said Wee Paulie with some authority. "It's all about money. The paramilitaries have had their day, you see. They're just a spent force these days and people are fed up with them, so now it's the hoods' turn to come forward. The future is ours for the taking.

"I reckon Mr McClelland and Mr Jippsen-Phillips have got big plans for the future, you know. They'll know exactly where the big opportunities are going to be, you can take my word for it. I would say they're really going to take off in the years to come, and guess who's going to be right there along with them."

"Ooh, let me think," said Gemma, laughing. She

knew she shouldn't get too carried away by Wee Paulie's wild flights of fancy, but maybe on this Saint Patrick's Day, as they strolled along to a fancy restaurant, looking their best, she could indulge him just a little.

She held him a little closer and allowed herself to dream that, just perhaps, the future really was theirs for the taking.

Seventeen

"And the bar was still open?" Tone was asking.

"Yeah, that's what I'm saying," said Seamus. "The bar was still open and there he was, out like a fucking light."

"Jesus!"

"I know!" Seamus exclaimed. They were trying to hold on to their place at the bar as the crowd jostled and swayed around them. "Do you not think he's been acting a bit weird lately?"

"More than usual, you mean?"

"Yeah, do you not think he's been a wee bit subdued, a bit quieter than normal?"

Tone glanced behind him to see Joker standing on a table. He was stomping his feet and clapping his hands while singing *The Star of The County Down.* Tone turned back to Jamesy.

"Now that you mention it," he said, "I suppose he has been a bit subdued. What do think it is then? Anything in particular?"

"Well, he was going on about Carol for a bit."

"Carol?" Tone finally caught the attention of one of the harassed-looking bar staff and was able to place his order. "You think he's still hung up on Carol?"

"Could be," said Seamus. "I mean, wouldn't you be?"

"Yeah, but…" Tone thought for second. "He hasn't said anything to me about it."

"I know, but this is Joker we're talking about. He probably doesn't even realise it himself, does he? He only mentioned her when he was totally out of it, probably doesn't even remember."

"So what was he saying about her then?".

"That's the funny thing," Seamus said, "he said she was far, far away."

"What?" Tone frowned. "Far, far away? What the fuck is that supposed to mean?"

"Who knows?"

The last two pints of the order were placed on the bar and Tone handed over his money. Once he had received his change, he and Seamus ferried the drinks back to their table.

"Get that eejit off the table," Tone demanded. "He's going to fucking spill something."

Joker, realising that beer had arrived, was only too happy to sit back down. He passed around some cigarettes and lit one for himself. The table served as a little island of relative calm in a stormy ocean of drunken, dancing revelry as a nation celebrated its conversion from one set of beliefs to another.

"Cheer up, Jamesy," said Joker. "You miserable wee bastard!"

"Yeah, so what the hell happened?" asked Sean. "I thought everything was going okay with you two."

Jamesy took a sip of his beer and shrugged. "I don't know," he said, "maybe I was moving things a bit too fast."

Joker nodded with understanding. "Did you slip the hand?" he asked.

Jamesy gave Joker a look. "No, I don't mean that," he said. "I was just trying to open her eyes a wee bit, you know?"

"What do you mean?" Seamus asked. "Open her

eyes? What, like in a sexual way?"

"What? No! What's wrong with you? There was nothing like that going on."

"Yeah," Bobby exclaimed, "this is my cousin we're talking about here, so just watch what you're saying." He turned to Jamesy "So, when you say there was nothing going on, do you mean absolutely nothing?"

"Yes," Jamesy sighed, "there was nothing going on."

"Told you!" Tone declared smugly.

"What?"

"Oh nothing, Jamesy," said Tone hurriedly. "What was it you were saying?"

"So what you're trying to say, Jamesy," Joker began, "is that, apart from you having a wee grope, there was absolutely no sex involved with you and Hannah? Is that right?"

Everyone at the table leaned forward. Jamesy rolled his eyes and took a drink.

"Well?" Gary prompted.

"Well what?" said Jamesy. "There's nothing to say about it. We never had sex, okay? Is that what you wanted to hear?"

"You mean apart from you-"

"No, Joker, there was nothing, okay? In fact, we never even…" Jamesy paused.

"Never even what?" asked Bobby.

"Well, we never even really had a kiss, to be honest."

Everyone stared at Jamesy. "So, when you say you've split up," said Tone, "you mean you were never really together in the first place."

"Not really," Jamesy replied glumly. "Not in the way that you mean anyway."

"So, what did you mean by 'opening her eyes' then?" asked Seamus.

"Well, I think it was at lunch the other day," Jamesy told him. "I was trying to explain the Theory of Evolution to her and I was probably-"

"Well, there's your problem," Joker exclaimed. "You've over-stimulated the poor wee girl. Jesus, it's no wonder she split up with you, is it? She probably couldn't handle any more excitement."

"She didn't take it well then?" Tone suggested.

"Obviously not," Jamesy reflected.

"Pity, that," said Tone. "I actually thought she had a bit of potential. She didn't come across as being completely brainwashed, you know? So how much reality did you explain to her? Did you point out all of the mass extinctions in history that the Bible fails to mention."

"No, Tone," Jamesy said miserably. "I didn't want to overwhelm her with talk of asteroids or Ice Ages, you know? I just thought it would be best to take it slow. Although, for all the good it's done me…"

"Well you know, Jamesy," Tone said decisively. "If you want to knock over a house of cards then it's best to just open a bloody window."

"Well, Jamesy," Joker suddenly exclaimed, "you know what you could with, don't you? You know what we all could do with, don't you?"

"Bobby," Tone said, "could you not have a word with Hannah?"

"Don't see what it has to do with me," Bobby told

him. "I don't really have much to do with that side of the family."

"Yeah I know, but-"

"Did nobody fucking hear me?" Joker said loudly.

"What the fuck is he waffling about?" asked Tone from the other end of the table.

Everyone around the table looked at Joker.

"Thank you," he said, straightening up. "Well," he went on, "I suggest that we could all do with a holiday." He paused to observe the expectant faces around the table.

"You've obviously got something in mind," said Gary.

"I certainly do," Joker proudly announced. "We all knew that the World Cup idea was never going to take off, didn't we? Well, it just so happens that I took it upon myself to make alternative arrangements." He calmly took a drink to build up a little bit of tension. "I've been talking to Johnny Gee," he continued, "and it turns out that-"

"Who?" asked Sean.

"Johnny Gee," Joker repeated. "You know Johnny Gee, he's the-"

"He means Weasel," Gary said to Sean.

"Yeah, well anyway-" said Joker.

"Who's Weasel?" Bobby asked Gary.

"Weasel was a guy we knew at school," Sean told Bobby. "He was sound enough, like. Can't remember where his nickname came from though."

"Aye," Bobby said thoughtfully, "nicknames are like that. I knew a guy once, from round our way, and he was-"

"Look, would you all just shut the fuck up and listen!" Everyone turned back to Joker. "Right," he said, "Where was I?"

"You were talking about Johnny Gee," Gary reminded him.

"Why are you calling Weasel Johnny Gee?" asked Tone. "His name's Kevin."

"Well, that's the thing," said Gary. "Me and Joker met him at-"

"Oh, for fuck's sake!" cried Joker. "Look, it doesn't fucking matter, okay? It doesn't matter what he's called. Johnny Gee, Weasel or whatever. He could be called Percy Fucking Titwhistle for all I care, but the point is-"

"Titwhistle?" asked Bobby. "Where the hell did that come from?"

"I think it was one of those old Ealing comedies," Sean said to Bobby. "*The Titwhistle Express* or something, it was called."

"No, Sean," Tone corrected. "You're thinking of *The Titfield Thunderbolt*, which starred Stanley Holloway. He was one of the-"

"Shut up!" Joker shouted. "Would you all just shut the fuck up, okay? Look, the point is this, right? The point I'm making is that Johnny…is that this wee mate of mine has got access to a beach-house in Spain."

That got everyone's attention. "A beach-house?" Gary asked. "What sort of beach-house?"

"Well, it's…" Joker hadn't been expecting the question, "it's, well it's, you know, it's just your normal sort of beach-house. It's got all the…What kind of stupid, fucking question is that? What sort of beach-house? It's in a tree, halfway up a bloody mountain, it's *that* sort of fucking beach-house!"

"When you say he has access," Tone began, "then what do-?"

"His parents actually own it."

"Well, this is starting to get interesting," said Tone, getting interested.

"Do you have anything specific in mind then?" Seamus asked Joker.

"As a matter of fact, I do." Joker leaned forward and rested his elbows on the table. Everyone else leant closer. "What I suggest is this," said Joker. "We're all going to be off on the Monday and Tuesday after Easter, right? So, I say we take off the rest of that week and head off for a holiday in the sun. The accommodation's already sorted, so we just need flights and beer money."

Everyone was silent as they mulled it over. The idea, everyone decided, had actual potential.

"And we can still use the stag do excuse, can't we?" Gary suggested.

"I don't see why not," said Joker.

"What does Kevin say about this?" asked Tone.

"Who?" said Bobby with a grin.

"Don't start that again," Joker groaned. "Anyway, you can ask him yourselves."

"What do you mean?"

"I told him to meet us here today, so he said he'd be along later."

"Well, I'm up for a week in Spain," Tone declared.

"Yeah," said Sean, "I'm free that week."

"And me," Bobby added.

"Count me in," said Seamus.

"Well," Gary joined in, "I'm hardly going to miss my own stag do, am I?"

Everyone looked at Jamesy. He looked at each of them in turn and shrugged. "I obviously have nothing on that week," he said.

"Right," Joker announced as he stood up. "This calls for a drink."

Johnny Gee arrived a few hours later and joined the company at the table.

"Right," said Tone, once a new round of drinks had been acquired, "first things first. There'll be no more of this Johnny Gee business, okay? It's either Kevin or Weasel. Your choice."

"Kevin," said Kevin.

"Kevin it is then," agreed Tone. He passed his cigarettes around the table and the smokers all lit up. "Right, so," Tone looked at Kevin, "presumably you're aware that Joker only asked you to come along today because of his shamelessly mercenary attitude with regards to a beach-house in Spain, is that right?"

"Well yeah, I'd figured that," said Kevin with a vague smile.

"Okay then," said Tone. "Now Joker has suggested the possibility of us all spending the week after Easter in this beach-house, and I want to hear what your opinion is on the matter."

"What do you mean by 'shamelessly mercenary attitude', Tone?" asked Joker, disgruntled. "Johnny Gee's a mate of mine."

"Kevin!" said everyone.

"Oh right, Kevin. Why does everybody keep changing their fucking names around here?"

"Never mind that," said Tone, turning back to Kevin. "Well, Kevin, what do you reckon?"

Kevin seemed a little nervous under Tone's interrogation. He shifted in his chair before answering. "Yeah," he said, "Joker's already talked to me about that week and it shouldn't be a problem. In fact," he went on, "it could actually work out well because my folks have just bought a townhouse in the area and I was supposed to go out there anyway to make a start on clearing it out. You could all give me a hand with it."

Tone nodded. He liked the sound of that. He had been feeling slightly uncomfortable with the thought that they would be taking advantage of someone with whom they would not normally socialise, just because of his parents' money, but now they would be doing him a favour and that, thought Tone, was something he could go along with.

"Sounds good to me," he said, and everyone agreed. "So, whereabouts is it then?"

Kevin explained that the beach-house was on the east coast of Spain, just south of Valencia, in a place called Tavernes de la Valldigna. The beach and the town, where Kevin's parents had bought their new townhouse, shared the same name, though the town lay several kilometres further inland.

Kevin went on to paint a picture of uninterrupted blue skies, of hot sands and lazy, lapping waves, and smiling señoritas and sangria and ice-cold San Miguel, and, while outside the gentle tears of Saint Patrick lovingly washed the Emerald Isle, the thoughts and dreams around the table turned south to the golden glow of Saint James.

To where the scents of jasmine and orange blossom mingled in the warm air and danced to the chirping of cicadas.

To Spain.

Eighteen

Africa 1963

As the weeks wore on, Benjamin became increasingly frustrated. The authorities at the university had finally consented to the allocation of some buildings he could use to set up his new facility, but when he had gone along to inspect them he realised they were totally unsuited to his needs. They were little more than dilapidated cattle sheds, but when Benjamin had raised his objections it was made to look like he was the one who was being unreasonable.

He had tried to explain the situation to his superiors in Lagos, but it was impossible to convey, over the telephone, the apparent lack of interest and the sometimes open hostility he faced from the university administration.

It also didn't help, he thought, that the whole initiative was so unwieldy. Although partly backed and co-funded by the World Health Organisation, the project was hugely ambitious as it tried to encompass the entire continent in a spirit of cooperation between the established and emerging African states. Which in itself, Benjamin believed, was based on deliriously unfounded optimism.

There seemed to be no coherent guidelines to follow, no proper set of protocols to abide by in what was little more than a chaotic structure, seemingly riddled with in-fighting and corruption.

In fact, it was a surprise to Benjamin that he was still able to draw a salary, and that was probably why he had held on for so long in Kano. But his patience was beginning to run out. He was contemplating taking a flight to Lagos to try to find someone in charge who could tell him exactly what was going on, and if he could get no satisfactory answers there then it might even be time to return to England.

This, he felt, would be a last resort however, for he had given up his job there and had sold his flat, so returning to London would be like starting from scratch.

He had learnt that his old friend, Henry, had also left London to go and care for his ailing parents back in his home town, so there was not much remaining in London to tempt Benjamin back there. And besides, he thought, he had come to love being in Africa.

These were the thoughts going round in his head when the door to his apartment shook with a furious hammering.

"Benjamin! Oh, Dr Maher! Please! Please!"

Benjamin pulled open the door and was surprised to see Zara standing, tearful and shaking on the threshold.

"Zara," he said as he led her inside and closed the door. "What is it? What's happening?"

"It is Odi," she managed to say between sobs, "I think that they will kill him."

"What do you mean?" Benjamin guided her to an armchair, while he knelt in front of her and held onto her hand. "Where is Odi?"

"We do not know," she cried. "He went out to try to help but he has not come back. Adanna is terrified. Odi has not come back and Adanna is afraid of what has happened."

"All right, Zara," Benjamin said soothingly. "Take it slowly. Try to calm down and explain what is going on."

Zara nodded, gave a weak smile through her tears, and tried to explain.

Whether the rumours were true or not was irrelevant. It was believed that a young Hausa woman had been attacked and raped in broad daylight by a gang of young men. According to the rumours, Zara told Benjamin, the young men were all Igbo from Sabon Gari and the Hausa were now looking for vengeance.

Zara explained that several groups of Hausa men had entered Sabon Gari and were attacking any Igbo that they found. As the Igbo tried to defend themselves, the violence had escalated and was threatening to engulf all of Sabon Gari, so Odi had gone to see if he could help to calm the situation.

"But he has not returned," cried Zara.

"Where is Adanna?" Benjamin asked calmly.

"She is in their apartment. She wanted to look for Odi but I said it was too dangerous. I said I would come and find you. I said that you would know what we should do."

"Yes, yes, Zara, you did the right thing." Benjamin tried to be reassuring but he wasn't sure what he was expected to do. "What about the police?" he asked.

Zara shook her head. "The police are mostly Hausa," she said, "and the crowds are too big for them to control. Oh, Benjamin, what should we do?"

Benjamin crossed the room and opened a window. Odi and Adanna's apartment was on the other side of Sabon Gari, but as he listened he could make out distant shouts and muffled crashes and bangs. A sudden terrified scream chilled him.

He closed the window and turned to Zara. "Come," he said. "We must go to Adanna. We'll make sure she is safe. Perhaps Odi has returned by now."

Zara, still shaking, took a tissue and wiped her face. Benjamin led her by the hand and they tentatively walked outside and into the madness of the night.

Adanna was frantically pacing the floor of her apartment, alert to every sound that rose from the streets, when there was a loud knock at the door.

"Adanna!" Zara called. "Let us in! Please!"

She opened the door, and Zara and Benjamin hurried inside. Zara, weeping, threw her arms around Adanna.

"What is happening?" Adanna pleaded. "Have you seen Odi?" She then noticed that Benjamin was holding a blood-stained handkerchief to his left ear. "You are hurt?" she cried. The desperation and panic were clear in her voice.

"It's nothing," Benjamin told her. "Some people were just throwing stones, that's all."

"Oh, Adanna," Zara cried, "we saw many places that had been set on fire. There are Hausa everywhere."

"Did you see any police?" Adanna asked.

"Some," said Benjamin, "but they seemed to be keeping well back. I don't think we can expect much help from them."

"And Odi?" she begged.

Benjamin shook his head. "It is impossible at the moment," he said. "There are too many crowds, too much chaos."

"Then what do we do?" she demanded, suddenly angry. "We have to do something. We can't just sit here."

"We have no choice," Benjamin insisted. "It is far too dangerous to go outside. The best thing we can do for Odi is to be here when he gets back. We would not be helping if we went outside and got…and got caught up in the violence."

Adanna slumped into a chair. Zara sat on the floor and put her head in Adanna's lap.

"Trust me," said Benjamin. "The only thing that we can do is to sit tight and hope that this insanity will run its course."

As they waited through the long night, the sounds of the unrest came clear and harsh from the streets and ensured that their eyes remained open and their nerves remained taut. On top of the screams and the crackling flames and the gunshots and the shattering glass, came the constant chanting of the Hausa.

"Allahu Akbar! Allahu Akbar!"

Benjamin sat with his head in his hands and prayed for the dawn.

After a sleepless night, they ventured out to a to scene of destruction, with smouldering fires and broken glass everywhere. Benjamin suggested they all go to the police station to see if they could garner any information regarding Odi's whereabouts. They first made their way to Benjamin's apartment to pick up his car and then Benjamin drove them to the station on Sabon Gari's southern fringe.

Zara preferred to wait in the car while Benjamin and Adanna went inside. They were greeted with crowds of angry people from Sabon Gari remonstrating with harassed police officers, demanding to know why the night's events had been allowed to rage unchecked.

Benjamin and Adanna made their way through the crowd and eventually encountered a senior official at a desk in the back. He appeared nonchalant and relaxed, and responded to Benjamin's enquiries about Odi with a wave of his hand.

"We are holding no one of that description," he told them.

"But, surely you must know something," Benjamin insisted. "It is most unusual for him not to return home all night."

"Then I suggest that you try the hospital," the official replied impatiently. "Many of the injured have been taken there."

"The hospital?" The thought had already crossed Benjamin's mind but he hadn't wanted to voice his fears to Adanna. She stood quietly by his side as he turned to face her. "Perhaps we should try the-"

"Or you could try the market," the official continued.

"The market?" asked Benjamin, puzzled.

"Yes," the official said, "some of the sheds there have been allocated to hold the bodies."

Benjamin sensed Adanna physically weaken at his

side. *Bodies?*

"Now as you can see, we are extremely busy so if you could just…" Benjamin and Adanna were ushered outside and they slowly made their way to the car.

"Well?" Zara asked as they climbed into the front seats. Her cheeks were still streaked with tears. "Did you find out anything?"

"Odi is dead," Adanna said flatly.

"We don't know that," said Benjamin. "We will try the hospital."

They went straight to the hospital, but after more than an hour of desperate searching they could find no trace of Odi. As they walked back to the car, Benjamin insisted they should eat something before they continued their search. He found a stall and bought them all some roasted corn which they took back to eat in the car.

"You look tired, Zara," Adanna said, looking in the mirror. "You should go home to try to get some sleep."

"How can I sleep?" Zara pleaded.

Adanna did not reply. She took small nibbles of food and stared blankly through the windscreen, already resigned to what she would find at the market.

She spotted Odi almost immediately. He lay close to the end of a row of broken and disfigured corpses. Despite the mutilation inflicted on his body, Adanna could recognise the shirt she had bought him at this very market, the wine stain still visible on the pocket. She made her way calmly through the hysterical wives and daughters and mothers who were crowding the shed, and identified Odi to one of the officials trying to impose some order.

Benjamin caught up to Adanna and stared in disbelief at the body of his friend. None of it seemed real.

"Very well then," the official was telling Adanna, "but you must take him. You cannot leave him here."

"Adanna," Benjamin put his hands on Adanna's shoulders and looked into her eyes. She gazed at him without seeing. The light in her eyes was gone. "Adanna," he repeated, "I'm going to take you and Zara home, you understand? You must go home and try to rest. I will come back here and see to all the…all the requirements. Do you hear me?"

Benjamin led her to the car and then drove her and Zara to Adanna's apartment where he left them both to their grief and shock. He got back in the car and, resting his forehead on the top of the steering wheel, he began to physically shake.

Once he had calmed down, he started the ignition and, with a deep sigh, headed back to the market.

After the attack on the Igbo, all of Kano felt heavy with menace. It was as if the true feelings of the North towards the people from the East were no longer held in check and were now exposed like an open wound. Adanna and Zara, on returning to work, had both felt an unspoken hostility in occasional glances or deliberate stares from the Northerners of Kano.

Benjamin made all the arrangements for Odi's burial, consulting occasionally with Adanna, who had been behaving in a resigned, almost serene, manner since the day at the market.

As the arrangements were being made, Zara asked Adanna if it would not be preferable to take Odi back to the East for burial in the Igbo homeland, but Adanna had said no.

Odi, she said, did not have any family back in the East and, besides, he had always regarded himself as Nigerian.

"This," she told Zara, as she gestured all around her, "this is Odi's homeland."

There were few mourners at the graveside. Some of Odi's workmates had come along, though none of them, Adanna noted, were Hausa. A few of Adanna's friends and colleagues were there, standing with Benjamin and Zara, as the pastor said the usual words of condolence and consolation, and then, before anyone truly had time to process the fact, Odi was gone.

It was in the days that followed that Benjamin made a decision to leave Kano. It wasn't just the intransigence of the university that had swayed him; he had also been witnessing a rise in patients at the surgery who had been victims of random attacks in and around Sabon Gari. They had all been Igbo and had suffered unprovoked beatings from groups of young Hausa men who had begun to roam the area. Benjamin felt that someone should make a direct report of the incidents to the authorities in Lagos.

Adanna also came to the conclusion that she could no longer stay in Kano. Without Odi's salary she would have to find a cheaper apartment and, even though Zara had suggested she could move in with her, Adanna decided it was time for her to return to her family in the East. It had always been her intention to return there with Odi once they had made enough money in the North, but now she could see no reason for her to remain in a city that was now pulsing with an atmosphere of dread and persecution.

When the day came for Adanna to leave, Benjamin and Zara placed her luggage in Benjamin's car and they drove to the train station together.

"I cannot believe you are going," Zara said as she hugged Adanna on the station concourse. "And Benjamin will be leaving too. What am I going to do without you both?"

"You will be fine," Adanna told her. "And you have my mother's address so we can keep in touch." She turned to Benjamin. "Thank you for everything you have done, Dr Maher," she said, shaking his hand. "I don't suppose I shall see you again."

"No," said Benjamin, "I hadn't thought of it but I don't suppose you shall. I'm not sure where I will end up after I've been to Lagos."

Zara wept as she watched her friend board the train while, beside her, Benjamin waved as he felt a sudden surge of admiration for the tall, stately figure who had unsettled him with her intensity.

Adanna found a seat, made herself comfortable, and then broke down in tears as the train took her south and east to the land of the Igbo, to her family and her people, and to where the Hausa could not reach.

Nineteen

"Well? What do you reckon?" asked Joker. He was holding up a pair of swimming briefs.

Tone gave them his consideration. The thought of those tiny, fluorescent yellow speedos stretched over Joker's pasty skin was making him feel queasy.

"Yeah," he said, "I can see you in those."

"Really?"

"Yeah, you'd look class."

"Not sure about the colour though."

"What, jaundice? You don't like jaundice?"

"Don't know if it would really bring out my eyes."

"Good point," said Tone. "You're looking for more of a bloodshot with a hint of nicotine shade, aren't you?"

"You're just taking the piss."

"I thought we both were."

Joker sighed and placed the briefs back on the rack. "It's important to make an impression on the beach, you know."

"I don't think you've got anything to worry about there," said Tone as they strolled down the swimwear aisle. "Not with your general demeanour."

"You think I've got a demeanour?"

"Well, it's more of a misdemeanour."

"What do you think of these?" Joker had stopped to look at a pair of shorts. Tone stared hard at the fluffy clouds and cartoon palm trees that were splashed all over the garishly coloured shorts, then turned to look at Joker.

"Seriously?" he asked. "Did you forget to bring

your eyes out with you today?"

"You're not helping, you know," said Joker.

"Well, what is it that you're looking for?"

"Oh, I don't know," Joker said wearily. "I was just thinking I should maybe shake things up a bit for going away, you know? Go for a new image. A new *me* type of thing."

"And you think that looking like a wanker is the way to go?"

"Is that your idea of constructive criticism?"

"It is actually, yes."

"Well, what have *you* got then?" Joker pointed to the two items of clothing that Tone was carrying. "A blue T-shirt and a white T-shirt? Do you not think you've gone a wee bit too crazy there, you flash bastard?"

"What's wrong with these?" said Tone defensively. "These are classics! You can't go wrong with classics!"

"There's nothing classic about playing it safe. It just means you can't be bothered to make an effort, that's all."

"Look, just pick a pair of bloody shorts, will you? It can't be that difficult."

Joker picked up a standard pair of blue shorts. "These'll have to do," he said grumpily.

"Right then, are we done?"

"Oh hang on," Joker said suddenly. "Now we're talking!" He walked over to a rail that held a row of short-sleeved shirts. "Now this is what I'm talking about."

"That's actually not a bad shirt," said Tone.

"Not a bad shirt? You're kidding me, aren't you? It's bloody spectacular."

"Right, okay then, just grab it and we'll go."

"You know what?" Joker was admiring the shirt as they walked to the tills. "They'd love this round at the Parliament. I'm actually going to feel sorry for all of you, having to walk beside me wearing this shirt. You're all going to look like a bunch of sad losers, aren't you?"

"Well, we all have our crosses to bear, don't we?"

"Is there anywhere else you wanted to go after Primark?"

"What, shopping wise you mean?" asked Tone. "Nah, I think I'm all shopped out for the day."

"Yeah," Joker agreed as they waited in the queue, "I know what you mean, makes you thirsty, doesn't it?"

"It certainly does."

They walked with their shopping through the centre of town until Joker, realising that Tone had come to an abrupt halt, stopped and looked behind him. He could see Tone staring through the window of a café, and, curious, he walked back towards him.

"Fancy a cup of tea?" Tone asked him. It wasn't what Joker fancied at all.

"A cup of tea? What do you…?" He looked in the window. "Oh," he said.

Hannah thought about pretending she hadn't seen them but it would have been pointless, as they walked straight over to the table.

"Hannah!" Tone cried happily. "And Greg too, my

old mate. How are you doing?"

"All right there, Hannah love?" said Joker. "Right there, Greg? Solved any mysteries lately?"

"What?"

"Oh, nothing, nothing," Joker said, as he pulled a chair over to the table. "Don't mind if we barge in, do you?"

"Actually, we were-"

"It's funny, so it is," Tone began as he sat down at the table, "but we were just talking about you, weren't we, Joker?"

"Were we?"

"We were just saying that..." A waitress came over and placed a teapot and two cups down on the table.

"Your food's on its way," she told Greg and Hannah, and then looked expectantly at Tone and Joker.

"I'll just have a cup of tea too please," Tone told her.

"Aye, me too," said Joker. The waitress went off, and Tone carried on.

"We were just saying that it's a real shame that you and Jamesy split up," he said to Hannah. "You seemed to get on well together."

"I know," said Hannah, "but it was never going to work."

"Why's that then?" Joker asked her.

"Well," she said, "I just think that we were too different. I don't think that James is able to accept the truth of the Bible."

"Yeah, he's a bugger for that, isn't he?" said Tone, slapping his knee. "I've always said that, haven't I,

Joker?"

"No."

"I've always said that Jamesy's a real bugger for not accepting the truth of things."

Greg gave Hannah a quick glance. He seemed uncomfortable, which surprised Tone. Tone had assumed that Greg would relish any opportunity to confront the ungodly, but he looked as if he wished he were elsewhere.

The waitress appeared with a tray. She placed two plates of food in front of Hannah and Greg, along with tea for Tone and Joker. Tone paid for the tea and turned back to Hannah as the waitress left.

"You know what you should do, you know?" he began, but then Greg interrupted.

"It sounds to me that James, whether he's aware of it or not, is being influenced by Satan."

"Why would Satan want to do that?" asked Tone.

Greg gave Tone a pitying look. "Satan is a constant force in the world," he explained. "We have to be vigilant for any signs of temptation. It was lucky that Hannah recognised her tempter before it was too late. It's possible that Satan was trying to work through James."

"You've really got it in for this Satan character, haven't you?" said Tone.

"Satan was never meant to be a proper noun, by the way," Joker interjected, sipping his tea. "It's just an old Hebrew word that means adversary, so you may want to slip a wee definite or indefinite article in there somewhere."

"Oh, I'm sure Greg knows that," Tone said, looking

at Greg. "The Bible even refers to an angel of the Lord being a satan at one point, isn't that right? Although, it does depend on what version of the Bible you're reading."

Greg gave a dismissive gesture with his cutlery as he chewed his sausage roll. "It has become a proper noun though, hasn't it?" he said.

"Yeah," said Joker. "Funny the way language evolves, isn't it?"

"The name isn't relevant anyway," Greg continued.

"No," Tone agreed, "but whatever you want to call him, I still think you're being a bit hard on him, you know. I mean, it's not as if he flooded the whole planet and drowned everybody on it now, is it?" Tone realised he was getting side-tracked. "Look," he said, "I'm not trying to stick up for Satan – we all need our bogeymen, don't we? – I just wanted to make a suggestion to you, that's all."

Hannah looked up from the salad she'd been picking at. "What suggestion?"

"Well," Tone explained, "I reckon you should take Jamesy on at his own game."

"What do you mean?"

"Does it not bother you," said Tone, addressing both Greg and Hannah, "that the world seems to be moving further and further away from God? I mean, society is a lot more secular these days than it was a couple of hundred years ago, isn't it? And despite both of your valiant efforts, secularism always seems to be on the rise."

Greg eyed Tone suspiciously. "What's your point?"

"My point is that you should try to find out why that

should be. You should make a point of learning about the stuff that's turning people away from God. You know, find out what it is they've been stuffing their heads with so you can combat it more easily. Know thine enemy, that sort of thing." Tone gestured to Greg with his cup as he lifted it to his lips. "Know thine enemy, Greg."

Greg, realising what Tone was getting at, gave a condescending smirk. "The Bible is very clear on that subject," he said. "In Ecclesiastes it states that 'he who increases knowledge increases suffering'."

"Well," said Tone, turning to Joker, "that's certainly pretty clear, isn't it?"

"Can't get much clearer than that," agreed Joker.

"How do we get around that then?" Tone pondered.

"We could do what everybody else does," Joker suggested.

"And what would that be?"

"We just ignore those bits of the Bible that don't suit us."

"You may be on to something there," said Tone, "and then we could find a bit in the Bible that does suit us, couldn't we?"

"If we were that way inclined, then yes, we certainly could."

"Like the bit in Proverbs that says, 'get wisdom, get understanding', perhaps?"

"Perhaps indeed."

"Wisdom and knowledge are two different things," said Greg.

"What about understanding?" Tone said, and then held up his hand as Greg was about to reply. "Look,

I'm just trying to help you out here," he insisted. "Put it this way; if you want to argue with a cosmologist about the age of the universe, then wouldn't it make sense to be familiar with where his arguments are coming from?" He turned to Hannah. "I'm only referring to the cosmologist as a *he* for the sake of convenience."

"And because you're a bit of a sexist as well," Joker pointed out.

"Well yes," Tone nodded, "there's that too."

Hannah smiled, while Greg gave a snort of bemusement.

"Are you suggesting I take a degree in cosmology then?" he asked derisively. "Hardly very practical, is it?"

"No, Greg," Tone explained patiently, "but it wouldn't take much research to find out why cosmologists have settled on such a definite age for the universe, now would it? They haven't just plucked a figure out of thin air, have they? There's a reason for the conclusion they've come to and all you have to do is find out what that reason is, you see? Know thine enemy, Greg."

Greg shook his head disdainfully. Tone, however, was not bothered about Greg. As far as Tone was concerned, Greg was a lost cause, and so, despite directing most of his arguments to Greg, it was Hannah that Tone was talking to.

"I don't see what difference it would make," Greg said. "It doesn't matter what the reasons are. If the conclusions conflict with Scripture then the conclusions are wrong, and that's all there is to it."

"But doesn't it bother you that poor wee kids in school are being taught all these things that contradict what the Bible says?" asked Tone.

"Of course," Hannah replied, "it's terrible."

"Well then, don't you think it would be easier to discuss the things they're being taught if you understood what those things were? What harm can it do?"

To Hannah, what Tone was saying made sense. She had often wondered what it was that had made society in general decide to turn its back on Scripture. It couldn't simply be because some scientists, influenced by Satan, had led everyone astray with a few outrageous lies.

There had to be something seductive in those lies, something subtle and sinister that had driven a wedge between God's Word and His people, and Hannah felt a need to understand what it was.

"But you're a non-believer, aren't you?" Greg said to Tone. "So why would you care what we should or shouldn't understand?"

Tone shrugged. "I'm familiar with both sides of the argument," he said, "so I just don't think you can make a convincing case for your own position if you don't fully understand the position of the other side."

"It's a fairly transparent ploy, isn't it?" Greg suggested, pointing out Tone's fairly transparent ploy. "You're expecting us to just abandon the teachings of the Lord once we've been exposed to the *truth* of the scientists, isn't that it?"

"Not at all, Greg," Tone said, half-truthfully, "I believe that your faith is too strong for that, I really do."

Greg eyed Tone thoughtfully. "It isn't just a matter of faith anyway," he said. "A lot of the claims made by scientists are just too spurious to be given any proper consideration in the first place."

"Well, how do you know that?"

"Because I have done the research," Greg explained. "At least I've done enough to know as much as I need to. For example, I know that scientists don't have a clue about how the universe began, do they?"

"I wouldn't say they don't have a clue," said Tone. "The most widely accepted theory at the minute is the inflationary model of the-"

"You mean the Big Bang Theory?" sneered Greg.

"That's the popular name for it, yeah."

"Well, don't you have to admit that it's nothing more than a guess? It's just the best guess that scientists have, isn't it?"

"That's one way of putting it, I suppose."

"Well then," Greg declared, "that's where their argument collapses, isn't it? You see, I don't have to *guess* how the universe began, because I already *know* how it began."

"You do?"

"Of course," Greg smugly went on. "Everything was created by God in six days in-"

"Why did it take him so long?" asked Joker.

"What?"

"Well, if this God of yours is so-"

"That's not the point, Joker," Tone said excitedly. "The point is that Greg here is about to make us all very rich."

Greg narrowed his eyes as he regarded Tone.

"Right, Greg, if you know how the universe began," Tone exclaimed, leaning forward, "this is what you should do. You first need to gather all of the evidence that you've accumulated to support your hypothesis, along with the results of any experiments you may have carried out, and then you need to assemble it all together into a manuscript that you can then submit to the relevant journals for a rigorous peer review.

"Then, once your findings have been verified and accepted, you'll become the most famous person in all of history. I would imagine the Nobel Committee will be tripping over themselves to bestow every award that's going."

"Yeah well," Greg said, wiping some ketchup from his mouth with a napkin, "it's easy to be sarcastic, isn't it?"

"I thought I was being facetious," said Tone.

"Anyway," Greg pushed his chair back from the table and looked at Hannah, "I think we need to get going here."

They both got up, gave some polite nods to Joker and Tone, and made their way to the door.

Joker watched them leave and then turned back to Tone. He stretched, raising his arms, and idly rubbed the stubble on the top of his head.

"If it's any consolation, Tone," he said, "I thought you were being facetious too."

Twenty

It was just like when they were kids, thought Seamus. They often used to find themselves shuffling reluctantly along to stand before an authority figure, steeling themselves to face the consequences after Gary's recklessness had, once again, dragged them both into trouble.

"I still don't see why I have to come," he moaned.

"Well it's safety in numbers, isn't it?" said Gary. "I wanted Sean to come too, but he told me to fuck off."

"At least you know who your friends are," Seamus told him as he wondered why it hadn't occurred to him to use Sean's tactic. 'That's the trouble with us gays,' he grumbled to himself. 'Too bloody nice!'

"It'll catch her off-guard, you see," Gary went on. "We can come at her from different directions, so she won't know where to turn."

Gary had earlier called to Seamus' house and they were now walking the short distance to Rosie and Ellie's place.

"It won't be that bad, will it?" Seamus asked nervously. "You make it sound like we're trying to corner some sort of angry bear."

"You're not scared of her, are you?"

"What sort of question's that? You know I'm fucking scared of her."

"Oh, you worry too much," said Gary. "Anyway, she's carrying a lot of weight at the minute, so she can't move all that fast."

They stopped at the garden gate and Gary turned to Seamus. "Right," he said, "let me do the talking. I'll just work my way up to it, gently like, and then you can weigh in and back me up. Okay?"

"Okay," Seamus mumbled, unconvinced. The squeal of the gate, as Gary pushed it open, made him jump. "Fuck!" he hissed.

"Yeah," Gary agreed thoughtfully, "I should probably oil that at some point."

They walked up the path and Gary opened the door to the front lounge. It came as a surprise to see his sister there.

"Oh, here's that useless fucker now!"

"Karen?" Gary stepped inside, followed by Seamus. "What are you doing here?"

"I don't need a fucking reason, do I?" said Karen. "I'm here to see Rosie."

Gary's mind began to race. This was an unexpected complication. There were two of them now. It would have been much simpler to tackle Rosie on her own, he thought, especially as Karen, who was known to be quite opinionated, could tip the delicate balance of Rosie's fickle moods. This, he realised, would require a lot more tact and subtlety than he had planned to employ.

"Well, how's it going?" he said cheerfully as he took a seat on the sofa beside Rosie. Seamus sat down on the chair by the window.

"Oh, the usual," Rosie replied. "Hiya, Seamus."

"All right there, Seamus?" said Karen.

Seamus panicked. "Gary wants to go to Spain!" he shouted. Gary stared at him in disbelief.

"What?" Rosie said.

Gary jumped to his feet. "I'm going to put the kettle on," he declared. "I don't know what the fuck he's talking about."

"What was that, Seamus?" asked Karen.

"Who wants tea?" said Gary, heading for the kitchen.

"You just hold your fucking horses!" Karen said to Gary. "What was that about Spain?"

"It's all *his* idea!" Gary exclaimed, pointing to Seamus.

"What?" cried Seamus.

"What the fuck is all this about Spain?" Rosie said loudly.

"He wants me to go Spain with him," Gary explained, looking accusingly at Seamus. "But I said I couldn't go. I've got too much to do here, I told him."

Rosie and Karen both turned to Seamus who was squirming in his seat and staring hatefully at Gary.

"Are you going to Spain, Seamus?" Rosie asked.

"What?" he exclaimed, startled. "Um, yeah," he said, "all the lads are going." He then pointed frantically at Gary. "He said we could use his stag do as an excuse!"

Rosie and Karen then turned to Gary. Gary glowered murderously at Seamus as he tried to think fast. He suddenly clasped his hands together and turned to face Karen and Rosie.

"So," he said happily, "what do you reckon?"

"What the fuck are you on about?" said Karen.

"Well, it was supposed to be a surprise," he said, "but bloody Seamus here…" Gary rolled his eyes and tutted unconvincingly.

"Gary," Rosie began menacingly, "what's going on?"

"Look," said Gary, thinking fast, "I was thinking that after the baby's born, you could probably do with a bit of a break, right? A wee holiday in the sun, you know? Well, a mate of ours has got a beach-house in Spain, and-"

"Who?" Karen demanded. "Who's got a fucking beach-house?"

"Oh, you wouldn't know him. He was from school, but anyway he-"

"What do mean, 'after the baby's born'?" said Rosie. "Do you not think we'll be a wee bit busy, Gary?"

"Well, I don't mean right away, do I?" Gary explained. "I'm not saying you should just drop the pup and then head off to the airport, am I?"

"I don't know, Gary. What exactly *are* you saying?"

"I'm just saying we can wait for a bit until my ma's happy to look after the kid for a couple of days and then we can-"

"Does my ma know this?" asked Karen.

"What? Um…yeah, yeah, I'm sure she'll be…You know what, Karen? You and Harry could probably do with a holiday as well."

Seamus considered sneaking off towards the door while the girls were distracted by Gary digging an ever-deeper hole for himself, but he was afraid to move.

"Oh," cried Karen, "don't you fucking think you can just…what sort of beach-house?"

"Well, that's the thing," said Gary, getting into his

stride. "Me and Seamus here, and the rest of the lads, were thinking that we could go over and suss it out, you know? Make sure it's up to scratch and all that."

"That's good of you," Rosie told him.

"I know," Gary continued, ignoring the sarcasm, "but that's just the type of guys we are. Selfless, we are, bloody selfless. It's just the sort of-"

"What was that about a stag do?" asked Rosie.

Seamus could not help but admire Gary's uncanny ability to adapt instantly to the fluidity of any situation. He didn't even blink.

"Well, that's what you call killing two birds with one stone," he told Rosie. "So when you think about it, we'd actually be saving money. In fact, not going would be an act of financial stupidity. We might as well be just throwing money away."

Both Karen and Rosie found themselves in a quandary. On one hand it felt unnatural not to be ripping into Gary for being an underhand, self-absorbed dickhead, but on the other hand they were both intrigued by the promise of a private beach-house in Spain.

"So, when were you planning to go and *suss it out*?" Rosie asked cautiously.

"The week after Easter," said Gary. "We're really only going to help out a mate, you see. He needs a hand moving some stuff from some other place he's got out there, so it's not like it's going to be a holiday at all really. The plan is to head over, suss out the beach-house, have a couple of beers for a quick stag-do, and then work the rest of the time. Not a holiday at all."

Seamus thought that Gary was probably stretching the concept of his selfless altruism a little too far, but the girls now seemed to be too enraptured by the idea of cheap holidays in the sun to pay Gary's ramblings any close attention.

As they left the house, having decided to call into the Star for a drink, Gary and Seamus had formed different opinions on how the encounter had gone.

Seamus thought that Gary had made a lot of promises he had no right to make. They had left the two girls excitedly making plans for long, leisurely breaks in the summer and beyond, but there could be no guarantee that Gary would be able to deliver any of the increasingly outlandish situations he had promised. Gary, as usual, was only thinking of the present. The thought that any of his words or actions would have any repercussions at a later date was little more than a vague and abstract notion that Gary had no time for.

"Well," Gary enthused, as he rubbed his hands together, "That went really well, didn't it?

Twenty One

Jamesy climbed the stairs to the Speakeasy Bar in the Student Union. It was Friday afternoon and his lectures were all finished for the day.

As he walked through the door to the bar, he nodded briefly to acknowledge a smile from a girl as she passed going the other way, and then made his way through the Friday crowd until he found Sean and Bobby at a table close to the bar. Putting his bag under the table, he sat down.

"All right there, Jamesy?" said Sean. "Perfect timing, Bobby was just about to go to the bar."

"Well, now that you mention it…" Bobby stood up. "The usual, Jamesy?"

Jamesy nodded and Bobby set off.

"How's it going?" asked Sean. "All set for Spain?" They had all gone into town the weekend before to buy their plane tickets. It had been decided that their best option would be to fly from Dublin to Barcelona, and then take a train to Valencia where they could then take another train on to Tavernes. It would be a long day, but they were all young enough to view the travel as part of the adventure.

"Yeah," Jamesy said. "Looking forward to it."

"I think it's already starting to get hot over there, so it should be roasting by the time we get there."

"Well, I've packed my shorts."

Bobby came back from the bar and set three pints down on the table.

"You've packed, did you say?" he asked Jamesy as he took his seat. "That's a bit organised, isn't it?"

"No, I mean I've only just started packing," Jamesy told him. "But I think I've bought everything that I need to take, so I'm near enough ready to go."

"Well," said Sean, taking a sip of beer, "there's not long to go now, is there? Though we still don't know how we're getting to the airport."

"I thought Gary had it all in hand," said Jamesy.

"Yeah, but that's just according to Gary, isn't it?"

"That's right," Bobby agreed. "You can just picture us all standing there early on Easter Monday with all our luggage, and Gary shows up on a fucking skateboard."

"You don't have a lot of faith in him then?"

"No!"

Jamesy shrugged and picked up his drink. He was sure they'd work something out, one way or another. A band started to set up on the stage over by the row of windows, and Jamesy watched them with little interest. It was the same band that played every Friday afternoon and Jamesy had heard the same set many times over the years. There was still something comforting though, in the familiarity. Jamesy turned to Bobby.

"Have you seen Hannah lately?" he asked nonchalantly.

"No, not at all. Why?"

"Just asking."

"That's definitely all over, is it?" asked Sean.

"Looks like it."

"Well then," said Bobby, "a holiday is just what you need to take your mind off things."

"Hope so."

"You feeling a bit low then, Jamesy?"

Jamesy looked thoughtful as he picked up his drink. "You could say that," he said, taking a sip. "But the worrying thing is I seem to be having trouble concentrating as well."

"In what way?" asked Bobby.

"Well, I'm supposed to be revising, but I just can't seem to focus on anything for more than a couple of minutes at a time. I'll just be like staring at a page and then realise I haven't actually been taking anything in. My head's all over the place at the minute, just don't know what I'm going to do, really."

"Well, that's not good," said Sean. "That's your one superpower, isn't it? Studying?"

"Yeah, let's face it, Jamesy," added Bobby, "you've got fuck all else going for you."

Jamesy didn't react, he just stared at his drink, so Bobby carried on. "It's weird, isn't it?" he said. "You and Hannah both go really well together. You belong together because you're both…well, you know…a wee bit dull. But a long time ago, a bunch of people, herding goats in a desert, wrote some stuff down, and now that means you and Hannah can't be together. Funny, when you think about it."

"Funny's not the word I would have used," Jamesy said glumly.

"Aye well, like I said," Bobby told him, "a holiday in the sun should cheer you up."

"Maybe it'll work for Joker too," Sean suggested.

"Yeah," said Bobby with sudden awareness, "he has been a bit miserable lately, hasn't he?"

"Aye, I don't know what the fuck's wrong with everybody at the minute."

"Tone seems to be in good form these days," Jamesy ventured.

"He does, doesn't he?" said Bobby. "And I've got a fair idea why."

Twenty Two

She had it all planned out. She was going to march straight in, call him an asshole, and march straight out again.

But when it came to the crunch, it was her face that let her down.

"You're an asshole," she told him through a beaming smile.

"Well, it took you long enough to work that out," said Tone as he rose to greet her. "What do you want to drink?"

Claire sat down at the table. "I'm not staying long," she said. "So, I'll just have a small red wine. I was sorry to hear about your daddy, by the way."

"Thanks," said Tone. He shrugged. "Just one of those things, really." He went off to the bar and Claire watched him as she put a light to her cigarette. She was surprised at how pleased she was to see him again. When he had suddenly broken off all contact just after Christmas, she had been, at first, confused, and then she had felt angry. She had no right, she knew, to feel that way, for their relationship had only ever been casual, but Tony's inexplicable silence still felt like a hurtful rejection and she wanted him to feel as bad as she had felt.

But now she was beginning to understand just how much she had missed him.

"There you go," Tone placed a glass of wine on the table and sat down. "So how have you been keeping?"

"Is that all you have to say?" she demanded, annoyed by his easy manner.

"Well, I didn't think I'd need to explain anything," said Tone. "I mean, hasn't Bobby told you all about it."

Claire was trying to maintain her irritation, but her stupid face broke out in another broad smile. "That was a shock, wasn't it?" she beamed.

"Jesus! You can say that again."

"When did you find out?"

"Christmas Eve. We have this-"

"Oh, Bobby's pub-crawl!" Claire exclaimed. "Of course. So you're one of his wee drinking buddies?"

"That's one way of putting it."

"It must have come as a real shock to Bobby too."

"He seems to be taking it well enough though."

"Well, I did tell you, didn't I?" Claire said as she stubbed out her cigarette. "He's a lovely guy."

"Have you seen him lately?"

"Not since St Patrick's day, no. Why?"

"Did you know we're going to Spain on Monday?"

"No. Who's *we*?"

"Me, Bobby and all our wee drinking buddies."

"What for?"

"Just a holiday. We got the chance of a cheap week in the sun, so we all just thought we could do with a break."

"It's all right for some."

"Well, like I said, it's just for a week."

There was a brief, stilted silence as they each sipped their drinks and wondered what they were doing there. Were they expecting to pick up from where they had left off, before Christmas, when they had torn each other's clothes off in a Dublin hotel room? Or was this an ending? Was this an opportunity to draw a conclusive line under something that had been little more than a passionate, but passing, fling, and could now be left forever back in a Dublin hotel?

"You've finished your drink," Tone pointed out needlessly when Claire placed her empty glass on the table. She didn't reply. She stared accusingly at her glass and wondered why she had asked for a small one. She never asked for a small glass of wine; she could never see the point.

But then she realised that this was her chance. This was her opportunity to stand up, to say something clever and final and to simply leave. 'Well, it's been nice knowing you,' she would say, and then maybe shake hands, as Tony looked into her eyes with longing and a desperate pleading. 'We'll always have Dublin,' she would tell him as their fingers slipped slowly apart and she turned and walked steadily away into the swirling black and white mist.

Tone was becoming uncomfortable as he looked at Claire. He had never been aroused by just a person's face before, but Claire's hilarious attempts to stifle her natural exuberance were turning him on. He had always felt vaguely unsettled by her irrepressible cheeriness, believing it to be somehow unnatural, but watching her now try to impose some sort of discipline to her face, he realised that her smile shone all the more brightly, and it now seemed right. It seemed right and natural and perfect. And undeniably sexy.

The tension between them began to grow. Claire raised her eyes from her glass to stare into Tone's face. She could see confusion and doubt in his eyes, and guessed that he could see the same in her eyes too. The silent tension stretched.

"Well," she said finally. "Are you just going to sit there?"

Tone grinned. "A large one this time, I take it?" he said. She lit another cigarette in reply and watched as he went back to the bar.

Later that night, Claire was still trying to convey a sense of aggrieved indignation, but as she peeled off her pants before climbing on top of Tony, she had to concede that she wasn't being entirely convincing.

Twenty Three

Hannah was having trouble with smallpox. She was in the reference section of Belfast Central Library and she was learning about one of the most devastating infectious diseases in human history.

Smallpox, it seemed, had a fatality rate of thirty percent, and those that survived were left heavily scarred and often blind. But that was not why Hannah was having trouble.

Hannah's problem was that smallpox was now in the past. It was a disease that had been officially eradicated, and that was giving Hannah some cause for concern.

She knew that all of the ailments of mankind could be traced back to God's displeasure at Adam and Eve's disobedience in Eden.

As well as being cast out from Paradise, humanity would have to face punishments in the form of illnesses for the remainder of its history.

She remembered the long and confusing discussions that she and her church group had had regarding the varying degrees of God's wrath. Bone cancer in children had raised a lot of harrowing debate. And malaria. And dysentery. And heart disease. But what about tooth decay? Was that one of God's punishments? Or dandruff even?

God had sprinkled His punishments seemingly at random throughout His creation, as if it were mankind as a whole, and not the individual, that mattered.

But His creation, it seemed, was fighting back.

What did God make, she wondered, of such disdain for His will? And what about medicine in general? Were doctors and nurses not constantly subverting His will? Hannah was worried that mankind was unwittingly fuelling God's anger. The story of the Tower of Babel was an example of how God viewed the hubris of humanity but then, for Hannah, it all came back to God's omniscience. God knew how every event in human history would play out. He must know; He's omniscient. So why, in Scripture, is He so often moved to anger?

The reference books she was browsing covered a wide range of topics, but none that she could see made any reference to Scripture. She had largely dismissed those books that dealt with evolution, for they were obviously just disgraceful propaganda, but there were other books that covered broad topics such as geography, geology, history, science and astronomy that seemed not only to ignore the Bible, but to go way beyond its scope, almost as if the Bible were not a comprehensive enough resource. For one thing, every subject seemed to make casual reference to the fact the Earth was older than six thousand years. Much older.

She flicked through some books dealing with the natural world of flora and fauna, and was astonished and appalled to learn that nature was little more than an unending struggle for survival, and was filled with slaughter, suffering and unimaginable cruelty. There were insects that laid their eggs in the eyes of mammals, and parasites that slowly devoured their hosts from the inside out; not to mention the teeth and slashing claws, ripping and tearing at terrified prey in every corner of the world. Nature was not in balance, it was at war.

She knew, of course, that all of this was a direct result of the Fall, but it seemed, to her, to be wildly disproportionate. All of this because some people ate a piece of fruit six thousand years ago?

It seemed that no matter where she turned she was faced with questions she couldn't answer.

A glimpse at a scientific magazine informed her that a new volcanic island had just appeared in the Pacific Ocean; a fact that left her dumbfounded. She had always believed that God had created the Earth fully formed, so why were new bits of it suddenly popping up from nowhere? Feeling perplexed, she was drawn to a glossy and colourful book on astronomy, attracted by the pictures that showed the jaw-dropping majesty of the full extent of God's creation. She was starting to read about the Solar System when she felt Jamesy's teeth nibble gentle at her earlobe and she had to close the book in frustration. She looked up and let her mind wander aimlessly while she allowed her body to have its moment as tiny prickles rippled across her skin in all sorts of confusing ways. The moment passed and she went back to her book.

The sun, she already knew, was a star. It was the only star in our Solar System, but was just one of at least a hundred billion other stars in the galaxy that was called the Milky Way. Hannah stopped. She had to read that again. At least a hundred *billion* other stars? She was barely beginning to comprehend such a number when she read about the distances involved in outer space.

The closest star to our own, she learned, was Proxima Centauri, but it would take over six thousand years to get there using current technology. Even travelling at the speed of light, which, she read with increasing incredulity, was more than six hundred *million* miles per hour, it would still take over four years to reach our closest stellar neighbour. And what about the hundred billion other stars? It was all on a scale that Hannah found impossible to grasp, but she found herself becoming intrigued.

She was just putting the fragments of her blown mind back together when her imagination exploded once more. She had had only a vague notion beforehand of there being other galaxies in the universe besides the Milky Way, but when she learned that there were at least a hundred billion other galaxies in the universe, each containing a hundred billion stars, she calmly closed the book and stared into the middle-distance.

God, it seemed, had been much busier than the Bible suggested. The Solar System was far more massive than she could comprehend, but it was a mere speck in the Milky Way galaxy, and that, in turn, was entirely insignificant in the wider universe.

She discovered that it was unlikely that humans would ever be able to travel very far within the Solar System, let alone being able to travel to another star. And the idea of humans travelling to another galaxy was far-fetched even for science fiction. The scale of everything was just so far beyond anything she could even begin to imagine that it begged a simple question in Hannah's mind.

Why?

Twenty Four

Africa 1963

The first time that Benjamin set foot on the campus he felt at home. He could sense a greater desire for new medical teaching and training, among both students and faculty at the university in Enugu, than he had ever felt in Kano.

When he had first gone to Lagos he had been met with blank indifference and a simple lack of understanding for the difficulties he had been facing in Kano, and he had begun to suspect that an ignominious return to London was now inevitable. It was during his second week in the capital, however, that a chance encounter with a university administrator from Enugu in the East had alerted him to a shortage of training staff in the Faculty of Medicine at Enugu University, and he had broached the subject with the committee that was overseeing his placement in Nigeria.

Even though Benjamin suspected the committee had seized upon the suggestion of his reassignment to Enugu as an ideal way of getting rid of him, he didn't mind because it meant he could finally step into the role that had tempted him to Nigeria in the first place.

His first tour of the facilities had confirmed to him that this was truly what he wanted to do with his time in Africa. The students he encountered at the Enugu University Faculty of Medicine possessed an almost manic eagerness to learn, and as Benjamin was helping to address the faculty's chronic under-staffing issues, he felt that he could make a real difference.

The position also provided him with accommodation on campus which, to Benjamin's surprise and delight, turned out to be a pretty little bungalow with sizeable gardens to the front and back. He bought a new car, having sold his old one back in Kano, and he set about furnishing the bungalow to his own, fairly traditional, tastes, with plenty of bookshelves and comfortable chairs for reading. He even decided that he could try his hand at gardening, now that he had been given some decent-sized plots to work with, and his mind raced ahead into the future with all sorts of plans for his gardens and his house. *His* house. His home. He smiled at the thought. He was home.

It was the enthusiasm of his students during his first weeks in the job that made Benjamin sadly reflect on the words of his friend, Odi. Odi, Benjamin realised, had been accurate when he had described the hunger for learning among the people of the East, and the memories of that beaming grin and infectious laugh made Benjamin smile and want to weep. He hated his grief. He hated missing Odi and he hated that Odi was gone, and it was thoughts of Odi that led him, one evening after several beers, to think of Adanna and where she had gone, and it was thoughts of Odi that had led him to pull an atlas from a bookshelf and to tearfully flick through the maps looking for the name of a village. A village that Odi had once told him about and which was, as far as Benjamin could remember, close to Enugu. After a while, he found it.

This coming Saturday, Benjamin decided, he would take a drive down there to look around, to perhaps get a sense of where Odi had come from and maybe even see if he could re-establish contact with Adanna, to see how she was doing.

He parked close to the village square and then strolled past the bars and cafés that bordered the square's western side. To the north of the little square was a church that huddled in the shade of a corkwood tree and, as Benjamin stood and looked around the Saturday afternoon crowds, walking, shopping, eating, drinking, he began to wonder why he had come.

He could feel no special connection to Odi here, and the chances of somehow bumping into Adanna in this busy little town now seemed slim. He sighed and sat down at a table outside the nearest café and ordered a tea. As he waited, he became aware of someone approaching him from the side and then a voice spoke to him in Igbo.

"*Ndeewo.*"

Benjamin turned and was surprised to see a white face smiling at him. The face belonged to a catholic priest.

"*Ndewo,*" Benjamin replied, "but I have to say," he went on, "that's about as far as my Igbo goes, I'm afraid."

The priest laughed. "Yes," he said in a strong Irish accent, "I didn't take you for a local. Are you waiting for someone?"

"No, I'm…I'm not sure why I'm here, actually."

"I'm Father Jerome," the priest said, holding out his hand for Benjamin to shake. "You don't mind if I join you, do you?"

"Oh no, of course not. Please do. I'm Benjamin, by the way."

Father Jerome sat down at the table. "Well, Benjamin," he explained, "it's just that I can tell you're not Nigerian, you see, but I can't quite place your accent and I'm a shockingly nosy man, so I am."

"I'm Egyptian," said Benjamin, smiling, "but I've spent several years in England."

"England, you say?" Father Jerome shuddered. "You have my condolences, but then I suppose we've all had our troubles."

Benjamin laughed. "I have a good friend who is Irish," he said. "We were students in London together. We still try to keep in touch."

"I'm very glad to hear it," Father Jerome told him. "So tell me, Benjamin, what brings an interesting and exotic man like yourself to this little backwater then? Like I said, I'm a very nosy man."

Father Jerome ordered a beer from the waitress who brought Benjamin's tea, and then listened intently as Benjamin explained what he was doing in Nigeria, how he was living and teaching at the university in Enugu, and how he had come, on a whim, to the village where his friends had grown up.

"Odi Mbanefo?" Father Jerome reflected sadly. "Yes, I knew him," he said, "though not terribly well. And Adanna too, of course. They were with the Anglican congregation in the village," he gestured to the church on the other side of the square. "The news of Odi's death came as a real shock to everyone. As you can imagine in a small place like this, everyone knows pretty much everyone else."

"I believe that Adanna has moved back here," said Benjamin.

"Yes, I believe so," agreed Father Jerome. "I can get you her mother's address, if you like."

Benjamin nodded as he finished his tea. He was beginning to have some doubts about tracking down Adanna now that it had become a possibility. They had never been friendly in the same way that he and Odi had been. His relationship with Adanna had always been stiff and formal, he felt, and he wasn't sure he wanted to reacquaint himself with the simmering ferocity that he sensed in her.

"That beer looks good," he said, gesturing to Father Jerome's almost empty bottle.

"Then why don't you join me in one?" Father Jerome suggested. "And we'll raise a toast to the memory of a fine man."

"Well, when you put it like that," said Benjamin with a smile.

They drank and chatted until well after dark when it occurred to Benjamin that it would be foolish for him to drive back to Enugu.

"Oh, you can stay with me tonight," Father Jerome assured him. "I've got a wee place, not far from here, over by St Patrick's."

"St Patrick's?" asked an amused Benjamin.

The café began to close so Father Jerome directed Benjamin to a nearby bar where they could continue their conversation.

"Yes, St Patrick's," Father Jerome said, "it's the chapel and the charitable mission for the Holy Ghost Fathers in the village. St Patrick, of course, is the patron saint of Nigeria."

"What, really?" asked Benjamin. He managed to prop himself up against the bar as Father Jerome ordered the next round.

"Yes, really," Father Jerome replied. "The British, you see, go around the world, planting their flag in places, while we Irish go around planting our saints."

Benjamin gave the priest a long look. "Well, tell me, Father," he said, "what's an interesting and exotic man like yourself doing in a backwater like this then?"

"Oh, there have always been missionaries in Africa," Father Jerome told him, "whether the Africans want them or not. I like to think that we do more good than harm though, but then I would say that, wouldn't I?"

Benjamin found it easier to raise his drink as a response rather than try to formulate words into a coherent sentence. He had been enjoying the company of this easy-going priest, but he was beginning to feel the evening slip away from him, as it slurred and stumbled into night.

It took a while for Benjamin to understand where he was when Father Jerome shook him awake the next morning.

"Good morning, Benjamin," the priest said as Benjamin opened his eyes. "I'm going to have to go soon, but you can stay as long as you like. There's some bread in the kitchen if you want breakfast."

The events of the previous day slowly assembled themselves in Benjamin's consciousness as he sat up in the small cot-bed. He was still fully dressed, his head hurt, his mouth was dry and he blinked uncontrollably in the harsh morning light.

"How are you feeling?" asked Father Jerome. Benjamin thought that the priest was looking obscenely bright and cheerful, considering the amount of alcohol he had consumed.

"Did you say you were going out?" he managed to ask.

"Yes," said Father Jerome, "I have to go and say Mass later on. I got that address that you were looking for, by the way. I left it on the kitchen table for you."

"Um, thanks," Benjamin said as he stood up. Father Jerome showed him where the bathroom and the kitchen were and then left him on his own in the house. After a trip to the bathroom, Benjamin sat down at the kitchen table, picked up the slip of paper that had been left for him and stared at the address. He did not think he was up to seeing anyone today, but it would be useful to have the address for the future.

He made himself a quick breakfast and a cup of coffee and spent some time in the bathroom trying to make himself look and feel more human. Eventually, though still queasy, he felt he could make his way to his car and then suffer the drive back to Enugu, where he planned to climb into bed and stay there for the rest of the day.

Before he left, he scribbled a thank-you note to Father Jerome and, adding his address and phone number to the bottom, he placed it on the table. He then stepped outside and, blinking in the sun, made his way to the village square.

He walked through the square, feeling glad that he didn't have to see anyone today for, despite his best efforts, he still looked dreadful. He was unshaven and his clothes were all wrinkled and beer-stained. He tried to focus his thoughts on his bath and his bed back in Enugu as he stumbled groggily towards his car.

"Dr Maher?" The woman's voice made Benjamin freeze. The congregation from the Anglican Church was pouring into the square, jostling Benjamin as he slowly turned to face the source of the inquiry. It was Adanna, though she now seemed to be a lot more blurry than Benjamin remembered.

"Adanna!" he exclaimed, struggling to convey surprised enthusiasm. She stepped towards him and gave him a tentative embrace.

"But…but what are you doing here?" she asked, and then took a step back. "And why are you…?" She gave him a quizzical look.

"Well, it's…um," Benjamin was only too aware of how he must look in a crowd of people who were dressed in their Sunday best. He probably smelt quite differently as well. "I'm living in Enugu now," he finally told her. "At the university."

"Enugu?" Adanna said, surprised. "Are you teaching then?"

"Adanna!" The voice came from behind her. "Who is this man you are talking to?" An older woman, heavier than Adanna, and not quite as tall, appeared at her side.

"This is Dr Maher, Momma," said Adanna, "I told you about him. He was in Kano with us."

"A doctor?" Adanna's mother cried in disbelief. "You are a doctor?"

Benjamin's discomfort was approaching a crescendo. He wished he could just slip away and crawl under the covers of his bed at home, but instead he was sweating uncomfortably under a mocking sun whilst trying to make small talk with two intimidating women in a crowd of chirruping churchgoers.

"It's nice to meet you, Mrs..." Benjamin realised, with horror, that he couldn't remember Adanna's surname. "Mrs...?"

"Obiaka," said Adanna with an amused grin.

"Oh yes, of course," he stammered, "Mrs Obiaka." He extended a hand which, after a hesitant pause, Adanna's mother briefly shook. "I know I'm not looking my best," he continued, "but I drove down here yesterday, you see, because I've been living in Enugu and, well, I had heard Odi speak of this place and I just thought that...well..." Benjamin was running out of words, though he wasn't sure what he was trying to say. "Well, I got talking to a Father Jerome, you see, and-"

"Father Jerome?" Mrs Obiaka gave a sudden burst of laughter, which made Benjamin wince in pain. "You do not have to say any more, Dr Maher," she said as she walked past him, still laughing, to go and speak to someone in the crowd.

"So you have had an interesting night with Father Jerome then?" Adanna asked, smiling.

"Well yes, you could say that," said Benjamin, mopping at his brow with a handkerchief. "It's good to see you again, Adanna."

"It is good to see you too, Dr Maher," she replied. "How are you finding Enugu? Did you say you were teaching?"

"Yes, yes," he said, suddenly enthused, "I'm teaching, and the faculty at Enugu is wonderful. Just what I had been hoping to establish in Kano, actually."

"I'm glad that you are happy in Enugu."

"And what about you?" asked Benjamin. "How have you settled back home?"

"Yes, I am well," Adanna said with a shrug. "Life goes on, does it not?"

Benjamin could sense the same lifelessness in Adanna that had settled within her after Odi had died, but now was not the time to probe deeper. They stood for a little while longer exchanging standard pleasantries until Benjamin saw a chance to take his leave.

"Well, Adanna," he said, "I must get back to Enugu, but I would be happy to visit you again if that is something you would like."

Adanna nodded without much enthusiasm. "Of course, Dr Maher. I would like that very much."

Benjamin gave her his telephone number, while she gave him the number of the bar where she worked, and he then set off to find his car.

As he drove back to Enugu, Benjamin reflected on the chance meeting and he realised with some surprise that he had actually told Adanna the truth. It *had* been good to see her again.

It was a few weeks later that Benjamin went back to the village. He had been invited by Father Jerome to inspect the little cross-congregational clinic that had recently opened in the square, so he drove down early one Saturday morning. He had not had any word from Adanna since his first trip to the village, but he was keen to renew his friendship with Father Jerome.

"Benjamin!" the priest called to him as he crossed the square. "Good to see you again."

"You too, Father," said Benjamin as they shook hands. "You've been busy, I see."

"Oh, we've all been involved in this," Father Jerome told him. "All the congregations from miles around have chipped in something. Come, have a look around."

The clinic, though small, was neat and professional, and Benjamin voiced his approval and made a few helpful suggestions to the staff. After the tour, Benjamin was invited to lunch with Father Jerome and a few of the protestant ministers.

"That sounds like an excellent idea," he said, "but do you think it would be possible for me to invite a friend?"

"Of course," said Father Jerome. "Are you talking about Adanna?"

"Yes, if that's all right? I fear I may have made a rather poor impression on her when last we met."

Benjamin made his way to the address he had been given and knocked on the door. Adanna's mother answered, and when she recognised who it was she stepped outside with a condescending smile.

"Dr Maher," she said. "How nice of you to call."

"Hello, Mrs Obiaka. I just called to see if-"

"Adanna!" Mrs Obiaka shouted back inside. "It's your drunken doctor friend!"

"Well, I…I…"

"Who?" Adanna appeared in the doorway. "Oh, Dr Maher. What are you-?"

"I think he has come to take you drinking with him," Mrs Obiaka suggested mockingly.

"Oh no, I just thought that…" Benjamin wavered. Mrs Obiaka folded her arms and glared at him.

"Momma," said Adanna, "why don't you go back inside?"

Adanna's mother hesitated, then, still staring at Benjamin, she walked slowly inside and closed the door.

"Yes, Dr Maher?" Adanna asked, raising an eyebrow.

"Adanna, I…I was wondering if you would like to come out for lunch. I mean, not just with me…with some of the local church leaders, I mean…"

"Church leaders? Have you found religion, Dr Maher?"

"Yes. I mean no…I mean…" Benjamin mopped at his forehead. "Adanna," he said, "won't you please call me Benjamin?"

She looked at him thoughtfully and then smiled. "Very well, Benjamin," she said. "Now, if you will give me a minute to get ready, then yes, I will have lunch with you."

Initially, it seemed odd to Benjamin to be joining a table of clergymen for lunch, but he knew Father Jerome, and Adanna was familiar with most of the others to varying degrees so they were able to blend in quite naturally.

The conversation around the table was dominated at first by the new clinic but during the meal it began to fracture into individual chats amongst the diners. Benjamin and Adanna talked among themselves.

"I have received several letters from Zara," she told him. "She says that the situation in Kano has settled down now. She wants to know if I would return there."

Benjamin nodded. "I went to the police headquarters when I was Lagos," he said. "I thought that they would want to have as much information as possible about what had happened, but they dismissed it all as a local disturbance. They showed no interest at all."

"Welcome to Nigeria," Adanna said with a sardonic smile.

"Yes," Benjamin returned her smile, "I have to say I have noticed a lot of differences between the regions. Especially between the North and the East. There does seem to be a much greater desire for change down here than in Kano."

"Of course, Dr…" she smiled. "Benjamin. Do you believe in national traits? Or racial traits? Or tribal traits?"

"Do certain groups of people behave inherently differently from other groups, is that what you mean?" he asked. Adanna nodded, and Benjamin seemed to consider it. "I don't think so," he said. "I mean, there are superficial differences, of course, but I believe that people are all essentially the same."

"What about cultural differences that have been ingrained for generations?"

"Well," Benjamin began. He was wondering how a light chat over lunch could have suddenly become so intense. "I think cultural differences are still superficial," he said. "The species *Homo Sapiens* is, after all, just one species."

"Then it depends on how deep you believe the superficiality descends."

The other conversations around the table had begun to tail off as theological ears pricked up at the hint of a philosophical discussion.

"Would you listen to you two!" said Father Jerome. "And here's me discussing the chances of Glasgow Celtic winning the league this year."

"Perhaps," suggested Benjamin, "it is not a suitable discussion to have over lunch."

"Oh, I don't know," ventured an elderly pastor at one end of the table. "If it saves us all from another one of Father Jerome's rants about some obscure football team, then I say we should give it a try."

"Obscure?" cried Father Jerome. "I'll have you know that-"

"So, Adanna," the elderly pastor continued, "I'm curious to hear your thoughts on the matter. It sounds like you have some firm opinions on the differences between people, is that right?"

"I'm sorry, Pastor Osawe," said Adanna, "I'm afraid I may have spoken out of turn."

"Not at all," the elderly pastor assured her. "We all know how much you have suffered, and how it is natural for you to bear ill will towards our neighbours in the North but, of course, you know what Our Lord has to say on the matter of turning the other cheek."

Adanna smiled. "If only it were that easy."

"No one ever said that forgiveness is easy," said a burly Methodist who sat facing Benjamin. "To do so means striving against our natural human impulses."

"Ah," Father Jerome interjected, "but from what I gathered earlier, it sounds like Adanna is saying that not all humans have the same impulses."

"I am only going by the evidence of my own eyes," Adanna said defiantly.

Benjamin sighed. He just wanted to have a nice lunch with pleasant company, but he could already tell that things were about to get heated.

"I would like to hear the argument from a scientific point of view," said Pastor Osawe, looking directly at Benjamin. "What does a doctor of medicine have to say on the matter?"

"What?" Benjamin said, taken by surprise. "What matter?"

"It's just the old question of nurture versus nature, isn't it?" said Father Jerome. "So, Benjamin, what's your take on it?"

"I've already said that there is only one human species," Benjamin explained. "That's simply from a biological point of view. Recent discoveries in molecular biology have only confirmed that viewpoint. Of course, some groups of humans will exhibit certain characteristics that differ from other groups but the same can be said of individual humans as well. It doesn't change the fact that on a very basic, fundamental level, we are all exactly the same."

"So, nurture then?" Father Jerome said with a smile.

"Of course," said Benjamin. "No child is born a Christian, or a Muslim or even a fan of Glasgow Celtic."

Everyone laughed, but Benjamin could sense that Adanna, beside him, remained tense. The conversation moved on and, when lunch was finished, Benjamin offered to walk Adanna back home.

"So, have you replied to Zara's question?" he asked her as they walked.

"Which question?"

"About returning to the North."

"Ah, no, I have not answered her yet, but I do not think I will return to the North."

"Why not? Wouldn't you make more money there?"

"Money is not everything," Adanna said softly, her head bowed.

"No, no, of course not," said Benjamin. It was obvious to him that Adanna was still suffering, still consumed by a grief that seemed to be dragging her down. He felt compelled to help.

"So, you're working at a bar in Ngwo?" he said. She turned to look at him, suspecting his disapproval, but his face was neutral.

"I am the manager there, yes," she said defensively. "Why? What of it?"

"Oh, nothing," said Benjamin hastily, "but I was just wondering if you had ever considered teaching, that's all."

"Teaching? Teaching what?"

"I don't know," he said, "it needn't be anything specific. You could teach children to read and write, for example. Or you could teach English, or geography, or anything you-"

Adanna stopped and stared at him. "What are you suggesting?" she demanded.

"Well," he explained, "there is a shortage of qualified teachers throughout Nigeria, so the university at Enugu is running several courses for anyone who wants to get into teaching. And I just happen to think that you would make an excellent teacher."

"Why?"

"Well, because you...um...well, you know...you have such strong opinions."

Adanna laughed as they walked on. "And that makes a good teacher, does it?"

"You know what I mean," he said. "You're smart, you could be a real help to children. You would certainly make them think, that's for sure." Benjamin smiled, but Adanna walked along with her head down, quiet and thoughtful. When they arrived at her home, she stopped, still silent, and then looked into his eyes.

"What do I have to do?" she asked.

Twenty Five

Michael was not a fan of sports, and rarely engaged in any form of physical activity, so Simon was surprised to see him in a pair of shorts, running around his back garden. He raised an eyebrow at Michael's wife, who had shown him through the patio doors.

"I know," said Maddy, laughing, "he thinks he's Maradona."

"What on Earth is he doing?"

"It's Peter," Maddy explained. "He loves his football, so his daddy said he'd have a wee kick-about with him. Michael's a bit crap though. He's getting hammered."

"Yes," Simon agreed, "he looks like he could do with some practice."

"What are you two gabbing about?" Michael called from the lawn.

"We're just admiring your fancy footwork," Simon shouted across the garden. "Poetry in motion, we were saying."

"Aye, very funny," said Michael, walking towards them. He picked up a towel from a chair on the patio and began to mop his sweating face. "Jesus!" he gasped. "That's bloody killing me."

"Do you have a few minutes?" asked Simon.

"Yeah, no problem," Michael turned back to his son. "Just going to take a wee break here, Peter," he said. Peter waved in acknowledgement and carried on practising his dribbling.

Michael and Simon went into the house and made their way to Michael's home office. Maddy offered to make them tea but they both declined.

"Well?" asked Michael as he closed the office door and went to sit at his desk.

"I've received some interesting information," Simon began, "regarding Hegarty and those other two…nuisances."

Michael sighed and ran a hand through his hair. "Go on," he said.

"An opportunity may have presented itself," Simon told him, "just after Easter."

"Easter? Why? What's happening?"

"Well, apparently, Anderson and Lingfield have arranged to go off to Spain for a week."

"Just those two?"

"No," Simon admitted, "there'll be a group of them going." Michael frowned at this, so Simon hurried on. "It isn't ideal, I know that, but hear me out."

Michael leaned back in his chair, waiting to be convinced.

"They're going to be flying from Dublin Airport," Simon continued, "and who do you think will be taking them there and back again?"

"Hegarty?"

"Yes," said Simon. "Hegarty has agreed to drive them all down in his van, and then pick them up again the Sunday after Easter."

Michael remained silent as he mulled over this new information. He had been half-hoping that the whole Hegarty business would just quietly go away as the months dragged on with no viable opportunity becoming obvious, but now it looked like he would have to give the matter some thought. He disliked the thought of others being involved, but the idea of the targets being grouped together on quiet Sunday roads in the Irish Republic was too tempting to be dismissed.

The fact that the matter could be dealt with, safely out of the way, on the other side of the border, held a strong appeal for Michael.

"What have you got in mind?" he asked.

"Well, I was thinking that the Sunday when they're coming back would give us more time to prepare," Simon told him. "The roads should be quieter too, so I was thinking we could slip over the border, early on Sunday morning, and pick our spot to wait for them coming by. Obviously, I'll have the area scouted out beforehand to make sure we choose the perfect place."

"Who do you have in mind for this?" Michael asked.

"Just you and I, and two others."

"Weapons?"

"Pistols only, I would have thought."

Michael pondered this, and then gave another nod. Pistols made sense, he thought, for they would be making their way through some of Northern Ireland's most sensitive regions to get to the border. It would be best to be discreet.

"Two others?" he asked. "Who are you thinking of?"

Simon seemed to hesitate. "Um…I'd thought of maybe Wee Paulie and Big Dennis," he muttered.

Michael exhaled slowly. "Not exactly the cream of the crop, is it?" he suggested.

"No," Simon admitted, "but they're both fairly dependable, and Big Dennis has just got that new car so it would be completely clean. There's no way it could be traced back to us."

"Big Dennis will be driving then?"

"Yes, it's still early days, of course, but that's the plan so far."

Michael thought some more, then came to a decision.

"Okay," he said, "you sort out the rest of the details, and let me know how you get on."

"Fine," said Simon, getting up and walking to the door. He turned at the door and smiled. "I'll let you get back to your football."

Twenty Six

The tiny ticking accusations of an unseen clock. Brooding, featureless walls of threatening blue. The cry of a child, shrieking like a thousand demons.

Martin had his eyes squeezed tightly shut, but it was no use. The voices were still there. He could still *see* the voices. But how was that even possible? How could he see-?

It's all for you!

He didn't want to scream. Screaming hurt. But screaming was so seductive. The shaking started again. He looked at his hands and they were motionless. Pale and still, like…

For you, Martin. All for you.

He didn't understand. But he did understand. He knew he deserved it all. The voices nodded. Everything was because of him. Because of his sins. Because of…the voices were nodding faster now. And laughing. And accusing. And they were…the bed shook violently as he jolted awake.

He lay still for a moment and listened to the ticking of his wristwatch on the bedside cabinet. The hotel room was small but comfortable with walls of soothing blue, washed pale by the streetlights from the road outside.

Martin sat up and looked at the digital display on the clock beside the bed. 4:33am. He was sleeping much better these days, he thought, and the nightmares were now confined to when he was asleep. He had made a lot of progress in the last six months. He got up and went to the bathroom.

He had spent his first few days in Belfast reacquainting himself with the city centre, and was surprised to find that not an awful lot had changed. The security gates that ringed the main retail area were, he supposed, inevitable, and the Grand Central Hotel that had once graced Royal Avenue was now a garish new shopping centre, but most other things were familiar to him.

The famous department stores of Robinson and Cleaver, and Anderson and McAuley had ceased trading, but the decorative old Victorian buildings were still there, now hosting new retail outlets for fashion and entertainment.

The City Hall still stood, unchanged, at the very heart of the city, and Martin was cheered by the sight of buses darting constantly around the pale grey building. He had once worked as a mechanic at the bus depot in Ardoyne and, even though these buses were updated versions of the ones he had worked on, they brought back some distant memories, and he looked on them fondly.

Ardoyne was now at the forefront of his mind as he stood looking out of his hotel window at the empty city. The streetlights still illuminated the roads outside, despite no one being around to appreciate their glow. Martin preferred this time of day. He preferred it to when the city had shaken itself awake to shatter the peaceful calm with the scurrying, shouting, insidious infestation of humanity. At this time of day it was just him and the redundant streetlights, and just as the lights would quietly fade as the city stirred, he would retreat a little into himself as the noise and the bustle of the day increased.

He sighed as he sat back on the bed. He was trying not to think of the day ahead, but he could avoid it no longer. Today was the day when he would go back to Ardoyne.

So, what would he find there? That was the question that was causing little ripples of anxiety to wash back and forth through his thoughts as he played out a host of scenarios in his mind. Would he be welcomed with open arms back into the happy warmth of his family? This, he felt, was the least likely of all the scenarios, but it was the one that he played with the most. What could he expect from their reactions, he wondered. Would it be disappointment? Anger? Disgust? Blame? Or would they be happy to see him? Would there be celebrations? Would there be joy?

Or would there be indifference? Would that be the worst reaction, he wondered. An apathetic shrug? He shuddered as he tortured himself with events that most likely would never happen. Not today at least.

Martin knew that it was unlikely he would find his family in the same little house that he had been dragged away from all those years ago, but he believed it could provide a start to his search. He had sent a speculative letter to the address several weeks ago but had received no reply, and he could find no listing in the phone book, so he decided he would simply call to the house, knock on the door, and see where it led him.

His fears, though, were crippling him. The clock told him it would soon be time for the brash day to sweep away the night that the steadfast little streetlights still pointlessly held at bay, so he forced himself to prepare for whatever he was about to face. He would have a wash and a shave. He would dress and he would have breakfast, and he would stride with confidence and with purpose into the coming day.

And he would go to Ardoyne.

There were two Ardoynes. There was the original village, built in the 1800s to house the workforce from the mills that wove flax plants into linen, with houses that were simple brick two-storey boxes packed tightly together in rows of tiny streets.

This village gradually expanded further from the mills, but the structure of the houses remained the same – four roomed, two storied dwellings, with a lavatory out in the backyard and a front door that opened straight onto the street.

This was 'old' Ardoyne, and by the time the McCann family had moved in, the mills had been abandoned and the homes adjacent to them, sitting on cobbled streets, were largely derelict. The McCann's house, however, was still in a vibrant part of the area, and from his front window, Martin was able to look straight up Elmfield Street and see the Saunders' Club on the left hand side. If he stepped outside his house and turned directly to his right he would see the little gap in a row of larger houses that led to the most recent part of Ardoyne that was known as the Glenard Estate.

Martin and his wife, Shauna, had once had ambitions to one day move the short distance to Glenard, where each house, though still terraced, had a spacious front garden and, more excitingly, an indoor bathroom. It was in Glenard where the bus depot was situated where Martin had once worked, and he had admired the gardens as he walked through the area every day on his way to and from work. And so, he decided, it might be pleasant to approach his old home by strolling through Glenard on his way to the little gap that led to the older terraces of Herbert Street and beyond.

It was a bright spring day when the bus dropped him at the Oldpark Road end of Alliance Avenue. The houses here were large, detached properties, surrounded by tall, established trees, and a world away from the terraces of Ardoyne that lay less than a mile away along the road.

The avenue itself ran through the leafy suburbs until it eventually became the eastern boundary of Glenard, running parallel to Brompton Park, a half a mile distant, that formed the western boundary. It was Brompton Park that was split in half by the gap through to Old Ardoyne. If Alliance Avenue and Brompton Park could be said to form the two uprights of the capital letter 'H' then the bar in the middle was formed by the arrow-straight Berwick Road, from which ran, left and right, the streets of Glenard.

As Glenard was built on the side of one of Belfast's many hills, then anyone walking along the Berwick Road from the Alliance Avenue end towards Brompton Park would see the streets on their left run steeply downhill and the streets to the right rise uphill. This was Martin's plan, to walk along the Berwick Road towards the Brompton Park gap.

As he made his way down Alliance Avenue towards the Berwick, he was saddened to see the tall corrugated iron barriers of the 'Peace Lines' filling in any possible gaps along the right hand side of the avenue and preventing any contact with the people of the Glenbryn Estate on the other side who were, judging by the Union flags showing just above the Peace Line, loyal to Britain and therefore hostile to the Irish nationalists of Ardoyne.

Martin could remember how these streets had once been all open, and how people could move freely wherever they liked. He felt, as well, that everything seemed cleaner back then, or more cared-for at least. Back in the sixties before that decade's end had ushered in the Troubles.

He reached the Berwick Road and paused. To his right, the gap in Alliance Avenue that echoed the gap at the other end of the Berwick was blocked off by a Peace Line. Ahead, the road carried on to eventually meet one of the main roads that circled Ardoyne, which meant that Martin turned left and set off towards the gap that he could just make out at the far end of the Berwick Road.

Many of the gable walls, Martin noted, of the end houses on the streets that ran at right angles to the Berwick Road contained colourful murals. These murals featured images either of nationalist politics, supporting the revolutionary efforts of Irish republicanism, or of Mary, the goddess of conservative Catholicism, which gave the impression that the Queen of Heaven was a passionate advocate of armed resistance.

This mixture of politics and religion was also evident in the Easter decorations that Martin could see in the streets to the right and to the left as he strolled along. The colours of the buntings that ran from the upper windows of many of the houses, down to the wall or fence at the front of their gardens, fell into one of two categories.

One of these was the green, white and orange of the Irish national flag which served to commemorate the Easter Rising in Dublin in 1916, when Irish Republicans had launched an armed insurrection against British rule. Though quashed by an overwhelming British military response, it would lead directly to the formation of an independent Irish Republic, and also to the partition of the island which left six counties still under British rule.

The other type of bunting was yellow and white. The colours of the Pope. This was to commemorate the most important date in the Christian calendar, when God sacrificed Himself, in human form, to atone for the sins of Man.

It all gave the district a colourful, festive air, thought Martin, which was only enhanced by the warm sunshine and the sense that spring had finally begun.

Walking along in the sunshine, Martin began to entertain all kinds of silly notions. He thought of taking Shauna for a drink at the Wheatfield, the bar they had frequented during their courting days. In his mind, Shauna was stunned but ecstatic to see him. She would catch a glimpse of him at the end of the street, but would look away and then slowly turn back as recognition widened her eyes and caused her to gasp aloud. She would walk towards him, and then run, and then she would throw herself into his arms and…he shook his head, bemused by his own foolishness. He knew that it was nothing more than a corny romantic fantasy, but still, he thought, he could dream at least, couldn't he?

As Martin got closer to the gap, he started to feel uneasy. This wasn't because of the apprehension he should have been feeling as he approached his old home, it was something else. Something was wrong.

He walked through the gap with growing disbelief. Where was Herbert Street? He could still see it in his mind. The pavement on the right hand side of the narrow street was higher than the pavement on the left, and had a kerb of large granite blocks that formed a double step. He could see Elaine and Rosemary sitting together on the step, sharing a bag of sweets. He could see the housewives, gossiping at their front doors as their children kicked a ball and chased each other around the street. He could see the corner shop at the bottom of Elmfield Street where he bought his cigarettes before going for a drink in the Saunders' and…where was Elmfield Street? Where was the Saunders'?

A street sign informed him he was in something called Butler Place, which made no sense to him. He could remember a Butler *Street*, but not a Butler Place. He then found a Butler *Walk* which made sense, he supposed, for the paving tiles beneath his feet seemed to be for pedestrians only. He walked on with increasing despair. The houses here were all clean and modern and, he imagined, perfectly pleasant, but why were they all placed in such a haphazard fashion? The straightforward system of one street after another had been abandoned for a more random placement of homes that seemed to follow no obvious pattern. He eventually found something called Elmfield Street, but it bore no resemblance to the one he remembered.

Martin became more and more disorientated as he made his way through the unfamiliar and surreal environment. Disillusioned, and in something of a daze, he eventually found the Oldpark Road where he turned to his right and trudged back towards the city centre.

Back at his hotel that evening, Martin lay on his bed and wondered what he should do. It all seemed hopeless to him at the moment, but maybe he just needed some advice. Someone he could talk to. He fished out the little piece of paper that the woman, Stephanie, had given him on the ferry, and stared at the phone number.

After a few moments of internal debate, he made a decision.

Why not?

Twenty Seven

There was no reason why Hannah should not meet up with Rosie but, as she approached the café in Great Victoria Street, she still felt a sense of unease about Rosie's connections to James.

It shouldn't matter, she told herself. She liked Rosie. She liked the thought of having Rosie as a friend, so she could see no reason at all for them not to meet.

Rosie had phoned to ask for more details on possible programming courses that she could take and it was decided that they should meet in town in order to speak face to face. Hannah had brought along some prospectuses and brochures that she thought might be of interest to Rosie, and she found herself warming to the idea of helping someone embark on a new career.

When Hannah had first met Rosie she had initially been wary of her terse manner, but she soon came to appreciate Rosie's sharp humour and shrewd intelligence, and was now only too happy to encourage her desire for improvement.

She pushed open the door to the café and was surprised to see Rosie seated at a table beside another girl.

"Hiya, Hannah," said Rosie. "You remember Karen, don't you? From the funeral? She gave me a lift into town today."

"Karen, yes of course," Hannah said, taking a seat. She gave Karen a warm smile. "Harry's wife, right? I could hardly forget your Harry."

"Aye, I know, Hannah, love," Karen replied, "he is hard to forget, isn't he? God knows I've tried."

They all laughed as the waitress came to take their order. Once the order of tea and pastries had been brought to the table, Hannah and Rosie discussed the pros and cons of various courses while Karen watched and listened with great interest.

"I might try one of these courses myself," Karen told them as she flicked through the brochures. "I mean, I don't mean computers, like, I don't have the brains, but some of these other courses sound class."

"Well, why not?" said Hannah. "It can't do any harm, can it?"

The conversation and the easy laughter flowed freely around the table until, inevitably, the subject of Jamesy came up.

"It's a real shame about you and Jamesy," Karen told Hannah. "You looked really well together."

"I know," Hannah sighed, "but I think there were just too many differences. I still think about him though." And then, to her surprise, Hannah began to reveal how she had been having inappropriate thoughts about James at inconvenient times of the day, and how they were making it difficult for her to concentrate.

"Awk, you're just horny, love," Karen told her. "Just have a wee wank. That'll sort you out."

Hannah could only gape, open-mouthed at Karen, as Rosie searched for somewhere to look. Rosie was no stranger to bawdy banter, but she believed there should be a time and a place for such remarks. Karen had no such filter.

"What?" asked Karen, puzzled by their reactions. "It's totally natural."

"I know," Rosie began, "but…"

"I…I…well…" Hannah was still wide-eyed and tongue-tied.

"I mean, I know it's not the same as having a-"

"Anyway, Karen," Rosie hastily interrupted, "I'm sure Hannah doesn't want to hear about all that."

"I'm only trying to help."

"But…but…" Hannah managed to stammer, "isn't it sinful?"

"Is it?" Karen asked with genuine curiosity. "Is it really?"

"Well, I…I…" Hannah thought about it. "I'm sure it must be," she concluded.

"So, are you saying then," Karen began, "that somewhere in the Bible, it says 'Thou shalt not finger yourself'?"

"Oh, holy fuck!" Rosie muttered under her breath, as she raised her eyes to the ceiling.

Hannah had got over her initial shock and was now, despite herself, becoming fascinated by the discussion. "Well, not those exact words," she said, "but then a lot of Scripture is implied."

"Implied?" asked Karen "What does that mean?"

"It means that you have to work out for yourself what a lot of the meanings are because it doesn't spell everything out for you."

"I still don't know what you mean."

"Well, for example," Hannah explained, "you're talking about female masturbation, aren't you?"

"No, I'm talking about having a wank."

Hannah laughed. "Okay then, that. But the Bible implies that male masturbation is a sin, so from that we can-"

"Does it really?" Karen was intrigued.

"Well, yes, it's called the sin of Onan."

"Why is it a sin?"

"Because it's wasteful to spill your seed on the ground."

"Hannah!" Rosie exclaimed with shock and amusement and some new-found admiration. "You dirty bitch!"

"Aye, Hannah, that's just shocking talk, so it is," Karen told her solemnly, and they laughed. "Anyway, women don't spill their seed, do they?"

"Well, no but…"

"It sounds like you're reading a wee bit too much into the Bible there," said Karen.

"Maybe it's all about having wicked thoughts though," Hannah suggested.

"Don't think about it then. Just do it."

"I don't think it's that easy."

"Then you're doing it wrong."

"Jesus!" said Rosie. "I can't believe I have to listen to this. Can you two hear yourselves?" She steered the conversation back to less contentious topics and later, once they had finished up, Karen offered Hannah a lift back to her flat at the university.

"No, it's all right thanks, Karen," Hannah told her, "it's not too far to walk."

They said their goodbyes and Hannah made her way thoughtfully back to her flat.

That night, in bed, Hannah lay awake thinking about the talk she had had with Karen. She couldn't fathom how Karen could be so unconcerned about the fate of her soul, and so uncaring about where she would be spending eternity. The words of Paul's letter to the Ephesians kept playing in her head:

But fornication, and all uncleanness, or covetousness, let it not be named among you.

Karen's liberal use of profanity was, according to Scripture, sinful in the eyes of God, and it bothered Hannah that anyone could be so dismissive of God's laws. Hannah, for most of her life had been terrified of incurring God's wrath.

There was a time in her childhood, she remembered, when she had been friendly with a little girl called Rebecca, who lived in the same street as her. At that time, they each owned a Sindy doll, a popular girls' toy, which they would play with constantly in each other's homes and gardens.

Rebecca though, Hannah noted, possessed a lot more of Sindy's accessories than Hannah. In particular, Rebecca owned Sindy's pony. A beautiful Palomino horse that Hannah craved. She never seemed able to persuade her parents to buy one for her though, so she would secretly burn with desire to possess Rebecca's pony. It was only later, when she had learnt the meaning of the word 'covet', that Hannah realised with horror that she had been continuously breaking the Tenth Commandment; *Thou shalt not covet thy neighbours' goods.*

She could still remember the sheer terror she had experienced as it became clear she would be going to

Hell. She knew that committing a sin was enough to arouse God's fury, but to repeatedly break an entire Commandment could have only one consequence. She was going to Hell. She was going to burn forever in everlasting agony. Her childhood was suddenly a nightmare of fear, her imagination feeding with increasing intensity the torments she was certain to face.

The paralysing anxiety that she had felt had led to a spate of bed-wetting, which only made things worse, for she knew that God must look with disapproval on such behaviour. It didn't matter that she could find no direct reference to bed-wetting in her Children's Bible, her paranoia was self-fulfilling. She was beyond redemption.

It had taken years for her to accept that there was a way for her to earn God's forgiveness, through the understanding and love of Jesus Christ, but the memories still haunted her. She still suffered from debilitating panic attacks, always fearful of causing some inadvertent offence.

As she lay on her back, her right hand resting on her lower abdomen, her fingertips lightly touching the skin through a gap in her pyjamas, she tried not to think of James. She tried not to think of Karen's frivolous words. She tried not to think at all. She knew that God was watching her. She knew that He could see and hear everything, but more than that, she knew despairingly, He could read her thoughts.

And how was she supposed to manage her thoughts, she wondered helplessly. Surely everyone experienced unwanted and unbidden thoughts that they could not control. She couldn't be the only one, could she?

She had been told, her whole life, that God's love was infinite and unconditional, but what were the Commandments, if not conditions? She felt God's disapproval more often than she felt His love. She felt His perpetual judgement, and, more than anything, she feared His wrath and His eternal damnation.

She turned over onto her side and tried to sleep, wondering if James felt as miserable as she did.

Twenty Eight

"The back of the bus is in the huff,
Barney Boo!
The back of the bus is in the huff,
Barney Boo!
The back of the bus is-"

"That's enough, Gary," Harry's voice was soft, and held no obvious hint of menace, but Gary stopped singing nonetheless.

"Aye, no problem, Harry," he said. He turned round to address the back of the van. "Just trying to get the holiday mood in full swing, isn't that right, lads?"

"Bit too early in the morning," said Seamus.

"Yeah, fuck off, Gary," Tone agreed. "Some of us are still asleep."

Gary grinned and turned back to look through the windscreen, tapping his fingers on his knee as he finished the song in his head.

Harry, in the driver's seat beside him, also stared ahead. The early morning roads were devoid of traffic, and they were making good time as they headed for Dublin Airport. Despite himself, Harry was quite enjoying the drive. He was pleased with his new van, which replaced the one he had lost at Christmas. It was larger than his previous van and, in the back, he had fitted wooden benches down the sides to accommodate his work crew as they went from job to job. Gary's friends now occupied the seating, with their luggage taking up the space in between.

The sun was shining and the road ahead was clear, so Harry was in good spirits. He was looking forward to the drive back, when it would just be him on his own, listening to the radio and lost in his own thoughts. Such tranquil moments were rare in Harry's life and so, when they did occur, he made a point of embracing them.

When they arrived at the airport, Harry stepped down from the driver's seat to help unload the luggage.

"Cheers for that, Harry." Everyone took turns to shake Harry's hand or pat him on the arm. Tone handed him a wad of notes. "Here you go, Harry," he said. "We did a wee whip-round for the petrol."

"Nah, don't worry about it," Harry told him. "That's too much anyway."

"Now look, Harry," Tone insisted, "we don't want to have to fucking slap you about a bit, but if you keep up that auld nonsense then-"

"All right, all right," said Harry with an exasperated smile. He took the money, got back in his van and drove off. Bobby, standing by Tone, watched the white van weave through the airport traffic until it was out of sight. He waited a little longer. Then a bit more. Then, when he felt sure that Harry was no longer in the same county, he turned to Tone.

"I reckon we could have taken him," he said.

"Aye, I know," said Tone. "Did you see the look on his face? Looked like he was going to shite himself, to be honest."

Everyone picked up their bags and walked into the airport. Once they had checked in their luggage, they all turned and automatically headed for the bar.

"Best thing about going on holiday," said Gary, lifting his pint, "is early morning drinking at the airport."

They all nodded in agreement.

"Got a long day ahead of us though," Kevin pointed out.

"Well, that's why it's important to get off to a good start," Gary told him. "So what's the deal then, Kevin, with this place in Spain?"

"My folks bought it a couple of years ago," Kevin explained. "They'd been going on holiday to Spain every year and they just thought it would make sense to buy their own place out there."

"Was it expensive?"

"Well, it wasn't cheap, but it was reasonable compared to other parts of Spain. That bit of the coast doesn't get the same number of tourists that you get in the Costa Blanca or the Costa Brava, you see."

"Why not?"

Kevin shrugged. "Don't know," he said. "It's got some spectacular beaches. Maybe it just hasn't been developed as a tourist spot yet. It's where the Spaniards go on holiday though. They come from all over Spain to the region, especially Gandia. That's the big holiday town there."

"So the Spanish people go on holiday to a place where they don't have to put up with drunken arseholes from the rest of Europe then, is that what you're saying?"

"They're going to love *us* then," said Seamus.

Kevin smiled. "It's not like that," he said. "Everybody's dead friendly there. It's all really relaxed, a lot more relaxed than all the mad tourist places anyway."

"Sounds like just what we need," Tone said, looking around him. "Somewhere we can all just chill out for a few days."

Joker stood up. "Well, I'm going to get a round in," he informed everyone. "Who wants to give me a hand?"

"I'll go with you," said Jamesy, standing up. "I want to have a look in the bookshop as well."

"You want to pick up some nudie books?" asked Joker, as they set off.

"What? No, no, I just…"

"It's all right, Jamesy, I'm not judging…"

Gary turned back to Kevin. "So, do you speak Spanish then?" he asked.

"I wouldn't say I'm fluent, but I can get by okay."

"I suppose it's still the Easter holidays there."

"Yeah, I think so."

"So, how do you say Easter in Spanish then?"

"Mmm…*Pascua*, I think."

"*Pascua*? Really?"

"Why, Gary?" said Tone. "Did you think it would be something like 'Eastero'?"

"Well yeah," Gary replied. "Or something a bit closer to Easter anyway. *Pascua* is completely different, isn't it? Where did *Pascua* come from?"

Kevin shrugged. "Never thought about it."

"Ask Joker," Sean suggested. "He'll know."

"Not that I'm all that curious," said Gary, "but it just seems a bit weird, that's all." He drained the last of his pint and put the empty glass on the table. "Now that's what I call timing," he said as Joker and Jamesy returned from the bar. Drinks were distributed and everyone settled down for the fresh round.

"Did you go to the bookshop, Jamesy?" asked Bobby.

"Yeah, I just had a quick look, I might go back later on."

"Are you looking for anything in particular?"

"I don't know," Jamesy sighed, "I just thought I might try a bit of light fiction."

"Fiction? Really?" Bobby was surprised. "That's not like you, Jamesy. I thought you'd be after something like a thousand-page account of what the Babylonians got up to."

"Well, I'm having a bit of trouble concentrating these days," Jamesy explained, "so I thought I could use this week to try and take it easy, you know? Just chill out a bit."

"Yeah," said Bobby, "I think that's the plan for us all."

"Right well, if you two have finished boring the shite out of everybody," said Gary, "I have an intellectual question I'd like to pose to Joker here."

Joker gave Gary a quizzical glance.

"Why is the Spanish word for Easter," Gary began, "so different from everybody else's word for Easter?"

"Everybody else's?" asked Joker, amused. "Do you know what the French word for Easter is?"

"No."

"It's *Les Pâques*," said Joker. "And what about Italian?"

Gary shook his head.

"*Pasqua,*" Joker told him.

"What?" asked Gary. "The same as Spanish?"

"Near enough."

"So, Easter is the odd one out then? Is that what you're saying?"

"Not quite," Joker explained. "French, Spanish and Italian are all classed as Romance languages, and the Romance languages take their names for the resurrection story from the Latin and Greek variations on the old Hebrew word for *Passover*."

"*Passover*? Isn't that a Jewish thing?"

"Yeah, *Passover* was already an established festival for that time of year, so the Christians just adapted it."

"Yeah," said Tone, "they did the same thing with Christmas."

"So, where the hell does the word Easter come from then?"

"Well," said Joker, "English is classed as one of the Germanic languages, you see, and it seems that, back in the day, the pre-Christian tribes of northern Europe had a load of different gods and goddesses, and one of these goddesses was called *Oestre*. That's spelt O, E, S, T, R, E. She was the goddess of spring, or the dawn or something. So anyway, when they all became Christians, they just said, 'Fuck it! We'll just use that.'

You know, because it had that whole rebirth, springtime sort of vibe going on."

"You could make a claim," Jamesy suggested, "that *Oestre* evolved from an earlier Mesopotamian goddess, *Inanna*, whose name later became *Ishtar*."

"Yeah well, we're not going to go down that rabbit hole, are we, Jamesy?"

"Just saying."

Kevin stared at Joker with a mixture of puzzlement and awe. "How do you know all that?" he asked.

"Oh, it's just a wee hobby of mine," Joker told him. "Languages, linguistics, that sort of thing."

"Sounds like you'll come in handy over in Spain then."

"Well, Castilian's not a problem," said Joker, "but I'm looking forward to finding out a bit more about Valencian."

"Valencian?" asked Seamus. "What the fuck is Valencian?"

"You've heard of Catalonia, haven't you?" Joker asked. "And the Basque Region?"

"Yeah but-"

"And you know they speak their own languages, don't you?" Joker carried on as Seamus nodded. "Well, as far as I know, in the region around Valencia, they speak their own language too. It's not as famous as Basque or Catalan, but it-"

"For fuck's sake!" Gary exclaimed. "Does *anybody* speak bloody Spanish in Spain?"

"Yes, Gary," Joker patiently explained. "Everybody speaks the official language of Castilian Spanish, but Castile is just the middle bit of Spain. The other regions have their own sense of identity, and some of them have their own language too."

"It all sounds a bit fucked up, if you ask me."

"It's like if you go to Wales," said Joker. "Everybody there speaks English, but a lot of the time they just talk to each other in Welsh."

"Or if you go to North Belfast," Tone suggested. "Everybody there talks bullshit."

"Fuck off!" the natives of North Belfast told Tone, who was grinning into his beer.

"I would imagine," Joker went on, "that Valencian isn't that much different from Catalan, which, as I'm sure you all know, is another Romance language from the Proto Indo-European root."

"Well, obviously!" tutted Bobby, rolling his eyes.

"Unlike the Basque language," said Joker. "Nobody knows where the fuck that comes from."

"You see, Kevin," said Tone. "And you thought this was just going to be a week of mindless boozing."

"It *is* just going to be a week of mindless boozing," insisted Gary. "All this educational bollocks needs to be nipped in the bud."

"Look," Tone explained hastily, "nobody is suggesting for a minute that there won't be any boozing going on, but you have to-"

"I don't know how you can say that," said Sean, holding up an empty glass. "I've run out of booze already."

"Oh, for fuck's sake!" cried Tone. "Right, okay, I'll get this round."

"They'll be calling the flight soon," Bobby pointed out, "so you should get a move on."

The flight to Barcelona was almost full, with the holiday mood in full swing, and the time passed quickly in a haze of vodka and beer and banter and sing-songs.

At Barcelona Airport, Kevin led them to the trains, where they boarded an Express to Valencia. This proved to be the perfect opportunity for everyone to catch up on some much-needed sleep as they were whisked, in air-conditioned comfort, down the east coast of Spain to the next stage in their journey.

At the train station in Valencia, they caught another train for the short trip to the station at Tavernes de la Valldigna. Where some confusion arose.

"What the fuck do you mean, 'we're not there yet'?"

"Well, I told you," Kevin tried to explain, "that Tavernes beach is obviously on the coast, but the actual town is a few miles further inland."

"So, what's your point?" asked Gary, as they walked outside the tiny train station to be greeted with…nothing. "Shit!"

"The train station," said Kevin, "is between the two."

"In the middle of nowhere, you mean?"

"Well," Kevin looked around him. The plain stretched wide and empty, and was bathed in a sumptuous, early-evening light that was a parting gift from the sun as it dipped behind the mountains in the distance off to the left. "You could say that."

Gary considered launching into a thoughtful tirade, laced with some choice expletives, but the sheer tranquillity of the scene demanded reverential silence, and so they simply stood and watched as the light faded gently away into an evening that rippled with cicada song.

It almost felt like an intrusion when the shuttle bus came rattling along the road, but they all clambered aboard and by the time they arrived at the beach, it was dark.

They were dropped off at one end of a palm tree-lined paseo that ran behind a row of buildings facing directly onto the beach. Many of the buildings were apartment blocks, but there were several among them that were just single, private properties, and it was to one of these that Kevin headed for.

"Jesus Christ!" said everyone at once when Kevin had unlocked the door and led them inside. The large interior was all open-plan, with marble floors and luxurious furnishings. A kitchen area, off to one side, was spacious enough to contain a grand, French-polished dining table, while the lounge area held lavish seating, all tastefully upholstered in cream-coloured leather. At the far end of the room was an impressive set of double doors that could be opened to provide direct access to a veranda and the beach beyond.

"All built on the backs of the workers, no doubt," sniffed Joker.

"Oh, that's right," said Tone. "I forgot that the multi-national corporation that you work for gives all their profits away to charity. Isn't that right, Joker?"

"Piss off, Tone."

"Well, stop being such a fucking hypocrite then."

Kevin led them on a tour of the house. Upstairs they were shown the bedrooms, the lavatory and a separate wet-room, where they could shower.

"Where do these stairs go?" asked Gary, pointing to a staircase at the end of a corridor.

"I'll show you." Kevin led them up the stairs and onto a wide terraced roof with a floor of terracotta tiles. There was a wall along one side of the roof that held the door to the stairway, and which had a wooden bench set against it. A table and chairs sat in the middle of the tiled floor, and around the other three sides of the roof ran a low, ornamental balustrade.

Beyond the balustrade directly opposite the wall with the stairwell lay the quietly shimmering Mediterranean Sea.

"All the shops," said Kevin, "are just on the other side of the paseo, behind us. There's a wee supermarket that'll still be open, so if anybody fancies some beer then-"

Joker shocked Kevin with a spontaneous hug, he then clapped his hands together. "Right," he said, "I'm away to the shops. Who's coming?"

"We'll all go," said Tone.

"Well," Bobby sighed, as he took a look around him. "this'll just have to do, I suppose."

Twenty Nine

Africa 1964-1967

Adanna decided to enrol at Enugu University to begin a course in teacher training. Initially she had planned to take the bus every day to and from the university, but after a while Benjamin persuaded her that it would make more practical and financial sense for her to move into the spare room in his bungalow on campus.

And it was there that the fates, inevitably, threw them together as lovers.

After several months of needy, clinging, almost dream-like lovemaking, Benjamin blurted out a clumsy proposal of marriage, and Adanna accepted.

Later though, she wondered why.

Even though she was now working towards a career in teaching, Adanna still felt listless and unsure of her place in the world, and had accepted Benjamin's proposal with the same unthinking compliance that had led her into accepting her previous job offer in bar management.

Her introspection reached heavenward.

Adanna had always had an informal relationship with God – rather than pray she would prefer to have a casual chat – and it was to Him she turned for answers.

Lying awake at night, Adanna discussed how the easy assumptions of her future had all been shattered in Kano, and how she had drifted onto an uncertain path with little sense of direction.

'Is this where my life is meant to go?' she asked God. 'Is this the purpose that You have for me now?' Feeling untethered, disconnected, from her life, Adanna no longer trusted her own decisions. What was it that she wanted, she wondered. She tried to examine her desires, but they were vague and fleeting; drifting, like herself, on an aimless breeze.

She was not expecting any answers from God, but she asked for them nevertheless.

Her feelings for Benjamin were just as hazy as everything else in her life. Was she simply fond of him? Was it nothing more than admiration? Was she confusing her gratitude for his help in Kano for something else? Or did she love him? Was she actually in love with him? She couldn't say.

There was one night, however, when all of her feelings towards Benjamin became focused and resolute, as they all formed together into a blistering furnace of hatred.

That night she had screamed obscenities at him, loathed the very thought of him. She had sworn and cursed his name, his birth and his very existence. She didn't love him at that moment, that was for sure.

But it was not much later – that very same night, in fact – when her daughter had slipped into the world, and mother and child had gazed upon each other in silent wonder, that Adanna had thought that maybe she did love Benjamin after all.

She certainly felt that, at that moment, she had more than enough love to go around.

"She will have an Igbo name," Adanna insisted.

"Of course," said Benjamin, as he cradled his daughter in his arms. "Did you have something in mind?"

"Chiaza," she said firmly. "It is short for Chiazacam."

"Chiaza," Benjamin said, testing the feel of the name on his lips. "I like it." He stared at the tiny, sleeping face and whispered.

"Chiaza."

Benjamin and Adanna were already a popular couple on campus, and that popularity was only cemented by Chiazacam's arrival.

As she grew, the entire university fell before her. It was an unfair contest after all, for not only was she blessed with a wistful blend of her father's Nilotic golden bronze and the dark fire of the sub-Sahara, she was also armed with a giggle that could squeeze hearts. No one stood a chance.

Benjamin arrived home one day from work, to find Chiaza in the kitchen, helping Adanna's mother to bake bread.

"Hello, Ijemma," he said to Mrs Obiaka as he lifted Chiaza into the air, "and how has my little girl been today?"

"She has been fine, Benjamin," Ijemma replied. "We've had a very busy day, haven't we, my sweet?"

"I thought that Adanna would be home by now," said Benjamin, as he lowered his daughter back to the floor.

"No, she told me she would be late getting back today. She said she had something to do after class."

"Did she say what?"

"No, not to me."

Benjamin shrugged and poured himself a glass of water. He leant against the kitchen worktop and chatted to Ijemma, while Chiaza tugged at his trouser leg for attention. After a while, they heard the front door, and then Adanna appeared.

"Good afternoon, everyone," she said, smiling. Chiaza ran to her and Adanna picked her up and carried her into the living room. Benjamin and Ijemma followed.

"Where have you been?" Ijemma asked Adanna as they sat down.

"Oh, Momma, that is my business."

"So, you have secrets from your mother?" Ijemma cried passionately. "From your husband, I can understand, but from your own mother?"

Benjamin was about to say something, but Ijemma motioned for him to shush.

"You will know soon enough," said Adanna, "but, Benjamin, you said this morning that you wanted to talk to me about something."

"What? Oh, yes," Benjamin said, "I was just thinking that we could go on holiday when the term is over. I thought it would be nice to visit Europe, perhaps see Paris, or London maybe. What do you think?"

"Does this include me?" asked Ijemma.

"Yes, of course," Benjamin told her.

"Then I think it is a very fine idea!"

They turned to Adanna who was playing on the sofa with Chiaza. She acted as if she hadn't heard.

"Well?" Ijemma prompted.

"Well," Adanna finally spoke. "That all sounds well and good, but what will we do with Chiazacam's baby brother?"

"Chiazacam's…?" Benjamin stared at her. "What?"

Adanna simply smiled, and Benjamin jumped up to cross the room and embrace her.

"But, how can you be sure it will be a boy?" he asked.

"It will be a boy," Adanna stated firmly.

It was a boy.

They named him Ikeobi, and Chiaza was delighted with her new toy, taking charge to fuss over him and to teach him all the things that he would need to know.

This was a happy time in Benjamin's life. Adanna was now teaching at a school in the centre of Enugu, and had found satisfaction and a contented peace in the role. Chiaza and Ikeobi thrived and Benjamin arranged for a young girl from a nearby village to look after them during the day while he and Adanna were at work.

In the evenings, after the children had gone to sleep, Benjamin and Adanna liked to take some drinks out to the back garden and sit at the little table on the lawn, quiet and comfortable in each other's company. They would often have friends call to the house as well. Adanna's mother, Ijemma, would drop by several times a week, and both Father Jerome and Pastor Osawe were regular visitors. Adanna would often leave Benjamin and Father Jerome chatting outside long into the night as they discussed everything from football to science and religion to the bewildering machinations of Nigerian politics.

It was not long after Ikeobi had taken his first steps in the world that the first reports of the massacres came in.

Adanna and Benjamin listened with growing disbelief to the confusing news bulletins, but it was the visit of Father Jerome that brought home to them the full horror of the events.

"It's bad all right," Father Jerome admitted as they sat at the table in the back garden, Chiaza and Ikeobi playing nearby. "The stories are coming in from all over the North. It seems to be mostly Igbo who are being attacked, but there are reports of other non-Hausa people also being killed."

"But why?" Benjamin asked.

"Do the Hausa need a reason?" Adanna said bitterly.

Father Jerome sighed as he shook his head. "They say it's to pay the Igbo back for the political killings at the start of the year, during the attempted coup."

"But that doesn't make sense," Benjamin insisted. "It was because of Igbo officers in the army that the coup failed."

"I know," said Father Jerome, "it's a flimsy excuse, and, in any case, it doesn't have the feel of simple acts of vengeance. It all seems to have been carefully planned. Many of the Igbo people in the army have been killed by their former comrades, and it's the

Hausa soldiers who have been responsible for many of the civilian deaths."

"Benjamin," Adanna suddenly cried, "Zara is still in Kano!"

Father Jerome looked at her. "If you have any Igbo friends in the North," he said, "then I would recommend that you urge them to leave as soon as possible. If you can reach them, that is."

"She should be at work at this time," Adanna said. "I should try to phone her." She got up and went inside.

"What does Gowon have to say about the killings?" Benjamin asked Father Jerome.

"Nothing that's any use," Father Jerome admitted. "You have to remember that Gowon is from the North, so there's not much chance of him cracking down on the troubles in the North, is there? Besides," he went on, "Gowon is an idiot. He may be nominally in charge at the moment, but I would say he's just a puppet for the Emirs in the North."

"But isn't Gowon a Christian?"

"He is, Benjamin, he is," said Father Jerome. "But like I said, the man is an idiot. There does seem to be an intelligence behind all of this, and intelligence is not something you can accuse Gowon of having."

"What about Ojukwu?" Benjamin asked. "Can Gowon recall him from the East?"

"I don't know," Father Jerome told him. "I'm not sure what the legal position is at the moment, but for now Ojukwu is still the governor in the East and I don't think that will change anytime soon."

"I can't get an answer at Zara's work," Adanna stated as she came back outside. "I don't know what we can do." She looked pleadingly at Father Jerome.

"Well, you can't go to Kano, that's for sure," said Father Jerome. "It's far too dangerous."

"They say on the radio that it is not just in the North," Benjamin said to Father Jerome. "Is that true?"

"I believe so," Father Jerome sighed. "I've heard of sporadic attacks against Igbo people even in Lagos. Ojukwu has demanded that Gowon do something, but I'm not convinced Gowon would be able to do anything even if he wanted to."

Adanna sat down and looked at Father Jerome. "What do you think Ojukwu will do?" she asked.

"It's hard to say, Adanna. It's hard to know what he *can* do. I've met Ojukwu, you know, and I believe he's a good man. Maybe too good, to be honest."

"What do you mean?"

"I mean that I think he's too honest to be a politician. He's a soldier, really, and that's fine up to a point I suppose, but when he assumed command of the East, I don't imagine that even *he* thought it would be anything other than temporary."

"What do you know about the reports of the refugees?" asked Benjamin.

Father Jerome paused as he scratched at his chin. He was a tall, well-built man, but Benjamin could swear he had shrunk since last they met. "Well," he said, "according to my colleagues, the reports, if anything, haven't gone far enough. People are coming in from all over the country, fleeing for their lives. The train stations of Onitsha, Nsukka and Port Harcourt are all swamped with walking wounded, all telling their stories and spreading the fear. I don't mind telling you both that I think it's just the beginning. I do believe it's going to get a lot worse."

The trickle of refugees became a flood. The Igbo fled from persecution from all corners of Nigeria. Even those who had never even been to the East, saw their traditional homeland as the only place where they could be safe.

The East buckled under the influx of over a million people, but managed to hold firm. The people who sought relief and sanctuary were seen as their own people, their family, and for the Igbo, family was everything. The refugees were welcomed and accommodated. But they brought with them tales that were fuel for nightmares.

"There is still no word from Zara," Adanna informed Benjamin.

"Have you spoken to her family in Port Harcourt?"

Adanna nodded. "Her father has driven to Kano to search for her."

"I don't know if that's wise," said Benjamin. "You've heard the stories, haven't you?"

"I know, but what else can her father do?"

Everyone in the East had now heard the stories. Of children being hacked to death. Of pregnant women being cut open, the contents of their wombs stomped into the ground. Of people being locked up without food or water and taunted as they died.

The systematic slaughter was seen as an attempted genocide against the entire Igbo race, and as 1967 began, the fear and the terror of the people in the East had turned to outrage. The demands began to grow for what many felt was the only option left open to them. Independence.

Benjamin was alone in the house when Father Jerome pulled up. They greeted each other warmly and then Benjamin took two bottles of beer from the fridge and led his friend out to the table in the back garden.

"Adanna not home then?" asked Father Jerome.

"She has taken the children to visit her mother," Benjamin told him.

"And how is Ijemma these days?"

"She is busy," said Benjamin. "You know how she has taken in some refugees, don't you?"

"Ah, yes," Father Jerome said with a smile. "The distant cousins."

"That's right."

"And how are you then, Benjamin? I haven't seen you in a while."

"Same as always really. Still teaching at the university."

"Mmm," Father Jerome said thoughtfully, "and what would you say is the mood there? Amongst your students, I mean."

"They all say the same thing," said Benjamin, "that we must have a country of our own. That the Igbo will never be safe in a Hausa-controlled Nigeria. That the East has no alternative but to secede and to forge a new destiny. But I am sure you have heard all the arguments yourself."

Father Jerome nodded. "Yes," he agreed, "no matter where you go, you hear the same things. The calls for independence grow louder every day."

"What do you think will happen?"

"Well, I know that Ojukwu will do everything in his power to keep Nigeria together." Father Jerome held up a hand as Benjamin was about to speak. "Oh, it's not that Ojukwu has any great idealistic notions about One Nigeria of course, but he's smart enough to know what the alternative would be. Gowon can't afford to let the East just walk away."

"Because of the oil, you mean?"

"The oil plays a big part of it, Benjamin, yes, but think of the bigger picture. Nigeria is not the only country in Africa to be cobbled together from the old colonies. There are borders all over the continent that cut through tribal lands that have existed for millennia. Ancient tribes have been thrown together here, there and everywhere and they've been told they're now part of this country or that country, and they're now called this or that. Did you know the name *Nigeria* was made up by an old British woman?"

"Yes," Benjamin smiled. "Thanks to my wife, I now know my history."

"So just imagine, Benjamin, if the Igbo were allowed to declare their independence and simply go off on their own. What message do you think that would send to the tribes all over Africa who feel persecuted, or unheard, or who just want to decide their own fate?"

"But it isn't just the Igbo, is it? Ojukwu has made a point of including all the tribes of the East. The East is a region, not a tribe."

"Yes, I know that, but that is not how it will be perceived by the outside world now, is it? No, Benjamin, it will be looked upon as nothing more than a rebellion by the ungrateful, upstart Igbo, and it could spark uprisings right across the continent."

"You don't agree with independence then?"

Father Jerome sighed and scratched his head. "Look," he said, "I'd be something of a hypocrite if I claimed that armed insurrection is morally unjustifiable – sure didn't my own father rise against the Brits in 1916? – but this would be suicide. Like I said, Gowon would have no choice but to go to war if the East declared independence, and the British would side with him. In fact, any European power with a vested interest in African stability would side with him too. Gowon would have access to whatever military hardware he needed to crush any uprising. And what do they have here in the East, Benjamin? Little more than shotguns and bloody muskets, that's what."

"It may be inevitable though," Benjamin said sadly.

"If that cretin, Gowon, reneges on the Aburi Accord," said Father Jerome, "then I would have to agree with you."

A diplomatic solution to the crisis had been sought at the neutral venue of Aburi in Ghana, where Colonel Ojukwu presented a set of proposals designed to pull Nigeria back from the brink of civil war.

These proposals were accepted by the delegation, led by Colonel Yakubu Gowon, representing the Federal Government of Nigeria. And war was averted.

Until Gowon returned to Lagos, where he reneged on the entire accord.

And the calls could no longer be ignored. A new nation would rise. A nation that would take her name from the bay that washed the southern shore. A nation that would stride onto the world stage, with her people filled with pride and hope and belief. A nation, alive with the glow of liberty, that would shine like a beacon for Africa and for the world.

An independent sovereign state with a burning urge for self-determination.

Biafra.

Thirty

Joker was the first one up. Standing at the bottom of the stairs he paused to take in, once again, the opulence of the room. He shook his head in wonder that this was considered just a little holiday get-away. He had been informed that Kevin's father had grown up impoverished in the working-class housing estate of Ballymurphy, and Joker had been forced to admit that his achievements since then had been worthy of appreciation and, indeed, praise.

Kevin had explained that his father made a point of using his chain of hair and beauty salons around Ireland to employ only the most vulnerable and the most disadvantaged from those sections of society that were generally overlooked, and had initiated a generous profit-sharing scheme that benefited the entire workforce. That information had certainly poured cold water on Joker's attempted rant about the callous exploitation of ordinary working people, and had led him to go into a bit of a sulk. He just wasn't prepared for altruistic capitalism.

He walked across the room and, turning the lock, pulled open the patio-style, double bi-fold doors to take a look at the beach. It was early and the sun had just cleared the horizon, smearing the sky with a chaotic mess of oranges and pinks and reds. He walked across the veranda and strode out onto the sand, enjoying the cool sensation on his bare feet.

The sea, whilst mimicking the sky in its silent surface, was making nonchalant little ripples against the shore, as if kicking its heels waiting for the world to wake up and come along to play. Joker sat down at the water's edge. As he gazed at the empty horizon, he wasn't sure that he liked all this peace and serenity. It seemed unnatural. The silence was almost unnerving.

"I could get used to this."

Joker turned to see Gary standing beside him, looking out across the water.

"Not missing Belfast then?"

"You're kidding, aren't you? It's going to be hard to go home," said Gary as he sat down. "In fact, I might squeal like a pig."

"Yeah," said Joker. "It's some place, isn't it?"

"Unbelievable," Gary agreed. "I was thinking of bringing Rosie here over the summer for a wee bit of a break."

"Bit presumptuous of you, isn't it? Anyway, aren't you and Rosie going to be busy this summer?"

"Fuck's sake, Joker, don't you start as well. It's just a baby we're having, it's not like it's the end of the world or anything."

Joker stared at Gary for a second, then turned away. "Yeah, maybe you're right," he said. He knew there was no point in trying to unveil the true nature of reality to Gary; it would be like trying to teach quantum theory to a bag of squirrels. "What about Kevin though? Or his folks even? Do you think they'll be happy with you just moving in?"

"Oh, I'm sure it won't be a big deal," Gary assured him. "Kevin seems sound these days, doesn't he? Totally different from the wee prick he used to be."

"Yeah, well he's not Johnny Gee anymore," Joker mused idly.

"Yeah, what was that all about? Did you ever find out?"

"Not that interested to be honest."

A few muffled noises of people stirring back at the house made them both turn around. Joker stood up and wiped the sand from his shorts.

"Well," he said, "I think we should go back and find out what the plan is for today."

After breakfast it was decided that, after the exertions of the previous day, they should take the opportunity to spend the day relaxing at the beach, and so by mid-morning they stepped onto the sand with their towels, and sunglasses, and swimming gear, and sun-tan lotion, and paperbacks, and bottles of water and sunhats and various inflatables.

They spent some time finding the optimum position before laying out their beach-towels in a long row and placing all the items required for a day at the beach in strategic places around the area.

It looked like the day would get hot, even though it was only late April, so they slapped on some sun-tan lotion and then, finally, they all lay down on their towels to gently sizzle in the golden Iberian sun. After ten seconds, Joker sat up.

"Fuck this," he said. "I'm going for a beer."

"I'll come with you."

"Yeah, me too."

"Yeah, this is boring."

"Yeah, I've had enough now."

They all stood up and spent some time packing away all of the beach paraphernalia – the paperbacks, the sunhats, the bottles of water, the sun-tan lotion, towels, etc., and marched off to find a bar.

Thirty One

India was once an island, apparently. But then, using something called *plate tectonics,* it crashed into Asia, causing the land to ruck up into the air and create a mountain range. And that's how the Himalayas were made.

Hannah shook her head in disbelief. How could such nonsense come to be written, she wondered. All of the land on Earth, she knew, had been created and fixed by God in a single day, but this book was trying to tell her that the land was moving about all over the place. And had been for hundreds of *millions* of years.

According to the book she was reading, the surface of the Earth was made up of different plates that moved around like lily pads on a pond. Sometimes these plates would rub against each other, causing earthquakes, and that made Hannah stop and think.

She knew that earthquakes were a powerful demonstration of God's wrath, and were sent as punishment for sinfulness, but she had never understood why earthquakes were prevalent in some parts of the world and not in others. The notion that earthquakes would occur mostly in those places where two of these plates met would explain that phenomenon, but that just raised all sorts of questions. Why, for example, would God create a world that was inherently unstable?

Hannah then noted with some disdain that the whole business of plate tectonics was just another scientific *theory*, and she closed the book with a sigh. Just more guesswork, she thought wearily, though she could see how the scientists would think it was a good explanation. She sat back in her chair and let her mind wander.

She had long known, of course, that much of society had dismissed Scripture as a reliable source of knowledge, but her time spent going through all these books at the library brought home to her just how pervasive the rejection of the Bible truly was. In fact, a lot of the information contained in these books flagrantly contradicted the facts given in the Bible. But then the Bible, Hannah thought guiltily, had a tendency to contradict itself.

It was the old conflict, she reflected miserably. The problems that she had with Scripture that pulled her in different directions. Biblical inconsistencies, Greg had told her, were probably just down to the scribes, who copied the original manuscripts, making silly mistakes, but why, she wondered, would God allow that to happen?

And besides, she thought, that might explain things like Saul's daughter, Michal, in the second book of Samuel, who remains childless all her life while, at the same time, having five sons, but it could not explain away the one obvious contradiction with which Hannah continued to struggle: the Sixth Commandment; *Thou shalt not kill.*

It is the most clear, the most straightforward, the least ambiguous guideline in all of Scripture, she thought, so why does God consistently ignore it? According to God, any woman who is not a virgin on her wedding night must be stoned to death. *Must!* Anyone caught working on the Sabbath *must* be stoned to death. Cursing your parents: death. Blasphemy: death. Adultery: death. Fortune-telling: death. Worship of other gods: death. The slaughter in Scripture is relentless.

Hannah stood up to clear her thoughts. Knowing she was under constant divine scrutiny always made her feel anxious when such nagging doubts crept into her head. She wandered over to what was becoming her favourite section in the library; astronomy.

The absurd scale of the cosmos seemed to speak to her on a level that she didn't fully understand, she just knew that it held her enthralled. She picked out a few books and went back to her desk.

They say that nothing in the universe can go faster than the speed of light, but there were no speed limits in Hannah's mind. Moving at a trillion miles per hour, she soared clear of the Milky Way and out into intergalactic space, heading for Andromeda. The tip of James' tongue circled slowly around her naval before moving down towards her...she brushed it away dismissively. This was getting interesting.

The Andromeda Galaxy was the closest galaxy to the Milky Way, and Hannah was looking forward to becoming more acquainted. Had she been plodding along at the sluggish old speed of light then it would have taken her over two million years to get there, so it was just as well she was really motoring.

She had learned that the galaxies themselves were not exactly standing still, they were positively racing through space. In fact, the Andromeda Galaxy, she discovered, was following a graceful arc that would send it crashing into the Milky Way in about…wait, what?

Hannah stared at the words on the page. The Milky Way Galaxy, it seemed – the galaxy in which she was currently living, where she kept all her stuff – was on a collision course with the Andromeda Galaxy. It wasn't due to happen anytime soon – she still had a few billion years in which to brace herself – but still, the idea of galaxies going around bumping into each other was a little unsettling. It suggested some fairly sloppy planning, for one thing.

Leafing further through the books, she came across the subject of asteroids, where she found even more food for thought. The asteroid belt was situated between Mars and Jupiter and was estimated to contain around a billion lumps of rock of all shapes and sizes. These were believed to have once been trying to form a planet, but had been pulled apart by the immense gravity of Jupiter, and again Hannah wondered at the purpose of such planning. She knew she had no place to go questioning God's divine plan, but a lot of His work was beginning to strike her as a little haphazard. Of course it was possible that God just wanted to have a handy source of ammunition floating around in space for when He was in the mood to do a bit of smiting, but Hannah was learning that even the direction of God's fury could be a little perplexing.

In 1908, Hannah read, one of these asteroids entered the Earth's atmosphere and exploded with a force of up to 30 megatons of TNT. That figure didn't mean much to Hannah, but it sounded like quite a lot.

So, what was the target of such violent retribution? Who or what had provoked God's fury to such a cataclysmic extent?

It was trees.

This catastrophic explosion had occurred in a remote and unpopulated region of Siberia and had done little more than wipe out a lot of trees. An awful lot of trees. Around eighty million, in fact.

Now Hannah knew that a lot of God's actions in Scripture could appear baffling to the mortal mind, but sending a thirty megaton fireball to destroy a forest in the middle of nowhere seemed quirky, even for God.

She shuddered as she realised her flippant thoughts could once again be construed as disrespectful, and she hurriedly closed her books and sat back, gripped with anxiety. She began to breathe faster and more heavily and, as she tried to bring her breathing under control, the image of James' smiling eyes came into her head and it seemed to calm her. To comfort her. She felt herself relax.

As she walked around the shelves, returning all the books she had taken, she thought again of James and it made her smile. She smiled at his gentle earnestness, his infectious passion for learning, his pompous assertion that he needed to know everything. She smiled at his gorgeous eyes, at his smile, at the way he would…she put her head down and walked quickly from the library, her mind clouded by discordant, confusing notions and the disapproving glare of God.

Making her way through town, she remembered Rosie telling her that James was in Spain this week and she imagined him drenched in warm sunshine.

What was he thinking right now, she wondered. Was he thinking of her? What was he doing today, and how was he getting on? She strode along Royal Avenue, anxious, and miserable, and smiling.

Thirty Two

"Squeal, little piggy! Squeal!" Joker was taunting the pork sausages, as they hissed in the hot oil, with his criminally underrated impression of an American hillbilly.

Although it was still early, Joker had already been to the supermarket on the other side of the paseo, and had now taken it upon himself to cook breakfast for everyone. Tone and Sean had yet to appear, but everyone else was up, sitting around the dining table, bleary-eyed and yawning, stretching and idly scratching bits of themselves.

"Who was on at the shop?" asked Kevin.

"Some wee redhead," Joker told him. "Funny looking bake, but in a sexy sort of way."

"Sounds like Gabriela," Kevin mused. "I know her."

Joker stopped tormenting the sausages for a second and looked at Kevin. "Know her?" he asked. "What? Like in a biblical way?"

"What?" Kevin flushed. "No...no...I was just..."

Gary leaned forward, intrigued by Kevin's reaction. "That hit a nerve, didn't it? Are you sure you're not slipping her a length?"

"Jesus! No! I only-"

"What's for breakfast?" Tone appeared at the bottom of the stairs wearing just a pair of shorts and some flip-flops.

"Sausages," said Joker. "Hey, did you know that Kevin and the wee redhead from the shop are blowing trumpets?"

"Good for them," remarked Tone, taking a seat at the table. "Sausages and what?"

"Sausages and ketchup," Joker replied.

"Genius!" said Tone appreciatively. "Absolute fucking genius! So who's this wee redhead then?"

"Gabriela," said Gary. He turned to Kevin. "That's her name, isn't it? Are you going to introduce us all later?"

"Seriously," Kevin stammered, "there's nothing going on. I've met her a couple of times and, like, we've said hello and all, but there's nothing going on."

"Well, far be it from me to question your veracity," said Tone as he lazily stretched his arms above his head, "but your redner would suggest otherwise."

"Yeah, what's the deal?" pressed Gary. "Do you fancy her, is that it?"

"If that's the case," said Joker, "then you've come to the-"

"For fuck's sake, leave the guy alone!" cried Bobby. He was concerned that Joker was becoming distracted from his breakfast-making duties.

"I'm just saying," Joker persisted, "that if Kevin needs a bit of relationship advice, then we're the very lads to come to. Isn't that right?"

"Yeah," said Bobby, "because we're all fucking experts in relationships, aren't we?"

"Exactly, Bobby."

"What's keeping those fucking sausages?" demanded Seamus. He felt he should try to deflect some of the attention away from Kevin, who was becoming more and more flustered.

"All right, Seamus," said Joker, "we all know how you love a good sausage, but don't panic. They won't be long."

"I've heard that Seamus likes them long," quipped Tone, and all attention shifted away from Kevin, as everyone dusted off their favourite old double-entendres, and held them up as breakfast-time entertainment.

Jamesy, sensing there was something unspoken in Kevin's suddenly subdued bearing, determined that he would try to have a casual chat with him at some point later. When it was quieter.

After breakfast, everyone was lounging around, smoking, drinking tea and making plans for the rest of the day. Sean had appeared earlier and had been surprised to learn that a vote had been taken to decide the person who would be doing all of the washing-up for that day.

"What can I say, Sean," said Tone, as he handed Sean a cloth, "it was completely unanimous."

"Wankers," Sean grumbled as he trudged off to the kitchen sink.

"So, what's the plan then?" asked Bobby.

"I reckon we should go and check out the town," Tone suggested. "We need to go there sometime this week anyway to sort that house out, so we might as well get it over with."

"Yeah," Kevin agreed, "I wouldn't mind doing that, to be honest."

"Sounds good to me," said Bobby, and everyone else nodded their approval.

"We could either go after lunch," Kevin said, "or go now, and get lunch in the town."

Tone turned to address Joker. "Did you get anything for lunch," he asked, "when you were at the shop earlier?"

"I did actually," Joker replied. "I got some stuff to make ham and cheese baguettes."

"Right then, we'll have lunch here, and then head off to the town after."

"And I even got some salad," Joker went on, "for Seamus here."

"What?" said Seamus, hearing his name. "What was that?"

"I got you some salad."

"And what the fuck is that supposed to mean?"

"Look, don't take this the wrong way," Joker began.

"Oh, fuck," muttered Gary. "Here we go..."

"But I was thinking that it's about time you started taking this whole gay thing a bit more seriously. You're just not making the effort, are you?"

"What? What are talking about?"

"Well, do you not think you should start by embracing your feminine side a bit more?"

"Fuck off, Joker!" cried Seamus. "I may be gay, but that doesn't make me a poof!"

"You see!" said Joker. "That's exactly what I'm talking about! How are you supposed to get your hole with that sort of attitude?"

"Get my hole?" gasped Seamus. "Jesus Christ! Not everything's about sex you know."

"Now you're getting the hang of it."

Seamus looked over at Tone with exasperation. "Can you have a fucking word with him?"

"Well, I don't know," said Tone, sipping his tea. "I think he might have a point."

"What?"

"It's all about being comfortable with your sexuality, isn't it?"

"Oh, for fuck's sake!"

"What's the salad got to do with anything though?" asked Kevin.

"Well, it's a woman's thing, isn't it?" said Joker.

"Is it?"

"Actually," Jamesy interjected, "if we're having ham and cheese baguettes, then I'd be happy with a wee bit of salad in mine."

"Well said, Jamesy," Joker enthused. "We can all have a bit of salad just to show there's no shame in it."

"What the fuck are you on about?" asked Seamus.

"Look, I'm only trying to help you out here, you know," Joker insisted. "I mean, think about it. You haven't told me that my shirt looks nice. You've never called me darling. You don't-"

"I'm sorry, which one of us is gay again?"

"You've never called me darling either," said Bobby, grinning. "My feelings are a wee bit hurt."

"Look," Joker said placatingly, "remember your man at the panadería yesterday?"

"Who?"

"You know who I mean. He called Jamesy his *hermosito*. Good-looking fella, he was."

"Oh yeah," said Seamus. "What about him?"

"Well, that's what I'm talking about," Joker explained. "Now you could tell that he was gay, couldn't you? He was completely at ease with his sexuality. And all that confidence really came across, didn't it? That's what I'm getting at, that's all. Actually I thought that you and him would look good together."

"Don't know about that," Seamus said thoughtfully. "He was a bit too gay for my liking."

"*Too* gay?" cried Joker. "*Too* gay? You don't like being too gay? What the fuck are planning to do then? Just stick it in a wee bit?"

"You don't know what the fuck you're talking about!" Seamus snapped. "You just think gay sex is all about the arse, don't you?"

"Well, isn't it?"

"No it fucking isn't!"

"How the fuck would you know?"

"Because I've…"

During the pause, everyone turned to stare at Seamus. Sean strolled over from the kitchen area. Tone's teacup was frozen halfway to his lips. Joker's right eyebrow rose slightly. A cheeky breeze flicked a few grains of sand through the open doors, and the sounds of the sea slapping the beach came along in slow regular beats.

Seamus looked around at the expectant faces and sighed. "Because I've already done the deed," he said.

Everyone erupted. "Good man yourself!" they cried as they patted Seamus on the back and shook his hand. "Good fucking lad!" Seamus, grinning, disappeared beneath all of the clamorous congratulations and the whoops of victory and joy.

The first thing that everyone noticed as they stepped off the bus, was the mountain. It dominated the town that sat at its base, and could be seen from miles around. Everyone stood at the side of the main road that ran through the town and gazed up at the distant peak.

"Can you see the cross?" asked Kevin.

"What? Oh fuck yeah, right enough." Right at the very top of the mountain, outlined against the blue sky, was a little black silhouette of a Christian cross.

"That's cool," said Sean, squinting up at the familiar shape.

"Right then, Kevin," said Tone. "Do you know where we're going?"

"Yeah, I've got a fair idea where it is," Kevin told him. He gestured across the road. "I think it's up that way."

The pavement on the street that Kevin led them to was only wide enough to accommodate two abreast, so they walked along in pairs as Kevin checked the house numbers. It was siesta time so the street was quiet, though a few residents could be seen sitting on the pavement by their front doors hoping to catch a cool breeze. Kevin halted.

"This is it, I think. Number Forty-Two."

"Bit creepy, isn't it?" said Bobby, looking up at the high façade.

"Atmospheric, you mean," Jamesy corrected. "Look at the size of those doors. Now why would they-?"

"Well, are we going to go in or what?" Tone asked impatiently.

"Right, right," said Kevin as he fumbled in his pocket for the key. Set in the huge double doors that made up a large proportion of the house-front was a small, single door. Kevin tried the key in the smaller door's lock and was mildly surprised when it turned and the door creaked open.

"Now we know how Howard Carter felt," said Bobby lightly.

"Who?" asked Kevin.

"Howard Carter," Bobby repeated. "Him and his mates opened the tomb of Tutankhamen."

"Yeah, and we all know what happened to them, don't we?" said Joker.

"What do you mean?"

"Well, it was the curse, wasn't it? Killed them all."

"Oh come on, Joker," said Jamesy. "That's a myth."

"They all died, didn't they?"

"Well, yes, eventually, but that-"

"Oh, for fuck's sake!" cried Tone. "Are we going to go in or not? I'm sure there's not going to be any mummies waiting to give us all a plague of fucking boils."

"You can't be sure though, can you?" said Joker.

"Jesus," muttered Tone, stepping through the door. The others filed in after him and then they all stood silently in the gloomy interior.

They were standing in a high-ceilinged reception area, with a door on their left, leading to the front room of the house, and an open dining area, complete with table and chairs further along, also on the left.

Straight ahead was another set of huge double doors, more ornate than the first pair, with decorative panels of painted glass. There was a sense of dark, oppressive age all around them, with the sun-bright street now reduced to an incongruous rectangle in the gloom behind them.

"Nice and cool in here," Joker whispered.

"Why are you whispering?" Tone whispered back.

"I don't know."

Tone caught a sudden movement in the corner of his eye on the wall to his right and he jumped.

"Shit!" he cried out, and everyone turned and bolted for the bright little rectangle in the door. They all crashed into the doorway at the same time, causing a jam until, one by one, they popped out onto the street, panting and cursing and shaking from the sudden release of tension.

A few doors down, a plump middle-aged woman sat on a chair on the pavement and watched impassively as they spilled out onto the road.

Sean looked accusingly at Tone. "That was just a lizard, wasn't it Tone?"

"A lizard?" asked Bobby. "A fucking lizard?"

"You fucking big Scaredy Baa!" said Joker.

"Okay, okay," said Tone. "Everybody calm down. It's no big deal. Right, I reckon we should have a quick look around the house and then go and explore the town for a bit. It looks like a lively wee place, so we could sit and have a beer somewhere and work out what our options are."

Everyone agreed and they all stepped back inside. As their vision adjusted to the gloom, they began to take more of an interest in their surroundings. Joker gave Kevin a hand to open the big interior doors and they discovered a small but functional kitchen that led to a third set of tall doors at the far end. Jamesy examined the grooves in the stone floor that ran from the front of the house to the back.

"Well that explains that," he muttered.

"Explains what?" asked Kevin.

"This would have led all the way through to some sort of courtyard at the back," Jamesy explained, gesturing from the doors at the front of the house to the third set at the back. "That's why these doors are all so tall. Whoever lived here would have brought their horse and cart, or wagon or whatever, all the way through the house to..." Jamesy unlocked the third set of doors and opened them onto a large courtyard with a two-storey outbuilding at the far end. "... to these stables."

"Why couldn't they just park it out the front?" asked Bobby.

"Joyriders," Joker told him.

"Well, something like that," said Jamesy. "It obviously would have made more sense to have your horse and cart safely tucked away for the night. It's fascinating when you think about-"

"Do you think we should check it out up there?" interrupted Tone, pointing to the upper floor of the stable block. "I'm only saying because I think Jamesy was about to bore the tits off everybody."

"The stairs look a bit rickety," said Kevin.

"Yeah," said Tone, "but the alternative is standing here listening to one of Jamesy's lectures on the social history of rural Spain, so come on."

They all crossed the courtyard towards the little wooden staircase at the side of the stables.

"Don't you listen to him, Jamesy," said Joker. "I thought it was very interesting."

Jamesy laughed as they made their way gingerly up the steps.

"Just a load of old crap, really," said Sean, and everyone agreed. The room above the stables was littered with ancient agricultural implements as well as old equestrian equipment. Nothing looked useful, or even usable.

"So what do you want to do, Kevin?" asked Tone.

"Well, I need to organise a van or something to come and take away a lot of this stuff. What we could do," said Kevin, "is have a bit of a look around today to see what can go and what can stay, and then come back tomorrow and pile all the stuff that's going in the hallway by the front doors. Then I'll make a couple of phone calls and that should be that."

"Sounds good to me," said Tone. "And we can get dinner around here this evening, can't we? Before we head back to the beach."

"Yeah, there are some really good bars around here."

"Perfect!" Tone declared, rubbing his hands. "Well, the sooner we get started…"

Later that night, the stable block was silent in the moonlight. The only movement came from the twitching ear of a ginger tomcat as it shuffled ever closer to a small lizard, dozing in the cool of the night. A sudden crash caused the cat to flinch and to turn, hissing, at the intrusion. Further loud noises persuaded the cat to abandon his hunt, and he sloped off over the wall of the courtyard to find somewhere less busy to indulge his passion for stealth and murder.

"What dickhead left that there?" Seamus winced as he rolled on the floor clutching his shin.

"It was you, wasn't it?" said Gary. "You were dead smug about it too, actually."

"Fuck's sake!"

"Yeah, you thought you were being dead clever," Gary reminded him, "putting all the stuff out today, to save having to do it tomorrow."

"Don't lie there too long," said Tone as everyone filed past Seamus. "You'll probably get covered in ants."

They all assembled around the old dining table, upon which they placed some carrier bags containing various bottles of alcohol.

"What made you buy gin?" Sean asked Joker. "You don't normally drink gin, do you?"

"650 pesetas for a litre of gin?" said Joker, "I could hardly leave it there at that price, now could I?"

"Yeah, but at that price," Sean pointed out, "it must be undrinkable."

"Well, that's what the lemon Fanta's for," Joker explained. "Really, Sean, you just don't think ahead, do you?"

Seamus limped over to the table. "Has anybody checked that the fridge is working?" he asked.

"Seems okay to me," said Bobby, coming through the open doors from the kitchen. "Well, it made a noise when I plugged it in so…"

"Well, you're the engineer," said Tone, "so that's good enough for me."

They had bought beer and vodka and whiskey, as well as some mixers, so they placed the beer in the fridge and then settled around the dining table and opened the bottles of spirits.

"Are we really going to stay here tonight?" asked Kevin. "We could always order some taxis."

"That would cost a fortune," said Tone. "And anyway, we fucked up, and when you find yourself in a situation like that, you just have accept it and make the best of it."

"How much did we miss the last bus by again?" asked Seamus.

"Four and a half hours."

"So, skin of our teeth really?"

"Yeah," said Bobby. "And Joker proved that we're in no fit state to hitchhike anywhere."

"Yeah, Joker! What the fuck?" Sean exclaimed.

"I'd just found a litre of gin for 650 pesetas, Sean," said Joker. "What was I supposed to do? *Not* dance in the middle of the road? Yeah, Sean, that's realistic, isn't it?"

"It doesn't matter now anyway," Tone said as he passed around some cigarettes. "We're stuck here and, to be honest, it's probably for the best. It means that tomorrow we can do what we need to do early on, and then we've got the rest of the day to ourselves. Jamesy, what's the bed situation?"

Jamesy came down the staircase that ran up the wall to one side of the dining area.

"Same as it was earlier," he said. "I can't find any sheets or anything, but there's no shortage of beds, and it's warm enough to not need sheets. Besides, I think we'll all be too comatose to care."

"That's settled then," Tone declared. "We'll hole up here for the night, and then we'll already be here first thing. Couldn't have worked out any better."

"I'll drink to that," said Joker, drinking to that. Gary got up and went over to a large wooden chest of drawers that had been pushed into an alcove under the stairs.

"Did we check out these drawers earlier?" he asked. "I can't actually remember."

No one else could remember so Gary began to pull open the drawers one by one. "Just more old crap," he said, picking up and examining various items. A hairbrush. Old newspapers and magazines. A framed monochrome photograph. "That's a weird picture to frame, isn't it?" He passed it to Tone who gave it a cursory glance. It depicted a simple, low-roofed building in a bleak, rocky environment, and with a tall black cross set against the sky in the background.

"Mmm," said Tone, "it is a bit weird." He set it down on the table and took a puff from his cigarette. "I was thinking if we get a chance tomorrow," he went on, "we could explore the town a bit more."

"We could do with getting back to the beach at some point though," Kevin pointed out.

"Yeah, no problem, Kevin. Don't worry about it."

"Some good wee bars around here," said Joker. "It seems like the proper, authentic sort of Spain around here, doesn't it? That *Tres Hermanas* bar was class earlier."

"Yeah," Gary agreed, "I reckon we should check out the rest of the town."

"But we do need to get-"

"Yes, yes, Kevin, all right," said Tone. "I said don't worry about it. What's that gin like, Joker?"

"It's going down well."

"So I see."

"It goes really well with lemon Fanta."

"Not the traditional mixer for gin though, is it?"

"No," Joker conceded, "but we'd all still be stuck in caves if nobody bothered to try anything new."

"So is that what you're doing then? Pushing back the boundaries of humanity?"

"I like to think so."

The night wore on into the early hours. The conversation around the table had slowed to intermittent mumblings. Tone sat quietly, staring at the photograph that Gary had found earlier. Sean nudged Bobby. "Do you think he's asleep there?" he asked, nodding to Joker who had one side of his face resting on the table top.

"Either that," said Bobby, "or he's wearing a really heavy, invisible hat."

Sean giggled drunkenly. Seamus took a closer look at Joker.

"He's definitely asleep," he said. "He's been doing that a lot lately."

"Well, he's knocked back most of that gin," said Gary. "Hardly surprising he's passed out."

"I know, but that's my point," said Seamus. "It's the fact that-"

"You know where I think this is?" Tone suddenly exclaimed. "I reckon this is up that mountain."

"What is?" asked Sean.

"This building." Tone passed the photograph around. He looked at Kevin. "What do you think, Kevin? Do you know anything about it?"

"No," Kevin told him. "First I've heard of it."

"There you go then!" Tone declared triumphantly. "That's settled it!"

"What are you talking about?" asked Jamesy.

"No, no. I think he's got a point," said Sean excitedly. "You see, from down here you can just make out the cross, right? But it looks exactly like the cross in this picture, doesn't it?"

"But all crosses look the-"

"So it's obvious that this building is up the mountain, isn't it?" Sean insisted. "On the other side of the cross."

Tone slapped the top of the table to confirm that Sean's logic was irrefutable.

"So?" asked Jamesy. "What's your point?"

"The point is, Jamesy Boy," said Sean firmly. "The point is…" He looked at Tone.

"The point is," said Tone as he took a gulp of beer. "The point is that it's got to be a monastery up there, hasn't it?"

"Has it?"

"Of course! What else can it be?"

"Well, it could be-"

"And you know what they've got in monasteries, don't you?"

"Monks?"

"Well yes, monks obviously. But you know what monks do, don't you?"

"What?"

"They make strong wine."

"Do they?"

"Of course," Tone insisted. "Everybody knows that. They're always at it. Let's face it, they've got fuck all else to do, have they? Especially stuck on top of a bloody mountain."

"Yeah, that makes sense," said Sean.

"Does it, Sean?" Jamesy demanded. "Does it really?"

"Right," said Tone, standing up and raising his glass, "so we're all decided then?"

No one around the table knew what Tone was talking about, but they held up their drinks and nodded in drunken agreement.

"Drink up, lads!" Tone exhorted. "For tomorrow, come the dawn, we rise!"

Thirty Three

Martin thought that Stephanie had sounded pleased on the phone and, as he waited in the city centre café for her to arrive for their arranged meeting, he realised he was looking forward to the encounter. He felt that he had run out of ideas in his search for his family, and he was hoping that sharing the burden with another person might unveil a fresh perspective.

Stephanie, he assumed, would also have a better understanding of what sort of official channels they could try that would be of use in pointing him in the right direction, but even just having someone to talk to, Martin felt, could prove to be beneficial.

Stephanie arrived on time and smiled when she saw Martin sitting at a table by the far wall.

"Hello, Martin," she said cheerfully. "Been waiting long?"

"Not at all," he replied as he stood to shake her hand. "Just got here really."

They both sat and a waitress came and took their order. They made general small talk about the weather while they waited for the waitress to return and then, once Martin had poured out two cups of tea from a little pot, Stephanie settled back in her seat and gave Martin a sympathetic look.

"So how have you been getting on then?" she asked.

"Not very well," he admitted. He explained how he had gone looking for his old home, only to discover it no longer existed, and how he had wandered around, bewildered, in a world he didn't recognise. "It's all been changed since I was last there," he told her.

"When were you last there?"

"Well, that's a bit of a long story." He said with a sigh, and then he went on to explain how he had arrived at his current situation. How, nearly twenty years before, he had been inadvertently caught up in the chaos of internment. How a subsequent mental collapse had thrown him into the confusing machinery of mental health treatment in the seventies, and how he had eventually found himself abandoned and lost on the streets. Of Glasgow.

"Glasgow?" cried Stephanie. "How did you end up in Glasgow?"

Martin gave a wan smile. "I'm probably not the best person to ask," he said. "Like I said, I wasn't exactly aware of what was going on at the time."

Stephanie nodded. "Yeah," she told him, "I recognised the look in your eyes when we were on the ferry. It didn't last very long, just a flash really, but it was there all the same."

"You recognised it?"

"Mmm," she said, sipping her tea. "My husband had a severe breakdown about ten years ago. Came as a real shock, I can tell you. It just came out of nowhere and was really bad for a while."

"How is he now?"

"Oh, he's okay these days," she assured him. "But even after all this time you still have to take it one day at a time, you know? You can't get complacent."

Martin smiled. "I know what you mean."

"What shocked me when it happened though," Stephanie went on, "was how nobody really seemed to know what they were doing. You know, the doctors and psychiatrists and all these people who you just expect to be experts, and who'll know exactly what to do; they didn't have a bloody clue. It was like 'try these drugs' and 'if these don't work, we'll try these ones'. It was like it was all trial and error."

"Yeah," Martin agreed, "I think I must have been under heavy medication for most of the time. There's just so much I don't remember."

"It's strange, isn't it? You just assume that the health experts all know everything, don't you? But when it comes to the brain, nobody has any idea. Or at least not much of an idea."

"That's true actually," said Martin. "It's only in the last year or so that I've really been making any progress, and that's only because I was lucky enough to get hooked up with this psychotherapist who's helped me out a lot. He's been doing a lot of new, experimental stuff, but he once told me that trying to cure mental health issues was like trying to rewire and solder an electrical circuit using only a lump hammer."

Stephanie laughed. "I know," she said. "It still amazes me how nobody seems to know how the mind works. So, where is this psychotherapist then? Is he in Glasgow?"

"No, no, I left Glasgow years ago," Martin told her. "I fell in with a couple of homeless alcoholics – which means I was a homeless alcoholic myself – and they came up with a plan for us all to make our way to London where we would all be, somehow, set for life. Of course, I didn't really know what was going on, I just went along with it, but eventually we must have made it to London because I have some vague memories of sleeping rough near King's Cross."

"So you don't remember much about it then?" asked Stephanie. "Is that because of the alcohol, or were you still suffering from mental health issues?"

"Probably a bit of both really," said Martin. "I mean, I was still having all sorts of hallucinations – they call them *psychotic episodes* apparently – but how much of that was down to the booze and the drugs, it's hard to say."

"You were taking drugs as well?"

"Yeah well, anything to make it through the day," he said. "Jesus! I don't know how I survived, to be honest. I think my two mates from Glasgow were looking out for me. They had their own problems, obviously, but they did see me through some bad times."

"Where are they now?"

"I've no idea."

"Why? What happened?"

"I had a bad overdose," Martin explained, "and ended up in hospital. It was touch and go for a while, but I managed to pull through and then I was placed in a homeless shelter that was being run by a mental health charity. That's probably what saved my life, because that's where I met Dr Sedgewick."

"Is this the psychotherapist?"

"Yeah, he happened to be working in London at that time, but he told me of a place in Sussex where he did most of his work. It was an old stately home that had been converted into a modern clinic devoted to mental health, co-funded, apparently, by charities and the private sector.

"Well anyway, to cut a long story short, Dr Sedgewick pulled some strings and the next thing I knew I was living in a stately home on the south coast of England. I mean, I was just a glorified guinea pig for some wacky, experimental therapies, but what did I have to lose?"

"Sounds like you were a very comfortable guinea pig."

"Oh yes, absolutely," laughed Martin. "It was lovely."

"You've only mentioned therapy," said Stephanie, "does that mean you weren't on any medication?"

"Oh no, I've had to go onto anti-depressants, but Alex doesn't like to-"

"Alex?"

"Oh yeah, sorry, Alex is Dr Sedgewick. We've spent so much time around each other that it's just easier to use first names."

"What were you going to say?"

"Oh, just that Alex doesn't like to focus on the medication side of things. His therapies are more geared towards practical exercises, you know? Almost as a way to retrain your brain, sort of."

"And you think it's helped?"

"I think so." Martin looked thoughtful. "Or it could just be the medication. Or coming off illegal drugs. Or just chilling out in a peaceful environment."

"Or a combination of them all," ventured Stephanie.

"Who knows?" said Martin, spreading his hands wide. "All I know is, I'm thinking clearly now, for the first time in years. And there's a family out there somewhere that could probably do with some answers."

"You've looked in the phone book, I take it."

"Yeah," Martin replied. "But I couldn't find anything obvious in there."

"Well then," said Stephanie decisively, "once we've finished this tea, maybe we should go about finding this family of yours."

Thirty Four

As they made their way through the town, it became obvious that the neighbourhoods were becoming less affluent the higher up they climbed, as if the poor were being pushed into the foothills to huddle out of sight of the prosperous town centre that languished on the valley floor.

Had Joker been more aware of his surroundings, then he may have held forth on the inherent inequalities of the capitalist system, and how the fat cats with the majority of the wealth could wallow in all the amenities the town centre could offer while the most vulnerable and the most in need were shoved to the fringes of society and forgotten.

But Joker was scarcely aware that he was even awake, and so the poor, huddled masses could only watch as their potential champion shuffled past in silence.

At the very top of the town, where the mountain could finally shake off the clinging attentions of man, and rise unhindered to meet the sky, the weary group arrived at a walled cemetery. It was silent here. The busy town centre was far below and the town itself had petered out into a few dusty and deserted alleyways that had almost made it to the walls of the cemetery, only to give up and now lie exhausted in the baking heat.

On the other side of the cemetery was a small grove of ancient olive trees, and it was here that Tone decided to make base camp, to rest and to make preparations for the final assault on the summit. He walked with Sean to the top of the grove to scout for possible pathways up the mountain. Everyone else collapsed onto the ground, grateful for the shade afforded by the trees. Plastic bottles of water were passed around to appreciative throats that were, despite the early hour, already parched.

"Why are we doing this again?" asked Gary.

"Doing what?" Joker mumbled. He was lying on his back with his forearm covering his eyes.

"Climbing a mountain," Gary said casually.

Joker wasn't sure that he had heard that correctly. Climbing a *what*?

"Right lads," said Tone, as he and Sean came back to stand in the middle of the group. "It looks like there's a path that winds up around the back of the mountain. It should take us up to the top."

There was that word again, thought Joker. *Mountain*. Just what the buggering fuck were they doing climbing a mountain? In this heat? He considered framing a question that might shed some light on the subject – something along the lines of 'what the buggering fuck are we doing climbing a mountain? In this heat? – but he needed his brain for that, and his brain, at the moment, seemed to be ignoring him.

"You know," said Jamesy, "I'm starting to wonder if this was such a good idea after all."

"Yeah," Seamus added, "it seemed reasonable enough last night, but that's because we were all-"

"What the fuck are you talking about?" Tone demanded. "This isn't a debate. We all agreed to do this, didn't we?"

"Well yeah, but-"

"And anyway," Tone went on, "think about the poor wee monk. He's probably sitting up there waiting for us with all that booze he's made. We can't just leave him hanging, can we? Think how happy he'll be when we all show up. And don't forget about all the buxom serving wenches there'll be. Come on! Don't be such fucking faders!"

Joker relaxed as he understood what was happening. He realised now that he wasn't actually lying on the lower slopes of some Spanish mountain in the blazing sun. He was still curled up somewhere, fast asleep, snoring and dreaming. Boozed-up monkeys? Swervy witches? It was a little more surreal and more vivid than his usual dreams, but he was still happy to go along with it. In fact, it occurred to him that now he knew it was a dream, he could do whatever he wanted. He could even fly up to the summit. He stood up, feeling altogether in a better frame of mind. Tone was still talking.

"I think we might have even sworn an oath on it."

"Well, I do remember a lot of swearing," said Bobby.

"Yes," Jamesy argued, "but look at how hot it is already. It's only going to get worse, isn't it? Do we even have enough water with us?"

"Typical Jamesy," laughed Joker, "always fucking moaning about something or other. Come on, Jamesy. We may as well get this over with."

"Right, are we all ready?" called Tone. He could tell there was a growing sense of mutiny in the ranks and, although Joker's attitude confused him, he decided to run with it. It was best to use the momentum to get everyone up and moving, and focused on the task in hand.

Which was what, exactly? Why had he become so intent on climbing this stupid mountain? He wasn't entirely convinced by the idea of an isolated monastery, but even if he was, would that justify what he was doing? All he knew was that he was determined to reach the summit and if sheer bloody-mindedness was his only reason for doing so, then so be it.

Everyone got up and, stretching their tired limbs, trudged out from the shaded grove and into the harsh and unforgiving sunshine.

It didn't take long for the truth to dawn on Joker and, struggling through his own little rainstorm as the last of the gin trickled through his pores and dripped onto the front of his shirt, he decided that something needed to be done.

Thirty Five

Ellie was at work, which meant that Rosie was free to wander around the house on her own. Even after all these months of abstinence she still craved a cigarette. It was bad enough, she thought, being so heavy and creaky, but not having the comfort of a little bit of nicotine was just making it all worse.

Of course, no one had forced her to stop smoking, but the risk of harming her child just about outweighed her cravings, and she reckoned that it only added to the sense of anticipation for the first cigarette she would have after the birth. She imagined slipping quietly away somewhere and putting a light to the tobacco and sucking in that first lungful of soothing smoke. Or maybe she wouldn't.

Maybe she would be able to build on this time during her pregnancy to finally quit once and for all. She had tried many times in the past but each time the addiction had proved too strong and her willpower had crumbled. This time might be different.

She roamed aimlessly around the front room, restless and irritable, wishing that Gary was with her so she could have a moan at him. The thought of him, though, made her smile.

She idly picked up a small glass ashtray from the mantelpiece and examined it. Why had Ellie kept this thing for so long, she wondered, though she knew the reason why.

It was a memory.

The colourful picture on the bottom of the ashtray was now faded and worn but the logo was still legible and it still told of a time before. A life before. The words *Butlin's at Mosney* tried to drag a resistant Rosie back to that summer, the summer that was the happiest time of her life and the summer that had torn her childhood into nightmarish shreds. *That* summer.

Rosie frowned at the memories that were trying to nudge their way through the armour she always wore. They were persistent, though, and to Rosie's dismay, and despite her best efforts, they came tumbling through.

Her heels bumped pleasantly against her father's chest. She was barefoot. Her white leather sandals were held in her right hand, while her left arm was wrapped tightly around her father's forehead. The buckles of her sandals jingled and glittered in the sunlight as her father strode across the expanse of manicured grass towards the building that filled Rosie with excitement and nervous anticipation.

Although she had been here for little more than a day, Rosie had firmly decided that this was the best place she had ever been. The holiday camp was in the Irish Republic, just north of Dublin, and was a world away from Ardoyne where, at the moment at least, everything seemed to be on fire.

The cute little shops along the pedestrianised streets were all filled with sweets and toys and comics, there were amusement arcades and playgrounds, a boating lake and a beach, a theatre and a free cinema that showed cartoons all day, a glamorous ballroom and cafés and restaurants and parks and happy people and music everywhere. And the building to which they were now headed. The swimming pool.

"You're not scared, are you?" Her father asked her as they got close enough to see the arms and legs of children thrashing around in the water behind the strengthened glass window panels.

"No," she shouted defiantly. She was terrified, but she refused to let her daddy know that. She could do this, she decided.

On arrival at the entrance, Martin lifted Rosie down from his shoulders and, taking her by the hand, led her inside. The sudden rise in the noise level made Rosie's heart beat faster as crowds of children ran here and there, shrieking and laughing and yelling.

They were both wearing their swimming costumes under their clothes so Martin led Rosie past the changing rooms to a row of plastic benches by the side of the pool. Rosie took off her top and her shorts and placed them on a bench. Martin also got undressed and then put all of their clothes into a hold-all that contained their towels.

"Just put your sandals under the bench there, Rosie," said Martin, "and I'll just stick the bag under there as well."

Rosie did as she was told, then turned with trepidation towards the pool.

"Those tiles might be a wee bit rough on your feet," Martin told her, "so, do you want me to carry you to the pool?"

Rosie took a few steps on the hard non-slip surface and grimaced. "It is a wee bit rough," she said.

"No problem." Martin scooped her up and carried her to the shallow end of the pool. He sat her down at the edge and eased himself into the water. He then reached up to lift Rosie and lower her into the pool beside him.

The cold water came as a shock. She had been told the pool was heated and had expected it to be warm, like a bath, but she gasped and struggled to catch her breath, which only added to her rising sense of panic.

"You're okay there, sweetheart," Martin assured her. "We're just going to take it easy now."

With the shock of cold and fear, Rosie could only nod. Her right hand was clasped in her father's as she allowed him to gently lead her further into the pool. The water level rose to her chest.

"Bend down a wee bit and splash your arms about," said Martin. "It'll warm you up a bit."

She realised she had been walking stiffly, her arms and legs held straight, and she had to make a conscious effort to loosen up. She bent her knees until the water came up to her neck and she made slow awkward movements with her left arm. The paralysing cold began to ease and she could feel herself start to relax. Her confidence was growing, but she still kept a firm grip of her father's hand.

They moved into deeper water until Rosie could barely feel the bottom with the tips of her toes and then, still holding on to her father's hand, she was treading water. With infinite patience and soothing encouragement, Martin would briefly let her go, proud of the fierce determination on his daughter's face, and she would splash about frantically until he held her again. After repeating the process for a while, Rosie was finally able to keep herself afloat with more controlled movements of her arms and legs, and a little later she felt confident enough to lie on her back and enjoy the sensation of floating.

They stayed in the pool long enough for Rosie to take a few strokes in the water and, knowing that her father was right beside her, she eventually could make her way from one side of the pool to the other. She could swim.

It didn't matter that her efforts were clumsy and ungainly. *She could swim.* And as they made their way back to where they had left their clothes and towels, Rosie's eyes shone with exhilaration. She couldn't wait to tell Ellie.

Outside, Martin looked at his watch. They were due to meet up with the rest of the family for lunch, but it was still early. He turned to his daughter.

"We've still got over an hour before we have to meet your mammy," he said, "so do you fancy going for a drink in Dan Lowry's?"

Rosie couldn't believe it. She and her brother and sister had been to Dan Lowry's Bar the night before, but they had just been running around playing, like all the other kids in there, while the adults sat at tables, chatting, smoking and drinking. This was different. She was being invited to go for a drink with her daddy. They would walk into the bar together, and they would sit at a table together, and they would talk and laugh as they sipped their drinks together. She had never felt so grown up.

Martin sat with a glass of Guinness on the table in front of him, and Rosie sat beside him with a glass of Coke which, she decided, looked almost like a glass of Guinness. She took delicate sips of her drink – not gulping it down like a child would do – as she surveyed, with a new-found pious detachment, the antics of the silly little children, rushing chaotically between the tables. She couldn't wait to tell Ellie.

The rest of the fortnight went by far too quickly. Before they left Belfast, Rosie and Ellie had both been given some holiday money to spend on treats for themselves during the two weeks they were at the camp, and as they were packing up to go home, Rosie rather ashamedly realised that Ellie had used some of her money to buy gifts for each of the family.

Jack had received a toy car, and Rosie, a doll. Their mother, Shauna, had been given a souvenir tea towel, and Martin had received a glass ashtray emblazoned with the Butlin's logo, set over some colourful pictures of the camp.

Rosie ran her fingertips over the long-faded image on the ashtray, and then gave an exasperated sigh as if to physically dislodge her memories. They didn't belong to her, she decided. They were the memories of a childhood that should have carried on, unbroken and uninterrupted. They were memories that should have been added to over the years as new experiences and happy times collected and accumulated on the carefree walk of a child through a world of comfort and wonder. But those few memories stood glaringly alone, and only served to highlight the scarcity of reckless joy from Rosie's past, like a few sugar grains sprinkled in coal dust.

Rosie had told Ellie that she hoped their father was dead, but that was not true. Rosie secretly hoped he was alive so that, one day, she could march right up to him and spit in his face. A dark anger had settled on Rosie's heart, an anger for the life she'd never lived and for the memories that never were.

Ellie insisted that their father could not be held responsible for what had happened, but Rosie didn't see it that way. She needed someone to blame. She could never hope to match Ellie's generosity of spirit, but she didn't want to. She embraced the darkness within her. More than that, she nourished it. It gave Rosie an almost perverse pleasure to feed her demons, to keep alive the notion that the day would come when she could stand in front of Martin McCann and cause his heart to break in the same way her own heart had been broken. In this, she was resolute.

A squeal from the garden reminded her to nag Gary, when he got back, to oil the hinges on the gate. She squinted through the window at the strange familiarity of the figure who stepped nervously into the garden. She frowned at the man's hair. There was grey in it now, she thought, but those hazel eyes of his were still…she froze in shock.

And the glass ashtray slipped from her grasp to bounce gently on the thick rug. It rolled crazily, wobbling and teetering, before coming to rest, with a tiny clink, against the cold marble of the hearth.

Thirty six

"Competitive?" scoffed Gary. "Is that what you call it? I call it a couple of stubborn wankers, that's what I call it."

"Well, it's all a question of semantics," said Bobby as he sipped his Coke. "Competitive. Dedication. Single-mindedness. Stubborn wankers. It's all much of a muchness really."

"Do you think they'll be okay?" Kevin asked, concerned.

"Probably not," said Seamus. "Jesus! This fucking ice cream is unbelievable. What's it called again?"

"*Turrón,*" Kevin told him. "You don't think they'll be okay then?" They were all sitting around a table on the town's paseo, enjoying drinks and ice cream from the nearby horchatería, though Joker had wandered off somewhere.

"No, they're fucked," Seamus answered. "If they don't actually fall off the mountain, then they'll just end up killing each other."

"The thing you have to remember about Tone and Sean," Jamesy began, "is that they-"

"What's that dickhead up to?" asked Bobby, gesturing across the paseo. They turned to see Joker apparently staring at a wall. After a while, he turned and walked back towards the group.

"What were you doing?" Gary asked as Joker joined them.

"I was just reading a poster on the wall there," Joker replied, "about a *Feria de la Pascua de Resurrección*, in a place called Benifairó."

"Benifairó?" said Seamus. He looked at Kevin. "Where's that then?"

"It's a wee village further down the valley. Not too far from here."

"*Feria de* what? That's an Easter Festival, isn't it?" said Gary.

"It is indeed," Joker told him, "and tomorrow night they've got something called a Dance with Cows."

"Well fuck," said Gary, "we didn't have to come to Spain to do that."

"What?"

"Shamrock disco on a Friday night," explained Gary. "You can dance with all the-"

"Yeah, ha, ha," said Joker, "but I reckon we should go. It sounds like it could be mental."

"It'll be our last night really, won't it?" Jamesy pointed out.

"Well yeah, we'll be travelling all the next night."

"It's got to be something to think about," Joker added. "Do you know much about these *ferias* then, Kevin?"

"Well, the ones in the summer are a good *craic*," said Kevin. "They're just big parties where everybody stays up all night drinking."

"Sounds like the *fleadh*," Gary suggested.

"Same sort of thing, yeah."

"Well, I'm up for a bit of that," said Seamus.

"An all-night party?" asked Bobby. "You can count me in too."

"Well," said Jamesy, "it does sound an authentic cultural experience."

"That's the spirit, Jamesy," cried Joker. "You mad old bastard!"

"What are we going to do about Hillary and Tensing though?" asked Gary.

"Yeah," said Kevin, "I'm a bit worried about them to be honest."

"No, it's not that," Gary told him, "we can't let them get away with not helping us move all this furniture, can we? I mean, I don't mind doing my bit, but if those lazy-"

"Well, we're not going to be doing anything before lunch now, are we?" said Joker. "I'm sure they'll be back by then, so we'll just meet them back at the house."

Thirty Seven

"I'm not going to lie, Sean," said Tone, "I'm a wee bit disappointed."

Sean didn't reply. He walked forward onto the rough, uneven plateau that formed the mountaintop. On the far side of the plateau, overlooking the town, stood a solitary cross.

Sean looked around. Aside from the cross and a few tendrils of mist that had drifted down from a low, passing cloud, there was nothing to be seen. No kindly old monk. No monastery. No building of any kind. Nothing but an eerie silence. He made his way over to the cross, quietly followed by Tone, then stopped and gazed up at the familiar silhouette, stark against the hazy blue of the sky.

"Buxom serving wenches?" he asked without turning round.

"Okay," said Tone, taking out a cigarette, "there's a chance I may have overstated things. But let's be honest, Sean, there were a lot of mitigating circumstances."

"You know what Joker has to say on that matter, don't you?"

Tone put a light to his cigarette. "What?"

"Under no circumstances," Sean expanded, "do you ever, ever blame the alcohol."

"Yeah, well," Tone looked over the edge of the plateau. "Hell of a view, isn't it?" he said, changing the subject.

Sean couldn't argue with that. The entire valley was spread out below them. Off to the right the valley floor was dotted with the occasional town or village as it wound its way through the mountains, while to the left the valley meandered to the Mediterranean which could be seen, glittering in the distance.

"Yes indeed," Tone concluded. "Well worth the effort, I would say."

Sean shook his head and took a closer look at the reason they were there. The cross stood about twenty feet tall and was embedded deep in the rock of the mountain. It was made of wood and had a patchy covering of a grey, weathered material that had a black, tar-like backing. It was clear that the cross had once been covered completely in the material which, after a closer examination, looked more silver than grey.

"Must have quite a sight, back in the day," Sean muttered.

Tone nodded as he pictured the cross fully attired in shining silver. It would have caught the Spanish sun and shone like a beacon for miles around. "Yeah," he agreed, "not quite Sugarloaf Mountain but still, it would have been something. Just looks a bit sorry for itself now though, doesn't it?"

The cross, Sean conceded, did look sorry for itself. Where the covering had peeled away, the bare wood had been exposed to the wind and the rain and the scorching sun, and had twisted and warped as if trying to dispense with its man-made guise and revert to its true origins.

"For the glory of God, eh?" said Tone. "Looks like nobody thinks it's worth the effort anymore."

"Suppose not."

"I could never understand why it's never occurred to Christians that Jesus probably wouldn't want to be reminded of the thing he was tortured to death on. Seems a bit insensitive really, like waving a noose around."

"Your cynicism gets a bit boring after a while, you know that, Tone?"

"Not to me it doesn't." Tone dropped his cigarette butt and stomped it out. "I can't let you Christians have it all your own way, can I? If I did, you'd all just lie there and have the Holy Men force-feed you bullshit all day."

To Tone's surprise, Sean did not react to this deliberate goading, but instead turned back to look down into the valley. Tone usually enjoyed provoking Sean into a passionate defence of the faith that was close to his heart, but there was nothing but a strange silence now between them.

"You all right there, Sean?"

"You don't know what you're talking about," Sean said quietly.

It wasn't like Sean to be so subdued, Tone thought, at least not on a topic like this, so he decided to give him a bit of a poke.

"Well, that's the thing," he said, "I do know what I'm talking about. I know how it works, you see. It's a business, well actually it's more of a scam than a business, with those self-righteous bastards selling something that-"

"Oh fuck off, Tone!" spat Sean as he spun around. "Fuck off! You don't know anything. You think you do, but you don't. You've got a fucking cheek calling anybody self-righteous. What does that make you then? You know fuck-all!"

Tone was shaken by the outburst. He was used to having heated debates with Sean, but this was different. This was raw, emotional, vitriolic. It was more than just anger. Sean turned away again and slumped down to sit at the base of the cross. He leaned forward to rest his elbows on his knees and gazed down at the town, silent and unreal on the distant valley floor.

Tone lit another cigarette and sat down next to Sean.

"Something on your mind, Sean?" he asked casually.

"Fuck off."

"Well, there's not much else to do up here, is there?" Tone said lightly. Sean remained silent. "You know I'm not going to let it go, don't you?"

Sean looked at Tone, then looked away again. The anger in Sean's eyes had gone, Tone thought, only to be replaced by something else. Something wistful. Something sad. The quietness of the scene intensified and Tone was about to say something else when Sean spoke up.

"I was only about eight or nine," he began, and Tone felt a sudden urge to hear no more. "It was in Donegal," Sean went on, "at one of those retreats, you know?" Tone nodded. "You know the deal, don't you? You book in for prayer and reflection and all that stuff."

"Yeah," said Tone, "I know the sort of thing you mean."

"It was my ma's idea. She thought we could all do with a weekend away, to get closer to God and all, so we all set off – me and Siobhan and my ma and da – and we got there one Friday evening.

"It was all really sound at the start. For me and Siobhan, it was just like a holiday really, and the place we were staying was dead cool. There was a seminary there as well, so there were loads of trainee priests knocking about, and me and Siobhan got friendly with one of them – Duncan, his name was – he was a good laugh like, always joking, you know?

"Well, on the Saturday night, I headed off to bed. I felt like a big lad because I had a room to myself, the boy's dormitory was full apparently, but anyway, I must have been knackered because I fell asleep right away." Sean paused as he tried to focus on the memory. Tone sat quietly and waited for him to continue.

"So then I wake up," said Sean, "because there's somebody beside the bed. It's Duncan, and he's kneeling down, and I think he's saying his prayers, and then I realise he's got my dick in his mouth."

"Fuck!" Tone exclaimed.

"When he saw I was awake, he just got up, dead calm like, and walked to the door. And then, before he left, he turned to me and smiled. That's what really got to me, Tone, the way he just fucking smiled."

"So what happened?"

"What do you mean, what happened? Nothing happened. We went home the next day and that was it."

"What did your ma and da say?"

"I didn't tell them. I didn't tell anybody. You're the first person I've ever told."

"Jesus Christ, Sean!" said Tone. "Why didn't you tell your folks?"

"Well, because…"

"Because what?"

"Because…" Sean hesitated. "Because I was…because I was ashamed, I don't know, I was only a kid, for fuck's sake!"

"So, that was what? Nearly twenty years ago?"

"Yeah, Tone," Sean said quietly, "I know what you're saying."

"So, how many kids do you think-?"

"Yeah, I know," Sean replied angrily. "I fucking know, okay? Do you think I haven't thought about it?"

"Jesus!" said Tone. He turned to look at the sunlight flickering on the distant sea. He then turned back to Sean. "So, why are you always sticking up for the Church then? I would have thought something like that would have put you off a wee bit, but you're always at Mass, aren't you?"

"You just don't get it, Tone, do you? That's just who we are."

"What? What the fuck does that mean?"

"It's our identity, isn't it? We're both Catholics, whether you like it or not. It's our heritage. Take away the Church, and what have we got?"

"Unmolested kids?"

"Yeah, very funny, but you went to your da's funeral Mass, didn't you? You can't stop being a Catholic, Tone, it's in your blood. It's who you are. It's the same for Joker and Bobby. They're

Protestants, and that's *their* heritage. That's who *they* are."

"That sounds just like the sort of sectarian bullshit that's got Northern Ireland into the fucking mess it's in today."

"You know me better than that."

"Yeah, but that's just Northern Ireland, Sean," Tone insisted. "It's Northern Ireland that's polarised people like that. Not everywhere is as fucked-up as that."

"Yes, Tone," Sean said patiently, "I know it's Northern Ireland but, let's face it, that happens to be where we live." He turned away to let his next words drift into the wind. "For the time being, at least."

"Is that why you're moving abroad then? To get away from it all?"

Sean stood up and brushed the dust from the back of his shorts. "That's part of it, I suppose," he said. "But it's a big world out there, Tone, and I fancy seeing at least some of it."

"Makes you one of the lucky ones then," Tone said, as he stood up to join Sean. "Getting out, I mean."

"Well, that remains to be seen," said Sean. "Who knows what the future will bring. Anyway, what about you? There's nothing keeping you in Northern Ireland, is there?"

Tone shrugged. "I suppose not," he said. "I mean, my ma's on her own now, but she's got all her mates to play with, so that's not a big deal, but...I don't know, maybe I'm just stuck in a rut."

Sean was about to mention Claire, but decided it was none of his business. Above them, the cross creaked mournfully in the stiffening wind. "Think we should get off this mountain?"

"Yeah," said Tone, "I don't know what possessed us to climb the fucking thing in the first place."

As they made their way to the path that led down the mountain, Sean glanced over at Tone.

"I can't believe I told you about Donegal," he said.

"Maybe you needed to get it off your chest."

"Can't think why though. I mean I haven't even thought about it in years. Obviously, it was a bit of a shock at the time. It took Gary and Seamus ripping the piss out of me to snap me out of it when I got back to Belfast."

"Good to know they're useful for something," said Tone. "So, why do you think you brought it up after all this time?"

"No idea," Sean replied. "Like I said, it's not something I've dwelt on all these years. Maybe it's a subconscious, Freudian sort of thing. Maybe I need to see a therapist."

"You could take Joker with you," Tone suggested, and Sean laughed.

"Yeah," he said, "what the hell was all that about earlier on, when he was running around flapping his arms up and down?"

"Who knows?" said Tone. "This is Joker we're talking about, so who the fuck knows?"

Jamesy and Kevin were clearing out the stable block. Seamus was in the house, rearranging the items he had tripped over the night before, while Joker, Gary and Bobby were seated around the dining table.

Jamesy decided to take the opportunity of being alone with Kevin to have a quiet chat.

"Everything okay with you then, Kevin?"

"Yeah, no problems," said Kevin. He stopped what he was doing and looked at Jamesy. "Why?" he asked.

"Just asking," Jamesy said nonchalantly. "So what's the deal with your woman at the shop? Gabriela, was it?"

Kevin coloured. "There is no deal," he muttered. "Like I said, there's nothing going on."

"Okay," said Jamesy, "it's just that you seemed to go very quiet when her name was mentioned."

Kevin took a deep breath and looked around him. He knew that if he could trust anyone, it would be Jamesy, but he still seemed unsure. Eventually he sighed and leaned back against a battered old cupboard. "You won't tell anybody, will you?" he asked.

Jamesy shrugged as if to suggest that it went without saying.

"It's just that," Kevin continued hesitantly, "it's just that I've never actually had a girlfriend."

Jamesy stared impassively ahead, but was then suddenly struck by the significance of what Kevin had just told him.

"What?" he said, stupefied. "*Never*?"

"No."

"So you've never actually…?"

"No," Kevin said miserably. "Never."

"Jesus!"

"Yeah, exactly."

"Mmm," Jamesy was thoughtful for a moment. "I'm probably not the best person to talk to about this," he said. "I don't have much success in that department myself."

Kevin stared at him. "You're kidding me, aren't you?" he said. "Women fall over themselves for you! It's actually embarrassing at times."

"Oh, well yeah," Jamesy stammered, "I mean, I don't have a problem *acquiring* women, it's just that I don't know what to do with them once I've got them." He tried to make light of it, but Kevin just looked away.

"I'd rather have your problem than mine," he said.

Jamesy wasn't sure how to respond. "You know," he said after a while, "it may be worth mentioning it to the lads."

Kevin shot him a look of disbelief. "Seriously? Wouldn't they just rip the piss out of me?"

"Oh yeah, they would," Jamesy assured him, "but then they'd all look at it as a problem that needed to be solved, and they'd all hunker down and try to find some way to help. I mean, okay, that help would probably be a bit cack-handed and misplaced, and totally inappropriate, but…actually forget I even mentioned it."

"Cack-handed? You mean like that whole salad business?"

"Yeah," said Jamesy. "Really though, just forget what I said."

"I don't know though," Kevin said thoughtfully. "I'm desperate enough to try anything at this stage."

"Well, just be sure you've thought it through," Jamesy told him. He turned his head towards the house. "They're being very quiet," he said. "Probably deeply involved in some heavy intellectual debate."

Kevin grinned. "I'm sure," he said.

"*Wacky races* was fucking shite, Bobby, and you know it!" Joker was standing up and pointing a finger across the table at Bobby.

"How the fuck can you hate *Wacky Races*?" cried Bobby. "It was a classic!"

Gary was chewing on a sandwich as he followed the discussion. "Yeah, I liked *Wacky Races* too," he said, "so I don't know what the hell you're on about."

"What the fuck's your problem, Joker?" added Seamus as he came over to the table. "*Wacky Races* was class."

"Oh, is that right?" Joker demanded. "Then tell me this; what was the coolest car in the whole show?"

They thought about it for a bit and then Gary piped up. "Well, the Double Zero, obviously."

"Yeah," Bobby agreed. "The Double Zero."

"Absolutely," said Seamus.

"Then tell me," Joker continued. "How many times did the Double Zero actually win a fucking race?"

"Well obviously it never won a race," said Bobby. "Dick Dastardly was the bad guy. You can't have the bad guy winning, can you? It sends the wrong message to kids."

"Fuck that, Bobby," said Joker passionately. "What about me then? I was a kid! And every week I'd be sitting there, cheering on the Double Zero, thinking;

Just this once! Just this once!, but every bloody week Dick Dastardly would get to within a couple of inches of the finish line, and then something would happen, and every other cunt would go flying past. *Every* fucking week! Broke my wee heart, it did."

"Yeah, now that you mention it," Seamus mused, "I remember that used to annoy me too."

"Yeah, fair point," said Gary.

"Actually, thinking about *Wacky Races*," Seamus added. "Wasn't Peter Perfect's car just one big phallic symbol? Or is that just me?"

Everyone looked at Seamus. "Yeah, I think that's just you," said Bobby.

"You fading bastards missed it all!"

"Well, if it isn't the wild men of the mountains," said Gary as Sean and Tone came through the door. "Hope you brought us some of that strong wine."

"What? Oh, the monastery was closed."

"Yeah," said Sean, "closed and non-existent."

"Yeah, that too," Tone conceded.

"Is there any food on the go?" asked Sean, heading for the kitchen.

"We got you some *bocadillos*," Joker told him. "They're in the fridge."

"Good lads."

Jamesy and Kevin came in from the courtyard and sat down at the table.

"How was it?" Jamesy asked Tone.

"Brilliant, Jamesy, you would have loved it."

Sean came back from the kitchen with a baguette each for him and Tone.

"We thought we'd wait till you two got back before we did any work," said Bobby.

"That's good of you."

"We're thinking of going dancing with cows tomorrow night," Joker declared.

Tone looked at Joker, then looked around the table, hoping that someone would translate.

"There's a festival on in a wee town along the valley," Bobby explained. "There was a poster in the paseo that said something about dancing with cows, whatever that means. We thought it would be something we could do for our last night."

"Dancing with cows?" asked Sean.

"I think there's a bullring in Benifairó," said Kevin, "so that might have something to do with it."

"Well, I'm not going to go and watch somebody stab an animal," Sean decided.

"Yeah, fuck that," said Joker.

"No, I don't think there'll be anything like that," Kevin told them. "They'll probably just run some cows around the ring and people can run around getting chased by them. You know, like the running of the bulls in Pamplona."

"But, cows though?" said Tone.

"Yeah, you all know what the big, black Spanish bulls look like, don't you?" Kevin explained. "Well the cows are the same as that, only smaller, faster and more agile."

"Sounds dangerous."

"It can be, yeah, but I think that's the point."

"Right then, I reckon we should check it out," said Tone. "What was the place called again?"

"Benifairó."

"Benifairó it is then. Right, that's tomorrow night sorted, what about tonight?"

"I'm happy to just chill out back at the beach-house," said Seamus, and everyone nodded in agreement. Tone looked around at all the furniture and bits and pieces lying around.

"This is going to take a while to sort out," he said. "We could end up missing the last bus again."

"It'll be easy enough to hitchhike," said Kevin. "If we split up into groups and go separately, it won't take long at all."

"Okay," said Tone as he finished his lunch. "We'd better get started then."

Thirty Eight

They started off at the City Hall, where they discovered they were in the wrong place. They were then redirected to a different building that was just a short walk away and Martin used the opportunity, as they walked, to voice his concerns.

"I've just got no idea what to expect," he explained. "I mean, technically I'm still married, but I'm sure that Shauna's found somebody else by now. The kids will all be grown up as well, and they'll be living their own lives. Probably without ever giving me a second thought."

"It's still best to know though, isn't it?"

"Oh yeah, absolutely," said Martin, "but I'm just not sure how I'll feel, if me turning up completely out of the blue turns out to be a real hassle for everybody, you know? What if I'm just an inconvenient embarrassment?"

"I think your children will want to know what happened to their father."

"You think so?"

"Of course!" Stephanie stopped and turned to Martin. "Don't you think they would have been curious? Surely they would have been wondering over the years what had happened to you."

"Yeah, I know," Martin said as they walked on, "but I just think that as time has gone on, they would have been more preoccupied with getting on with their own lives, you know? Maybe they'd think about me from time to time, but that would be less and less over the years, wouldn't it?"

"Maybe, but like I said, it's still best to know."

They entered a large office block and were directed by the receptionist to a room where they could access the electoral roll for Belfast. At first it was looking promising as they found several matches for Elaine McCann, Rosemary McCann and Jack McCann, but none of the dates of birth were the right ones. After half an hour of fruitless searching, Martin stood back and stretched in exasperation.

"It's looking a bit hopeless, isn't it?" he suggested.

Stephanie chewed on her lower lip with frustration. "There must be a way," she declared helplessly. She went over to talk to someone sitting at a desk on the other side of the room as Martin paced thoughtfully back and forth. He was felling increasingly torn by his desire to see his family and by his fear of what he would find.

"We could try the Land Registry," said Stephanie, striding back with her new suggestion.

"How do we go about doing that?"

"Well, it's in another building," she said, "but it's not far from here."

Martin looked at her. "Look, I'm really sorry for dragging you into all this. I'm sure this is the last thing you could be doing with."

"Nonsense!" Stephanie told him happily. "I'm just as desperate to get to the bottom of this as you are. It's turning into a bit of a quest, isn't it?"

"Well anyway, I appreciate it."

"I should tell you though," Stephanie said as they made for the exit, "this is probably a long shot. I don't know what the deal will be for Housing Executive properties." She paused. "Actually, that's not a bad idea. We could try the Housing Executive."

"What's the Housing Executive?"

"Well, it's just council housing really. The Executive organises all of the affordable rental properties in Northern Ireland. They might have a list of their tenants we can have a look at."

"That sounds well worth a look," said Martin. "We'll give it a try if we don't have any luck with this Land Registry thing. And I'm not sure we will, to be honest. I can't imagine Shauna or any of the kids being able to buy their own place."

"We should still try every option we can think of," Stephanie decided. "Leave no stone unturned, that's what I say!"

Her enthusiasm was contagious, and Martin was feeling quite optimistic by the time they pushed open the smoked glass double-doors of the imposing office block, and stepped into the offices of the Land Registry for Northern Ireland. Where they found Elaine McCann.

Martin stared at the name, next to an Ardoyne address, and tried not get too hopeful.

"There's no date of birth," he pointed out.

"No, but…" Stephanie gave him a glance. She could tell he was trying to suppress his excitement. "there's no harm in trying it out."

"No, I suppose not," he said as he noted the address. "I could call up this afternoon. You're welcome to come too if you want."

Stephanie smiled. "No, Martin," she told him gently, "if this turns out to be your daughter then I'll only be in the way. This is something that should be private, with just the two of you."

"Yeah, you're probably right," he admitted. "You've been a huge help though. I don't know how I can thank you."

"It's been a pleasure." She reached out and patted his arm. "Just be sure and let me know how it goes, okay?"

"Of course," he said. "Absolutely."

As he made his way along the street, counting down the house numbers, he could see that his destination lay just ahead. Just a few more houses along. Nearly there. He started to feel anxious. The tension was building in him, and his heart was thumping in his chest.

He stopped at the gate and, pushing it open, he almost cried out at the unexpected squeal of the iron hinge. He stared ahead to the front door at the end of the path as he hesitatingly put one foot into the garden.

He took one step at a time along the path, half-hoping it would be a false alarm. Half-hoping the encounter would end with an apologetic smile, and a shrug and a 'sorry to have bothered-' the front door crashed open causing his heart to jump. He stopped as a crazed figure burst into the garden. Martin's eyes bulged in his head and he instinctively stepped backwards as the pregnant woman hurtled towards him, with black hair flailing behind her and blazing eyes that were wild and wide and spilling tears that threatened to choke the cry that fell from her lips.

Daddy.

Thirty Nine

Africa 1968

The war had been raging for a year when Father Jerome disembarked at Lagos airport. After a brief spell in Portugal he had taken a direct flight from Lisbon and was planning to meet with representatives of Caritas, an amalgamation of Catholic charities, as well as interdenominational groups who were attempting to provide help to the people of Biafra. He had also been granted an audience with the Papal Legate to Western Africa.

The Biafran Army had shocked the world by not immediately capitulating to the superior Nigerian forces, but had instead pushed the Federal Army back almost as far as Lagos itself. Eventually, though, the greater numbers and the far greater firepower of Nigeria began to take their toll and the war had shrunk back to within the borders of Biafra, where the Biafrans were forced to rely on hit-and-run guerrilla tactics against the encroaching enemy.

As the noose tightened around the neck of the independent little nation, it became increasingly obvious that a crisis was looming. Biafra had already struggled to feed the millions of refugees that had poured across her borders since the massacres of 1966, but the war and the almost total blockade of supplies into the country by the Nigerian Armed Forces meant that the deprivation only accelerated and, by now, people were starving.

"What the hell do you mean he doesn't trust the Red Cross?" Father Jerome raged across the table at the Papal Legate. The legate looked impassively at the agitated priest and then waved his hand dismissively.

"Commander Gowon is understandably concerned about military supplies being smuggled to the rebel forces under the cover of humanitarian aid," he said. "It is an unfortunate situation, of course, but until a way can be found to guarantee that only supplies of sustenance are being transported to the East, and then that they are only being supplied to the civilian population and not to the military then there is little that can be done."

"Supplies of sustenance?" roared Father Jerome. "You mean food? You mean food that can prevent innocent people from dying, is that what you mean?"

"There is no need to become so emotional, Father. Negotiations are still ongoing, but the situation is delicate."

"I know what the situation is! People are starving to death, that's what the situation is! And you're worried about Gowon?"

"Commander Gowon has shown great restraint as he tries to contain an armed insurrection, and there is absolutely nothing that…" The Papal Legate stared open-mouthed as Father Jerome, in a shocking breach of protocol, stormed from the room.

The rest of Father Jerome's appointments proved equally fruitless and he was in a sombre frame of mind as he drove back to Biafra. He was held up on several occasions at military checkpoints, but his clerical status, as well as his white face, allowed him to cross the border without too much trouble. He was keen to reach Enugu.

Father Jerome knew that the Nigerian Army had captured Enugu a few months earlier, and he had been hearing some disturbing, if unconfirmed, reports of massacres committed against the civilian population. He hadn't heard from Benjamin in months.

He pulled up outside the bungalow and his heart sank. Benjamin's house and all of the houses around had clearly been abandoned. They stood silently derelict, in overgrown gardens, with broken windows and a few sad possessions scattered on the ground. Father Jerome walked thoughtfully around his friend's former home and tried listing the possible events that could have led to the sorry state he had discovered.

The worst case scenario was that the residents of the university campus had all been rounded up and taken off somewhere to be shot, but Father Jerome refused to countenance such a possibility. It was more likely, he decided, that they would have fled in advance of the Nigerians' approach, and were now staying at one of the refugee camps that Father Jerome knew had been set up around those parts of the country still under Biafran control.

He got back in his car and decided he would make his way to Umuahia, which he understood to be the current capital of Biafra, and where he hoped he would find some answers.

"You're looking a wee bit lost there, Father, if you don't mind me saying."

Father Jerome stopped and looked behind him. He saw a young white man wearing the uniform of the Biafran Army's 4th Commando Brigade.

"You're Irish?" Father Jerome asked.

"Awk, sure isn't that a grand accent you've got yourself there, Father." The young man walked forward and held out his hand. "Put it there, Father. The name's Mulrooney, Louis Mulrooney."

They shook hands, then Father Jerome took a step back to look the young man up and down.

"You're a long way from home, Mulrooney," he said.

"Sure didn't I hear there was a fight to be had?"

Father Jerome laughed. "Well, you got that right."

"So, what is it you're after, Father? If you don't mind me asking."

Father Jerome explained how his friends had been living in Enugu before the war, but now seemed to have disappeared since that city's occupation.

"I think you're right, Father," said Mulrooney, "they're more than likely at one of the camps." They walked, side by side, along the main corridor of the Government building in Umuahia. "I don't know if there's any sort of official list you could have a look at, but I do know someone you should probably talk to." Mulrooney led Father Jerome to a large office that was filled with noise and confusion. They made their way through the chaos until Mulrooney stopped at the desk of a harassed-looking, young woman.

"Now, Father," he said with a grin, "if this gorgeous creature here can't help you, then I don't think there'll be anyone else in all of Biafra who can."

The woman looked coldly at Mulrooney, then gave Father Jerome a quick glance.

"Yes, Father," she said politely. "What can I help you with?"

"Well, I'm looking for some people that may have been evacuated from Enugu," Father Jerome told her. "If I were to give you their names, would that be helpful at all?"

"No, Father," she said. "We don't have the time or the resources to file the names of everyone who is in transit at any given time."

"In transit?"

"But I can get you the locations of several centres where the civilians from that region may have been taken."

"That would be very helpful, thank you."

The girl got up and searched through one of many large filing cabinets that lined the wall. She pulled out three folders and returned to her desk. As she wrote down the names and locations of the relevant refugee centres, she glanced at Mulrooney.

"Are you still sober, Mulrooney?" she asked. "And it's almost eleven am. Are you ill?"

"Oh, my sweetheart," said Mulrooney. "Just to look into those eyes is intoxication enough for me."

She folded the paper she had written on and handed it to Father Jerome. "These are the places where your friends are most likely to be, Father," she said. "I wish you luck. Oh and Father, you may want to reconsider the company you keep in Umuahia."

"I'll bear that in mind, my dear. And thank you. Thank you very much."

As they walked towards the exit, Father Jerome turned to Mulrooney. "She seemed nice," he said. "And she seemed very taken with you."

"Oh, they all are Father. It's my Irish charm."

"What's her name?"

"Now don't be getting me bogged down with details, Father," Mulrooney said dismissively. "And did I just hear her say it was nearly eleven o clock?"

"You did."

"Well now, Father. Do you fancy a drink?"

It was in the second refugee centre that he visited that Father Jerome spotted Adanna. She was sitting on the ground, reading a newspaper, at the doorway to one of several long, low huts.

"Adanna?"

She looked up and gave a shriek of surprise. She got to her feet and rushed over to give him a warm embrace.

"Father Jerome," she cried, "it is so good to see you."

"And it's great to see you too, Adanna. Is Benjamin here as well?"

Adanna shook her head. "He is with the army."

"He hasn't been conscripted, has he?"

"He volunteered," she told him as she led him to a makeshift bench where they could sit. "He is a medic with the army now, but I don't know any more than that. I don't even know where he is."

"I could do some snooping around if you'd like. See what I can find out."

"Thank you, Father, but I don't think it will be necessary. I'm sure Benjamin is fine. He knows that we have been relocated to this camp, so he knows where we are at least. Actually, now that you've mentioned it, I haven't had any news from my mother in a while, so if you could…"

"Ijemma? Yes, of course. Consider it done."

"Thank you."

"So, how have you been keeping, Adanna? Are you all right?"

"Yes, we are doing fine," she said. "Of course I worry about the children not getting enough to eat, but I think we are doing better than most, so I won't complain."

"Where are the kids?"

"Oh, they'll be off playing somewhere with the other children of the camp."

Father Jerome looked around at the camp's residents. It was just the same as in the first camp he had gone to; people brought to the very brink of starvation. He had been shocked by Adanna's almost skeletal appearance, but he had thought it best not to comment on it.

"What's the food situation like at the moment?" he asked casually.

"We are allowed a handful of boiled rice, twice, sometimes three times a day."

"And that's it?"

"That's it."

He shook his head. "The bloody food is there, Adanna, do you know that? The Red Cross and the other relief agencies have stockpiled all the food you need, but the Nigerians won't let them bring it in."

"Well, what would you expect, Father?" Adanna said wearily. "They are trying to win the war."

"That's a fairly sober view of things."

"I just want it to be over now, that's all. They keep telling us that we are winning, but look around you, Father. Does it look like we are winning?"

"No," he said softly. "No, it doesn't look like that at all."

It wasn't the ripped and shredded limbs that bothered Benjamin. It wasn't the eyeballs torn from sockets or the heads blown from bodies. It wasn't the dribbling ravings of the shell-shocked or the senseless mutilations. It wasn't even the bodies of small children impaled on the spikes of iron railings, designed to taunt and to terrorise the beleaguered Biafran populace. As horrific as these things were, there was something else, something more sinister, more insidious, that stalked the misty edges of Benjamin's consciousness. It was called *kwashiorkor*.

As he travelled around the war-weary nation, Benjamin began to realise the true import of what was going on. He knew that, even though food supplies were desperately low, there was still enough rice to make sure that most people could get something to eat most days. But, for Benjamin, that wasn't the problem.

The problem was the lack of protein. Most of Biafra's protein-rich foods were imported, but that supply had now been cut off by the Nigerian blockade, which meant that the diet for much of the population was almost exclusively starch. Over any extended period of time this was unsustainable. The result was kwashiorkor.

The obvious effects of kwashiorkor, caused by protein deficiency, were wasted limbs and a grotesquely swollen abdomen, leading ultimately to death. Children were especially vulnerable.

Benjamin could see the signs of the affliction everywhere he went, and he knew that if the issue were not addressed soon then Biafra would face a disaster of unimaginable proportions.

But no one would listen.

He had tried on numerous occasions to raise the matter with his superiors, but the few who were sympathetic had insisted there was nothing they could do. The only realistic answer, it seemed, would be the lifting of the blockade, but that appeared to be increasingly unlikely.

If anything, the noose was tightening.

Father Jerome, now working as part of an inter-faith action group, was touring Uli airport, west of Umuahia, in order to learn how some of the stockpiled aid was managing to get through the blockade. It was only a tiny fraction of what was needed, but just the fact that it was able to break the Federal stranglehold gave Father Jerome some cause to hope.

He spoke to the construction gangs who kept the runway serviceable, despite constant attention from Nigerian bombers, then met with the flight administrator for the airport.

"Yes, Father," the administrator told him with a smile. "The Federals blow holes in the runway during the day, then we hurry to fill in the holes before the night comes."

"So the flights come in at night then?"

"They have to, Father. They would be shot down otherwise."

"Even planes that are clearly marked as humanitarian aid?"

"That is correct. The Federals have said as much."

"Is there a flight scheduled for tonight?"

The administrator looked uneasy and Father Jerome raised his hands. "No, no, of course, you don't have to tell me. I'm being far too nosy."

"Oh no, Father, it isn't that. There is nothing officially scheduled, but we do have pilots that will decide to come if they believe there is no activity from the Nigerian aircraft. Then, at the last minute, they will send us a radio signal and we will turn on the airport lights just long enough for them to land."

"The lights are kept off at night?"

"It is safer that way."

"Mmm, it all sounds very risky."

"Of course, Father, we are at war. And now that Port Harcourt has fallen, it is essential that we remain operational. We are Biafra's only real lifeline now."

The administrator appeared cheerful, but Father Jerome could sense the strain he was under and just how precarious his position was. The loss of Port Harcourt was a major blow to the Biafrans. The territory that was still in Biafran hands had now contracted to the interior of the country and was becoming ever more bloated with refugees.

"Thank you for your time," Father Jerome told him. "You're doing an excellent job under difficult circumstances."

"Thank you, Father."

Later that night, the dark airport bloomed suddenly and shockingly bright in the pitch-black Biafran night and, moments later, a Lockheed Super Constellation swooped in low from the surrounding gloom. Once the plane had landed, the airport went dark once more.

Father Jerome could appreciate the delicate timing. Once lit, the airport would be visible from the sky for miles around, easy prey for one of the Russian MiGs that Nigeria sent regularly into the skies over Biafra.

The Lockheed taxied into a waiting hangar and Father Jerome headed that way, hoping to intercept the pilot. The young man climbed down from his cockpit and walked towards the administration desk. Father Jerome watched him approach and grinned.

"Andrew," he called. "It is Andrew, isn't it? We met in Lisbon."

"Yes, Father," Andrew replied with a smile. His accent had a strong Australian lilt to it. "How are you doing?"

"I'm good. Would it be possible to have a word once you've finished here?"

When Andrew had completed his paperwork, he went with Father Jerome to a small reception area where they sat down at a table.

"It's good to see you again, Father," said Andrew, "but I think you're crazy for coming back here."

"I sometimes think we're all crazy, Andrew. Every last one of us. But I wanted to ask you about all that food we saw being stored back in Lisbon. What are the chances of it getting here anytime soon?"

"Very little, I would say. There just aren't enough aircraft."

"But doesn't your boss have-?"

"Oh, hold on there, Father," Andrew interrupted. "Hank is being paid to fly in equipment for the Biafran Army, and that's what he's doing. He's got three planes at the moment and their space is mostly taken up with arms shipments."

"Mostly?"

"Well yeah, the relief agencies keep putting pressure on us to carry aid on our flights and, to be honest, Father, we do what we can, but it isn't what the Biafran Government pays us for. If they paid us to bring food, then we'd bring food."

"I've heard that the charities are trying to purchase their own planes, how is that going?"

"Not as quickly as they'd like," Andrew told him. "I think the Canadians might have offered something, or the Yanks, maybe, but who knows?"

"Yes, I see."

"And there's always the added complication of the Nigerian Air Force, Father. Having enough aircraft won't solve that little problem."

"Dr Maher, is it?"

Benjamin turned to see a Biafran soldier, clearly a mercenary, sitting on a camp bed in the hospital tent.

His left hand was heavily bandaged, and in his right was a bottle of wine.

"Yes, I'm Dr Maher," said Benjamin. "Have we…um…?"

"Put it there, Doc," the soldier said, placing the bottle on the floor and holding out his hand. "I believe we have a mutual friend. I had a wee chat with a Father Jerome back in Umuahia," the soldier explained as Benjamin shook his hand. "He was having a hard time finding you, you know."

"Father Jerome?" asked Benjamin excitedly. "He's back in Biafra?"

"He is indeed. The name's Mulrooney, by the way. Louis Mulrooney, though everyone just calls me Paddy."

"It's good to meet you, um, Paddy. How is your hand?"

"Oh this?" scoffed Mulrooney. "It's nothing at all. A wee bit of shrapnel just took a chunk out of it, that's all."

"And how was Father Jerome?" asked Benjamin. "What's he up to now?"

"Father Jerome," Mulrooney began, "is a man who likes to keep himself busy. He's here, there and bloody everywhere." Mulrooney picked up his wine and offered a swig to Benjamin.

"No, thank you."

"Yes, indeed," Mulrooney went on, glugging from the bottle, "trying to save the whole damned world, if you ask me."

"Do you know where he is?"

"Not at this very minute, no. Like I said, Doc, he's a man who gets around."

"Do you think there is any chance you will see him again soon?"

"Anything's possible, Doc," said Mulrooney. "I'll be happy to keep a woe eye out for him, if that's what you're after."

"I'd appreciate it, thanks."

"Don't mention it. And you'll be based around here for a while, is that right?"

"Yes. At least I believe so."

Mulrooney held up the wine. "Then here's to the impending renewal of your acquaintance," he said as he took a swig. Benjamin thanked him again, then moved on down the long row of beds. His mind raced at this stroke of good fortune. If he could meet up with his old friend to let him know how things stood at the moment then he felt sure that Father Jerome would do everything he could to help. And Benjamin needed help, for he had arrived at a fateful decision.

He needed to save his young family, he realised. He needed to pluck them from the nightmare, from the apocalypse that he knew was coming, and to do that he knew they had only one choice.

They would have to flee Biafra.

Adanna no longer had the strength to scream. Nor to cry. Nor even to grieve. She stood, fragile and numb, as Ikeobi, her baby boy, was lowered into the shallow grave, just one of several children to succumb in the night.

She put an arm around the little girl standing quiet by her side and wondered when it would be her daughter's turn to weaken, and to collapse and to slip sadly away. Or would it be herself who deteriorated first? Would the little four-year-old Chiazacam have to sit in the squalid, overcrowded hut and watch her mother slowly die? And did it even matter?

Adanna had watched the population of the camp grow day by day, as people swarmed in from the countryside, desperate for food. The various charity groups, spurred on by a tireless Father Jerome, had lobbied for all available resources to be directed immediately to the refugees, but it was not enough. It would never be enough. They would all die.

She knelt down in front of Chiaza, and her broken heart broke a little more, for she could see that the light in her daughter's eyes, a light that once blazed with fiery intensity, was now little more than a ghostly flicker.

Benjamin had to wipe away a tear as he greeted Father Jerome. It was more than just the meeting of an old friend, it was a hopeful embrace of happier times. Of times before the war. Of cold beer and warm nights. Of meandering conversation and boisterous debate. Of giggling children and future plans, of hope, and friendship, and joy, and laughter and love.

"It's so good to see you again, Benjamin," Father Jerome said happily.

"You too, Father," said Benjamin. "A lot has happened, as you can see."

"Yes, yes, a shocking business entirely."

"I hear you've been keeping busy."

"I do what I can, Benjamin, but I fear it is nowhere near enough."

They sat at a table in an open plaza, close to the army base where Benjamin was currently deployed, and talked of the war.

"There is no war," said Father Jerome, "at least not as far as the rest of the world is concerned. I was at a big football match in Lisbon and I got chatting to loads of Scottish and Irish lads. Most had never even heard of Biafra, to be honest."

Benjamin nodded sadly. "It's understandable, I suppose. The world has got its own problems, but it still seems hard to believe that all this madness can go unnoticed."

"Have you seen Adanna lately?" Father Jerome asked.

"No," Benjamin admitted, "I haven't been able to get away for months now, but I heard she's been moved to a different camp."

"Yes, I managed to catch up with her there a few weeks ago. She seemed fine but, Jesus, Benjamin, she looked awful thin."

Benjamin leaned forward and lowered his head. "Well, that is kind of what I wanted to see you about, Father," he said, and then paused as if unsure about how to proceed. "I know that I don't need to explain to an Irishman anything about the word famine, but I believe that famine is exactly what Biafra is facing."

"Yes, Benjamin," Father Jerome agreed, "I can see it everywhere I go."

"And I don't think the war will end anytime soon," Benjamin continued, "which means that everything will only get much, much worse."

Father Jerome nodded, but said nothing.

"I have to get them out, Father," Benjamin stated flatly. "My wife and my children need to get out of Biafra. If they stay they will die."

Father Jerome showed no reaction as he considered Benjamin's words. "What have you got in mind?" he asked finally.

"Well, it means deserting from the army," Benjamin said quietly. "I thought of taking my car to pick up Adanna and the children, and then trying to make it across the border into Cameroon."

"That would be suicide, Benjamin, and I think you're well aware of that," said Father Jerome. "You would be trying to get through hundreds of miles of enemy held territory."

"I hold a British passport," Benjamin explained. "I had hoped that maybe it would be enough to confuse any checkpoint we came across."

"No piece of paper is going to hold any sway out there in the bush, Benjamin. You know that."

"Well, I don't know what else I can do, Father. I'm open to suggestions."

Father Jerome was thoughtful for a moment, then he grasped Benjamin's arm.

Adanna was lying listless and dozing with Chiaza by her side when she felt herself being shaken.

"Adanna," a voice hissed in her ear.

"Benjamin?"

"Come on, we're leaving."

She sat up and stared at her husband. "What do you mean?"

"There's no time, come on. Where's Ikeobi?"

Adanna lowered her gaze and slowly shook her head. Benjamin's heart froze.

"No!"

"I'm sorry, Benjamin. I'm so sorry. I couldn't save him. I tried, I…"

"Later, Adanna," Benjamin urged. "We need to go now!" He carefully picked up Chiaza, wrapped in a shawl, and was shocked by how weightless she felt. He then led Adanna out to the waiting car and helped her into the passenger seat before placing Chiaza in her lap. He jumped into the driver's seat and started the engine.

"Where are we going?" Adanna asked as they drove out of the camp.

"If we can make it to the airport by two am," Benjamin told her, "then Father Jerome believes he can get us on a flight to Lisbon."

"Lisbon? But what about passports? We don't-"

"We'll worry about that when we get there. Maybe the British Consulate can help. I don't know, we'll think of something, I'm sure. At least we'll be safe, that's the main thing."

"Benjamin. Ikeobi…I…"

"It's all right, Adanna," he assured her. "It's all right." But he knew he was lying. How could it be all right? His son was dead. It would never be all right.

They drove through the night, skirting the ever-changing front line, with the ghost of their little boy stifling their words and clouding their thoughts.

Benjamin spun round a sharp bend, only to see a Land Rover parked across the road just up ahead. He slammed on his brakes to avoid a collision, then watched in dismay as Nigerian troops jumped from the Land Rover and surrounded the car. They wrenched open the car doors and dragged out Benjamin and Adanna. One of the soldiers yanked the bundle from Adanna's arms and threw it onto the roadway where it rolled in the dust. As Adanna rushed forward to save it, a bayonet was thrust into her midriff and she folded over in shock. She slowly slumped to the ground. Someone was screaming.

Benjamin tried to run around the car to reach his wife, but a rifle butt smashed into his glasses causing his vision to explode in searing red agony. The screaming stopped, and Benjamin could hear the soldiers laughing as he scrambled through the blood and dust to get to Adanna. His blurred vision could just make out the look in Adanna's eyes as her wasted body succumbed to the appalling violation and her lifeforce seeped away into the Biafran soil. The screaming started again and continued through the bursts of automatic gunfire that ripped through the night.

"Come on, man, she's gone!" Benjamin felt someone tug at his shoulder. "Come on, you need to be quiet now."

Benjamin stopped screaming. He turned to see a young soldier in a Biafran Army uniform standing over him. Behind him, his colleagues were looting the bodies of the ambushed Nigerians, taking all of their weapons and ammunition. Benjamin made a hurried shuffle over to snatch up the bundle that lay lifeless in the moonlight.

The young soldier made to stop him, but then paused and turned away. The soldiers had all borne witness to the very worst that humanity had to offer over the last year, but there was something especially unbearable in the sight of a broken father clinging with wretched determination to the corpse of a child.

Forty

London 1969

Winter's weary end threw some half-hearted snowflakes at the window of Benjamin's rented apartment in South London. He watched them flutter moth-like against the warm glass as he replaced the phone receiver in its cradle. He had a decision to make.

He stood at the window and stared down at the sad dusting of snow trying to persuade an unconvinced Streatham Common to cling to winter and to ignore the cheerful inevitability of the coming spring. Reaching up to scratch an imaginary itch beneath his eyepatch, he considered the offer that his old friend, Henry Rafferty, had just made him.

The Biafrans were still fighting, he knew. Still dying. But his war was over. He had sacrificed enough for a country that was never his, for a struggle that was never his, and all he wanted now was to find some peace.

He had already made up his mind. He craved a refuge. He needed a place where he could begin again, a place to shelter and a place to heal his wounds, both in body and spirit, and so he would turn away from the all the anger and the hatred, all the bigotry and pain, and he would go and find his peace.

In Belfast.

In the spring of 1969.

Forty One

Tone and Joker made their way up the steps and onto a rooftop made bright by a mournful moon that blemished the star-freckled face of night.

"'O sovereign mistress of true melancholy," Tone quoted in praise of the plump, silvery orb that reflected on the still water of the Mediterranean. "The poisonous damp of night disponge upon me'."

"Reminds me of the Albert Clock," said Joker, following Tone's gaze.

Tone nodded but remained silent. He knew from experience not to pry too deeply into the dark, twisting spirals of Joker's mind. Confusion and doubt and screaming madness were the rewards for anyone taking a step in that direction, so Tone decided to redirect the conversation onto safer ground.

"Right," he said, "break out the beer."

Joker pulled out two bottles from the bag he was carrying and placed them on the table.

"We won't need any more for a while, will we?" he said.

"Nah, these'll last us for a bit," Tone told him as he took out his cigarettes. Joker brought the other bottles of beer back down the stairs to the kitchen and placed them in the fridge. He came back upstairs and accepted a cigarette from Tone.

"Still really warm, isn't it?" he said as he stood sipping his beer and looking out across the water.

"Yeah," Tone agreed, "makes you wonder why our ancestors left the Med. I mean, what the hell were they thinking?"

"You'd need to ask Jamesy that question. He'd probably give you a long and detailed explanation about all the environmental and migratory pressures faced by Neolithic tribes of hunter-gatherers in their great quest for who the fuck knows what."

"Remind me to never, ever to ask Jamesy that question."

Joker turned from the edge of the little terrace and walked back to sit down on the bench. He seemed restless, Tone thought. Distracted almost.

"What's your verdict on Valencian then?" Tone asked.

"It's just Catalan," Joker replied with a shrug. "Don't know why they call it Valencian."

"I've noticed they seem to be fond of the letter 'x'. It pops up everywhere."

"Yeah," agreed Joker, "though it's probably more noticeable because it isn't used much in Castilian. What about tomorrow night then? Are you up for a bit of cow dancing?"

"Yeah, it sounds like a laugh," said Tone. "It's our last night, so we might as well do something different." He hesitated as he tried to think of the best way to approach the question of Joker's, increasingly obvious, lack of motivation. "You know," he began, "I was talking-"

"Best fucking lift ever!" The exclamation accompanied loud footsteps at the bottom of the stairs.

"Yeah," said Seamus, "but it was only because we had Jamesy with us."

"Fuck off!" Gary retorted, as he, Seamus and Jamesy made their way onto the rooftop. "Your woman was all over me."

"You?" Seamus demanded. "You? Then why did she make Jamesy sit in the front?"

"Well, that's just-"

"Why did she stare at him the whole way here?"

"Because-"

"Why did she talk to him the whole time? And we just sat in the back like a couple of fucking gooseberries."

"You really don't know much about women, do you?" said Gary in a condescending manner. "She was just trying to make me jealous. Anybody could see that. Isn't that right, Jamesy?"

"What? Um...yeah, probably," Jamesy replied, sitting down at the table.

"And who did she give her phone number to?" asked Seamus.

"Jesus! Are you really that fucking dense?" cried Gary. "She was shy! She didn't want to make it too obvious, did she?"

"Well, you've got a point there," said Seamus. "She didn't make it fucking obvious at all."

"Did you dickheads get any beer on the way?" asked Tone. "I mean, as fascinating as this discussion is, don't you think that-"

"Yeah, we got beer," Gary told him. "It's in the fridge. Why?"

"Didn't occur to you to bring any up here then?"

Gary and Seamus looked at each other, then shook their heads and trudged back down the steps, grumbling at each other under their breath.

"Get me one too!" Jamesy called after them.

"Good lift, was it?" Tone turned to Jamesy.

"Good-looking German girl in a convertible BMW?" said Jamesy, smiling. "So, yeah, you could say that."

Seamus and Gary reappeared and, handing a beer to Jamesy, sat at the table. After a while Sean, Bobby and Kevin arrived with more beer and grabbed some folding chairs from a storage container that sat to one side of the rooftop.

"Jammy bastards!" Bobby exclaimed. "Did you see the fucking car they got into?" he asked Tone.

"Heard about it."

"Jammy bastards!" Bobby repeated. "And your woman driving it? Jesus Christ! Jammy bastards!"

"Marta, she was called," Seamus told him. "German girl. She gave Jamesy her phone number because she fancied Gary, apparently."

"Really?" asked Sean. He looked at Jamesy. "Are you going to call her?"

"Not much point, is there?" Jamesy replied. "Besides, it was Gary she was after."

Gary gave Jamesy a salute with his beer. "Too fucking right!" he said.

"You looking for the meaning of life there, Joker?" Kevin asked. Everyone turned to see Joker, lying on his back on the bench and staring up at the night sky. His bottle of beer on the terracotta tiles beside him.

"What makes you think there's a meaning to life?" he said.

"Isn't there?"

"You can sum life up in four words," said Joker, still staring at the stars, "but you won't find much meaning in them."

"What four words?" asked Seamus.

"Born, eat, shag, die," Joker answered. "Anything else is just killing time."

"Well, that's fucking bleak," said Sean. "So you're just dismissing everything that anybody's ever done in all of history? Michelangelo shouldn't have bothered painting the Sistine Chapel then? Just killing time, was he?"

"Do you think that ten thousand years from now, the Sistine Chapel will still be there?" asked Joker. "Or Rome even?"

"Well, Rome's the eternal city," Kevin suggested.

"'We are butterflies that flutter for a day'," Joker quoted, "'and think it is forever'."

"What?"

"Nothing's eternal," Joker expanded. "Nothing's permanent. Everything dies."

"And that, Ladies and Gentlemen," said Sean, "is the Second Law of Thermodynamics."

"Jesus Christ, Joker!" cried Gary. "What the fuck is wrong with *you*?"

"Yeah," said Bobby, "that doesn't sound like the Joker we know and tolerate."

Joker lay on the bench and gazed at infinity. Lost in his own thoughts, he elected not to answer.

So Tone decided to answer for him.

"He's missing Carol, that's what's wrong with him."

Joker sat bolt upright. "What?" he cried. "What the fuck did you say that for?"

"It's true, isn't it?"

Joker glared at Tone, then sighed and shook his head. He picked up his beer, stood up and walked to the edge of the rooftop to look out upon the empty sea.

"You're a bit of a dickhead, Tone," he pointed out. "You know that, don't you?"

"Yeah," replied Tone, "but is it true about Carol?"

"Probably," Joker admitted. He then turned to face Tone. "But there's fuck-all I can do about it."

"Why not?" Bobby asked.

"Because the last I heard," Joker explained, "was that she'd gone to Nigeria, which is just a wee bit out of the way."

"Has she finished her training then?" asked Tone.

"I don't think so," said Joker. "At least not completely, but I think she once said she could finish her training in Africa."

"Do you think she's gone for good then?" asked Seamus, and Joker shrugged in reply.

"For a while, anyway," he said. "So it's a bit pointless me missing her, isn't it?"

Kevin looked around at the others' faces. "I don't know Carol," he began, "so I may be missing something here, but why Africa?"

Joker walked back to the bench and sat down. He took a sip of beer and looked at Kevin. "Carol is her middle name," he informed him. "She was christened

Chiazacam, which as I'm sure you know, is an Igbo name."

"Eeboh?" asked Kevin, confused.

"Yes," Joker continued, "Carol was one of those wee Biafran kids we all used to make jokes about when we were at school. Nearly died, too, apparently. Anyway, she'd always talked about going back there at some point. Don't know why exactly, but I'm sure she's got her reasons."

"I've always thought that Chiazacam was a fucking cool name," mused Gary.

"Yeah," Kevin agreed, "does it mean anything?"

"The closest English translation," Joker said, "would be *God has answered me well*."

"That makes it even cooler," said Gary.

"So, what are you going to do, Joker?" Bobby asked. "You can't just keep on moping about her, can you?"

"Why not?" Joker smiled, but it was unconvincing. He gave another sigh. "I don't know, Bobby," he said. "I just have to get over it, I suppose. Just takes time, that's all."

"How do you know she's in Africa?" asked Jamesy.

"I bumped into one of her mates a while back – Susie, remember her? – and she told me that Carol had buggered off to Africa. It was probably then that I started feeling some sort of…oh, I don't know…regret?...is that the word?"

"Actually, I think I know who you mean," Kevin said. "Was she at Charlie's party?"

"Yeah, she was there for a bit," said Joker. "That was the night we split up. I think I was annoyed that she made me leave early so I made up some excuse to pick a fight with her."

"You're a dickhead," Tone told him, and everyone nodded in agreement.

"You think I don't know that?"

"Well," Tone decided, "nothing is insurmountable. We've got enough beer to help us come up with some sort of solution to Joker's wee problem, so let's get to it."

Forty Two

Rosie was almost hugging herself with anticipation. She couldn't be sure how long she and her father had spent sobbing in each other's arms as they stood in the garden, but now she was energized with forming a plan.

"You know what to do now, don't you?" she asked.

"Yes, love," said Martin. He was still trying to process the flood of information he had received from his daughter – *his daughter!* – after they had eventually made it into the house and had sat in the front room, babbling incessantly, trying to fill a twenty year gap in their lives.

Shauna was dead. Martin was stunned by this. In every scenario he had played out in his mind, Shauna was alive. She was alive, and she was angry. She was smiling. She was confused, she was crying, she was laughing, she was yelling, swearing, blaming. She was alive.

But Shauna was dead.

Rosie had held him as they both stood and sobbed once more until their shared grief tip-toed quietly into the background to leave them alone with new possibilities in an unexpected new future.

Ellie would come first, Rosie decided. Miss Goody-Two-Shoes was about to get the shock of her life. Rosie loved her sister dearly, but she struggled to match Ellie's simple goodness, resorting instead to teasing her relentlessly. She couldn't live up to her sister's piety, but then who could? Ellie was the very best of souls. Gentle and caring and kind.

"She'll fucking shit a brick!" Rosie declared happily, and Martin winced as he tried to reconcile his little Rosemary with this brash, feisty fully-grown woman who could swear with the best of them. And she was *pregnant*.

"I think you'll like Gary," Rosie told him. "I mean, he'll drive you mad sometimes, but I think you'll like him. I'm not sure if you would remember the Lingfields."

Martin shook his head.

"No, I didn't think so," said Rosie. "I knew them because Karen was in my class at school."

"And you were saying Gary's in Spain at the minute?"

"Aye," said Rosie. "He's another one who's in for a bit of a shock."

"So, what about Jack?" asked Martin. "Are you sure you don't want to give him a ring yet?"

"No, we'll ring him later," Rosie insisted. "Ellie should be the first to know – well, after me anyway. She never gave up trying to find you, you know. Not for a minute."

The emotions brought on by the thought of his eldest child's quiet but dogged determination threatened to overwhelm Martin. He cursed the wasted years. The years he had spent lost in a maelstrom of psychosis, clinging to whatever would quell the waves of anxiety and fear that ebbed and flowed and threatened to pull him under the surface, to darkness and madness and oblivion.

"You found us again," Rosie said softly as she understood his anguish, "and we've got our whole lives ahead of us. And anyway, you've got this wee thing to look forward to." She gestured to the bump that strained against her T-shirt.

Martin looked at her and smiled. "Yeah, you're right, love." He was going to be a grandfather. He was stupefied by the abrupt turn his life had just taken.

"Right!" Rosie suddenly exclaimed. "She won't be long now, so you'd better get ready."

"Right you are," Martin laughed as he made his way into the kitchen. It somehow did not feel unnatural to be bossed around by his youngest daughter. He was fine with it. It felt good. He was happy. And he was about to meet Ellie.

It was only natural she felt tired. She had just completed a twelve-hour shift at the hospital, so it would be surprising if she didn't feel some fatigue, but as she stepped off the bus for the short walk home, Ellie felt almost crushed by weariness.

She was off work for the next few days, as her shifts rotated, but rather than look forward to the time off, she was hoping to spend as much time as possible curled up in bed under the covers and seeing no one. She was beginning to feel some concern for her own well-being as her natural optimism seemed to drain more quickly these days.

Rosie's mood swings did not help, but it would be wrong to blame her little sister's volatile hormones on the fact that Ellie was no longer able to find joy. She simply no longer looked.

As she listened to the garden gate shriek in protest at her audacity in wanting to enter her own garden,

Ellie hoped that Rosie would be in a mellow mood. She didn't think she could face any angry sarcasm this evening. She could do without the sullen grumblings, the dark disdain and the constant, pointless arguing.

Ellie had long felt there was a lot more to Rosie's moods than just the shock of pregnancy, but on those occasions when whatever was eating at Rosie would shatter into brittle shards of emotion, she had found rational discussion impossible.

She pushed open the door and, as she stepped into the front room, she saw Rosie sitting on one side of the sofa with a grim, hard look on her face. Ellie sighed and walked across the floor to sit in the armchair against the far wall. As she sat down, she failed to notice the little glance that Rosie flicked towards the kitchen door that was set in the wall to Ellie's left.

"What do you fancy doing for dinner tonight?" Ellie asked Rosie.

"Oh, I don't know," Rosie replied distractedly. "We could get something from the chippy."

"Sounds good to me," said Ellie.

"Have you got any plans for later on?"

"No, I could really just do with an early night, to be honest."

"Mmm," muttered Rosie. "You're not planning on doing any more of your stupid searching tonight, are you?"

"What? No!" Ellie sounded exasperated. "In fact, I don't think-"

"I don't see the bloody point of it myself," spat Rosie, her voice harsh and cold.

"Okay, Rosie. Look, I just want to-"

"Just a bloody waste of everybody's time."

"I know, Rosie, it's just that I-"

"I mean," Rosie exclaimed indignantly, "he can't even make a bloody decent cup of tea!"

Ellie sighed and closed her eyes. She leant back in her chair. "Oh, Rosie," she said wearily, "I don't know what you're talk-"

"Not enough milk, apparently," declared Martin as he stepped through the kitchen doorway.

Rosie pushed herself tight against the back of the sofa to fully appreciate the chaos that was erupting on her sister's face.

It was as if Ellie's emotions had all gathered together at once, uncertain as to which one was due to take precedence over her features.

Surprise, of course, made the smug assumption that it would be taking charge from here on in, but anger made an unexpected early bid, only to trip over confusion, which was curled up in a ball, whimpering.

Panic, running around in circles, was tackled from behind by belligerence, and they tumbled off to the side, while scepticism raised a tentative finger before getting tangled up with anxiety and fear. At this point, apathy strolled casually onto the scene, but on realising its presence would not be required, sauntered nonchalantly away.

"Hello, Elaine," said Martin. "How have you been keeping?"

Joy romped home unopposed.

Forty Three

For countless aeons, the driving force behind life on Earth has often been envisioned as a benevolent, maternal figure, so it is possible to imagine a wizened crone, gnarled and weary from three and a half billion years of ceaseless toil, shuffling around in her slippers, in a front parlour lit only by a crackling wood-fire.

And it is then but a small step to picture this ancient, twisted old biddy cast a glance in the direction of Carol and then, nodding with satisfaction, stretch her worn and jaded limbs, put a light to her pipe – ornately carved, perhaps, from the horn of a Triceratops – and settle into a comfortable armchair with a final contented sigh.

'Job's a good'un.'

Possessed of a languid elegance that slipped, almost lazily, in and out of poetry, Carol was an obvious target for the envious, spiteful bullies that seem to infest all schools but, in this respect, Carol's schooldays were trouble-free. The snide put-downs, the subtle shoves, the insidious intimidation, all simply failed to materialise. Perhaps it was just that everyone could see in Carol something they recognised – or hoped they recognised – in themselves.

The dour misunderstood, the cool kids, the rebels; they all could see, in Carol's exotic appearance, the mark of the true outsider, shunned by the mainstream and forced to lurk on the fringe of society, with head held defiantly high in haughty, independent disdain. It was only Carol's enormous popularity, they reasoned, that held her back from her true calling as the lonely outcast.

And the beautiful people recognised Carol as someone who could truly appreciate the pressure that afflicts those cursed with perfect features. They looked to her as the one person who could understand their torment, someone who could listen to their woes with empathy and understanding. A queen of calm surrounded by delicate princesses.

For the jocks, Carol embodied the African stereotype of lithe athleticism, panther-like in her supple muscularity, loping with easy grace from class to class.

The bright kids worshipped her. The high-achievers, the swots, the nerds, the dweebs, the geeks and the dorks were all enchanted by Carol's intellect. And her sexuality, of course. Many an inadvertent emission had been caused by her overt sexuality, though it was considered vulgar to dwell on such things. It was her mind that mattered. It was Carol's sharp intelligence that was deemed the greatest stimulation for the school's top performers.

And so, the potentially stormy seas of adolescence were, for Carol, a millpond upon which she sailed serenely towards the beckoning haven of further education where she coasted, unflustered, into harbour on half-sail and dropped anchor before the metaphor became tortuous and unwieldy.

It was here that she could no longer ignore the glaring, Joker-shaped void in her existence, and so entered a tall, broodingly handsome stranger. A majestic mountain of a man with piercing gunmetal grey eyes and cheekbones that...

"Okay, okay, we get the bloody point! Jesus Christ, Joker!"

"Who's telling the story?" Joker asked indignantly.

"I know," said Bobby, "but you're going a wee bit over the top, aren't you? So, Mother Nature smokes a pipe, does she?"

"Well, she's hardly going to smoke fucking roll-ups, is she?"

"Okay, but you still need to tone it down a bit."

"I liked the bit about the metaphor though," said Jamesy, smiling.

"Thank you, Jamesy. Now where was I?"

"I'm still wondering about Biafra," Kevin interjected. "I mean, I can remember the name from when I was a kid and all, but that's about it. I don't know anything else about it."

"That's true," said Seamus thoughtfully. He turned to Jamesy. "Well, Jamesy," he said, "what's the story? You must know about it."

"Modern history isn't really my thing," Jamesy told him. "Anyway, I'm sure Joker knows more about it than me."

"Yes," said Tone as he put a light to a cigarette, "but I think we've all heard enough of Joker's flights of fancy for one evening. Go ahead, Jamesy. Fill us all in on the details."

"Well," Jamesy began, "as far as I know, the people of one part of Nigeria-"

"The Igbo people," said Joker.

"Yeah," said Jamesy, "the Igbo. Well, they started to get persecuted in some of the other parts of the country not long after Nigeria became independent from Britain in the sixties. I think a lot of them were killed actually. Thousands even. Anyway, the survivors all headed back to the region where the Igbo originally came from, to get away from the persecution. We're talking about millions of people here, so it caused a bit of a refugee problem.

"Well then they reckoned that they were never going to be safe in Nigeria so they formed their own country, Biafra, and tried to go it alone. The rest of Nigeria refused to let them go though, so they ended up going to war. Britain, and a lot of other countries, backed the Nigerians, so the Biafrans never stood a chance. Even so, it took a couple of years and it was only when Nigeria surrounded the Biafrans and cut off their food supplies that Biafra fell."

"Wait a minute," said Sean, "are you saying that the starvation was deliberate?"

"Yeah," Jamesy said, "the Nigerian government even said that starvation was a legitimate tactic of war."

"Fuck!"

"How many died then, Jamesy?" asked Gary. "Do you know?"

"All together? About two million."

Everyone stared at Jamesy.

"Two fucking *million*?"

"Give or take," said Jamesy. "And most of them were children."

"Kids? Why?"

"Adults can survive longer without protein than children can, so it was the kids who died first."

"Jesus!" Bobby muttered.

"Well, that explains why you don't hear about Biafra anymore," said Sean. "It doesn't exist."

"So, what about these days, Jamesy?" Seamus wanted to know. "There must still be a lot of tension there. I mean, you don't easily forget two million dead, do you? Do you think Carol will be okay there?"

Jamesy took a sip of beer and let out a sigh. "Hard to say," he said. "It just seems to be one coup after another in Nigeria, so you don't really know where you stand. I wouldn't fancy it myself, to be honest."

Joker, who had been sitting quietly listening, jumped to his feet. "That's it," he decided, "I'm going to Africa!"

"Well, finish your beer first," said Tone.

"I'm serious."

"Well, if you're going," Gary exclaimed, standing up to add emphasis, "then so am I."

"What about Rosie?"

"I won't tell her."

"Good man!"

"You two wankers will only get into trouble in Africa," said Seamus, also standing up, "so I'll have to go too."

Bobby stood up. "I'm Spartacus!" he said.

"What the hell," Tone declared. "Count me in too."

Sean and Jamesy, who both understood that it was all just drunken bluster, stood and raised their bottles in solidarity. Everyone turned to Kevin.

"Well, Kevin?" asked Sean. "It wouldn't be the same without you."

"No," said Gary with a grin, "it would be much better."

Kevin felt moved by the realisation that he was being fully accepted into the group, and the fact that it was happening without him having to pretend to be someone else made it all the more emotional. He stood and raised his beer.

"To Africa!" he said, and everyone answered.

"To Africa!"

But first, they had a date with some cows.

Forty Four

Calling it a bullring, thought Sean as he and Bobby made their way through the crowds, was a bit of a stretch.

The circular arena of bare earth was surrounded by a series of vertical steel poles that were placed just far enough apart to allow one person to squeeze through. Behind this barrier, and circling the round space in the centre, was an area where the public could stand and where several little bars, spaced at regular intervals, were selling cold beer and strong local spirits.

Above this area, and running around the entire ring, several rows of tiered seating had been constructed, and it was to these seats that Sean and Bobby were heading. They were the last to arrive and had been dropped off close to Benifairó by a bad-tempered old Spanish man.

"How come we have such shit luck with lifts?" asked Bobby. "Your man looked like he wanted to kill the two of us."

"Yeah, makes you wonder why he even bothered to pick us up."

"It just seems to be the natural thing to do around here. Sort of expected like."

"Well, maybe on the way back we can stay close to Jamesy and get a lift with him."

"That's an idea. Jesus! This is all a bit ramshackle, isn't it?" Bobby and Sean would soon be graduating as civil engineers and their sensibilities were somewhat offended by the rough and ready construction of the 'bullring'.

"It's seen better days," Sean agreed, "but it seems functional enough."

They purchased some beer from one of the bars and climbed the steps to the rows of seats. It was busy upstairs and it took them a while to pinpoint Tone and the others.

"There they are," said Bobby, "right round the other bloody side."

They made their way around to join the group.

"You made it then?" exclaimed Tone. "Class wee place, isn't it?"

"Seems like it," said Sean as they both sat down. "Really good atmosphere. All the bars were packed when we came through the town, loads of music too. So, what's going on here then?"

"There's a bit of a lull at the minute," Tone told him, "but every now and then they seem to let some cow into the ring, evil-looking bastard it is too, and all the young Spanish lads try to slap it on the arse. They've got a wee three-wheeled van as well and they drive that around the ring with a couple of lads standing in the back. It's all a mad bit of *craic*."

"A wee van?"

"Aye, Kevin reckons it's normally used to get around the citrus groves or the olive groves or whatever, but tonight they're using it to irritate a cow."

Suddenly the crowds that were milling around the centre of the arena rushed off to the perimeter and ducked behind the barrier of steel poles.

"Oh, here we go," said Tone. "Looks like they're starting up again."

The ring below was momentarily deserted, and then a lean, jet-black beast strutted into the centre and shook its head angrily from side to side. It snorted as it pawed at the ground, and then it stood still and raised its head, displaying a particularly vicious set of horns. A young man rushed into the ring, but the beast turned quickly to meet him and he had to veer away and scramble, just in time, through one of the gaps between the poles. The crowd jeered.

Several more attempts were made to touch the back of the cow, but she seemed fresh and fast, and only a few intrepid souls were successful. After a while Tone nudged Sean.

"Here's that wee van I was telling you about," he said.

Sean looked down to see a tiny Citroën van appear below him. It had an open back that was crowded with just five or six revellers, standing and waving and drinking beer. Suddenly, Gary jumped to his feet.

"What the fuck does that dickhead think he's doing?" he demanded.

Joker was celebrating. He had come to a decision, he was going to Africa. He was going to go and snatch the lovely Carol from the perils of the dark continent, and then... well, he hadn't got that far yet, but his brain seemed happy enough with the plan as it stood, and that was what mattered.

He had just acquired a bottle of beer from the bar and had then got caught up in the joyous atmosphere of the excited crowd. He had felt a sudden, warm affinity with these mad, drunken bastards and had not taken much persuading to join them on their quest to vanquish the beast in its lair.

He stood, exhilarated, in the back of the little van alongside his Spanish comrades as they trundled towards the centre of the ring. The crowd applauded their noble endeavours and Joker raised his bottle in salute. The cow eyed the strange vehicle cautiously as it trotted around the edge of the ring and then, shockingly, it burst into a sudden charge at the intruder.

The van driver swerved in panic and just managed to avoid a collision as the cow roared past. The van carried on, careering wildly, and Joker, clutching his beer rather than the side rail of the van was thrown clear. He landed on his side and rolled along the sand before jumping to his feet. He was laughing as he noted with satisfaction that he had spilled none of his drink. He spotted his friends in the seating area upstairs and, smiling, walked towards them.

He could see they were all waving and chanting his name, and he acknowledged their appreciation by raising his beer. As he got closer, however, it began to dawn on him that they were not so much waving, as gesticulating wildly. And they were not so much chanting his name, as yelling. "Run, you dopey wanker!"

Forty Five

Any misgivings that Martin may have had about accompanying Rosie faded away when he saw the baby moving around on the ultrasound monitor.

Despite his doubts, Rosie had insisted he come with her for her six-month scan and, as he was beginning to understand, his daughter could be very persuasive.

"But shouldn't it be Gary who goes with you?" he had argued.

"Yes it should," she had retorted, "but he's not bloody here, is he? So come on, don't you want to see your grandchild?"

"Yes, Daddy," said Ellie, relishing the word on her lips, "and we can all head into town afterwards and make a day of it." Ellie's reinvigoration, Rosie thought, had been astonishing. She no longer walked with her shoulders slumped, and her eyes, once dulled and defeated, now shone with a happy resolution. Rosie felt cheered by the transformation in her sister, and she had to acknowledge that she herself could sense that a cloud had lifted. Her overall mood was lighter somehow. Less intense. It was a confusing sensation but not, she had to admit, unwelcome.

"Yes, all right," said Martin, "but I just want to use your phone before we go."

"Oooh," the girls teased. "Phoning your girlfriend, are you?"

Martin reddened but smiled. "Don't be silly," he said. "I told you she's married. I just want to let her know that I'm going to see my grandchild. Why aren't you in the phone book, by the way? I had a look, but I couldn't see you."

"I only had the phone put in a couple of months ago," Ellie explained. "So it won't be in until the new book comes out."

Rosie's friend and Gary's sister, Karen, had driven them across town to the new tower block at the City Hospital, and then let them go off to the appointment.

"I'll just meet you back at the wee cafeteria," she told them, before giving Martin a playful slap on the arm. "I still can't believe Rosie and Ellie have got their daddy back," she said.

"Can't believe it myself," said Martin.

In the treatment room, they stared at the grey, fuzzy blob on the screen, and Martin had to fight back a tear when he felt his little girl squeeze his hand.

"Would you like to know if it's a boy or a girl?" asked the nurse.

"No," said Rosie. "I'm happy to wait. And I really don't mind either way."

They all walked back to the cafeteria and as they approached, Rosie could see Karen standing by a corridor on the far side of the open area. She was talking to a young doctor that Rosie felt she recognised. Karen spotted them appear on the other side of the room and broke off her conversation to come and join them. The young doctor disappeared down the corridor.

"Who was that you were talking to?" Rosie asked when Karen came over.

"What? Oh, that was Dr Maher," said Karen. "She used to go out with that stupid cunt, Joseph."

Forty Six

A person traditionally has fewer legs than a cow, but this was not Joker's only disadvantage. His reflexes were rendered sluggish by alcohol, and he was also slowed by having to set off from a standing start, so he should have been much less surprised than he was when the cow's horn punctured his right buttock and hoisted him into the air to balance precariously like some grotesque cow ornament.

He bounced and flailed with shock and pain as the triumphant cow thundered across the arena with her trophy held high until, feeling that her point had been made, she came to an abrupt halt in front of the steel barrier that circled the ring. Joker's momentum carried him onward towards the row of uprights, where he managed to miss every one of the gaps between the poles.

His forehead struck one of the uprights with a loud, vibrating *bong* and he rebounded back into the arena to land heavily on his back. Joker's nemesis, her blood fired up from her recent victory, sensed an easy kill and spun around with her head lowered to make the final charge. The people in the crowd closest to the action rushed forward to grab Joker's helpless, writhing form and were able to pull him back behind the barrier just as the cow raced past in snorting fury.

Joker, lying on his back surrounded by anxious Spanish faces, saw Tone appear, then Sean and Gary and everyone else. He noted with some surprise that he still held the bottle of beer in his right hand and he smiled as he looked up at his friends.

"Didn't spill any," he said, as the world turned blissfully black.

Joker spent the night in the emergency room at the Tavernes paramedic station, where bovine related injuries were apparently not uncommon. His wounds were cleansed and treated, and he was pumped so full of painkillers that, when Tone and Kevin picked him up in a taxi the next morning, he was smiling.

"So what's the plan for today?" he slurred happily.

"Remember," said Tone, "we're catching the train tonight, so you need to get some sleep back at the beach-house while we all pack."

"Are we going to Africa now?"

"Not yet, Joker, no. We have to go home first."

"That's good," said Joker. "Home is good."

"How's your arse?"

"Are you flirting with me?"

"Never mind."

Back at the beach-house, they carefully put Joker to bed, where he soon nodded off, and then everyone assembled around the dining table. The atmosphere was subdued.

"Hopefully he'll sleep for a couple of hours before we have to shoot off," said Tone.

"What was the verdict?" asked Gary.

"Well, the medics seemed more concerned about his head injury than what the cow did to his arsehole, but it's not fractured at least, and I think they were happy enough with it. He'll need to get it looked at when we get home though."

"Stupid bastard," Sean muttered.

"Yeah well," said Tone, "we need to get this place tidied up before we leave, and we still need to pack, so we can get all that done while he's out of the way."

A little while later, Joker appeared at the bottom of the stairs, looking confused.

"You're alive then?" Seamus shouted over to him.

"Is that what it's called?"

"How do you feel?" asked Bobby.

"Sore."

"Are you not sitting down?"

"I don't think I will actually, thanks all the same."

"Oh, you're up," said Tone, as he walked past holding a broom, heading for the veranda. "Don't forget, you need to pack at some point."

"Yeah, I know."

Jamesy was in the kitchen area. "Do you want a cup of tea, Joker?" he asked.

"Love one, Jamesy. Thanks." Jamesy filled the kettle while Joker stood by the stairs as if lost in thought.

"Actually," said Joker, "I could go and get my packing done while you're making the tea. It won't take me long."

"Yeah, no problem. I'll just have it here for you."

Joker turned and went back upstairs while Jamesy carried on making the tea. Kevin, quietly observing, felt moved by the unspoken concern the group of friends had for Joker's wounds. Despite the laddish banter, he thought, and the barbed comments and insults, it was obvious they were all gently grieving for their stricken comrade.

"Where's Ermintrude's hat?" asked Tone, returning from the veranda.

"He went back upstairs to pack," Jamesy told him. Tone set down the broom and climbed the stairs. A few moments later, the subsequent exchange, though muted, could still be heard downstairs.

"Hey, Joker!"

"What?"

"Mooooo!"

Kevin sighed and went back to tidying up.

Forty Seven

Gemma walked into the living room and placed her bags of shopping on the floor. Wee Paulie was lying on the sofa watching the football results on the television. Gemma gave him a quick kiss.

"How's the birthday boy?" she asked.

"Okay," he told her. "How was work?"

"Oh, the usual," Gemma said as she carried some of the shopping through to the kitchen. "I got you a couple of presents in the town."

"Thanks," Wee Paulie called after her. He sat up on the sofa and tried not to look at the remaining bags of shopping that Gemma had left on the floor. "But remember," he said when Gemma came back to sit beside him, "we can't really celebrate tonight because I need to be up early in the morning. Big day tomorrow."

"No problem. What do you fancy doing tonight then?"

"Just an early night," he suggested, "but then we can have a proper celebration tomorrow night."

"Sounds good," said Gemma, "I booked Monday off, so we can even go out somewhere if we want."

"Yeah, we could," said Wee Paulie, his gaze wandering over to the mysterious bags on the floor. "You know," he said, looking back at Gemma, "tomorrow could turn out to be a bit of a double celebration."

"Why?"

"It could be a big step up in my career," he declared. "All going well, that is."

"Is that right?"

"Yeah. Mr Jippsen-Phillips thinks I've got a lot of potential. There's a big shake-up coming, and he said I can expect big things to come my way."

"That probably just means you'll have heavier stuff to carry," said Gemma, but then regretted it when she saw the crestfallen look on his face. She squeezed his leg. "I'm only messing you," she told him. "Look, I got some lasagne for dinner, and there's some wine there as well. We can have a glass of wine with our dinner, can't we?"

Wee Paulie brightened up. "I don't see why not," he said.

"Right then, I'll stick the dinner on and then we'll sit down and you can tell me all about it."

"Okay, but I won't be able to tell you too much, you know. It's all a bit top secret."

"Oooh, sounds important," said Gemma as she got up and headed into the kitchen.

"Well, it's just about knowing what your options are," said Wee Paulie. "About being in the right place at the right time."

"This is going to take about forty minutes," Gemma informed him. "Why don't you open the wine?"

Wee Paulie got up and joined Gemma in the kitchen. He grabbed a bottle opener from the drawer and picked up the bottle of Shiraz. "You know," he began as he twisted the corkscrew into the top of the bottle, "it is my birthday today, so I don't see why I can't open at least one of my presents."

Gemma laughed. "Well, we'll see," she told him, "but it'll have to wait till after dinner. Now pour me a glass of that wine."

After dinner, they sat together on the sofa and Gemma teased him that they should wait until the proper celebration tomorrow night before any presents could be handed out. Wee Paulie began to whine so much that she relented, laughing. She reached down beside the sofa and began to feel around in one of the bags until she found what she was looking for.

"Happy Birthday!" she said as she handed Wee Paulie a small package.

"Thanks, love," he said, pulling away the wrapping to reveal a pair of boxer shorts.

"Boxers!" he exclaimed. "Very sexy."

"I know he's your favourite."

Wee Paulie gave the boxers a closer inspection. "Daffy Duck boxers!" he cried happily. "They're class, love. Cheers!"

"You're welcome."

"Yeah," he said, "Daffy Duck was the best of all the Looney Tunes characters."

Gemma had heard all this before, but she nodded and smiled, then settled back in the sofa to sip her wine.

"Not like that smug bastard, Bugs Bunny," Wee Paulie continued. "Daffy was more for the man in the street, you know. He had to put up with all sorts of shit too. And remember, all those old Warner Brothers' cartoons were never meant to be for kids. They were made to be shown in cinemas with the main film. For grown-ups, like." He was warming to one of his favourite themes, so Gemma thought she should intervene.

"Why don't you try them on?" she suggested.

"Try them on?" Wee Paulie repeated, holding up his new underwear shorts. They were made of a white, sheer material covered with little pictures of Daffy Duck in a series of action poses. "Aye, why not?" he decided. He stood up and started to unbuckle his jeans. "Do you know what my favourite Daffy quote is?" he asked.

Gemma knew exactly what his favourite quote was, but she shook her head and smiled indulgently.

"'With me, it's not the principle that counts; it's the money'," Wee Paulie grinned. "Fucking genius!"

"Yeah," said Gemma, "very good."

"Well, what do you think?" Wee Paulie stood, modelling his new boxers, in front of Gemma. He had taken off his top to let her have the full effect. "Sexy, or what?"

"Aye, dead sexy," Gemma laughed. She picked up the wine bottle and stared at it. "Jesus!" she exclaimed. "That went down well!"

Wee Paulie stopped striking sexy poses and looked, perplexed, at the empty bottle. The wine had just got him warmed up, but he was only too aware of the importance of having all his wits about him in the morning. He decided to be sensible.

"Right," he said firmly, "there's a ten-glass bottle of vodka in the kitchen, but we can only have one drink each out of it, okay? And then we need to have an early night."

"I got another bottle of vodka in town today," Gemma told him, "so that can do for tomorrow night." She set off to find the vodka while Wee Paulie went to admire himself in the full-length mirror in the hall.

Forty Eight

Fergal surveyed his troops with some dismay. He felt that things had slipped beyond his control but – he was reluctant to admit – he only had himself to blame.

It had only been a suggestion, he was sure, rather than a direct command that had come down from the Army Council a few weeks ago, but Fergal was shrewd enough to know that such distinctions were negligible.

The Irish Republican Army had decided to create a short promotional video to showcase some of their latest acquisitions, and Fergal had been offered the chance to volunteer for the job. He had accepted readily enough, considering it a simple enough task, but now he was having some doubts. Not about his ability to do the job, but because he knew that he had left it all too late.

He had believed the project to be of such low priority that he had put it to the back of his mind while he attended to matters that he felt were more pressing. In truth, he had largely forgotten about the whole thing until yesterday when he had been informed that a video cassette was expected to be delivered by 3.00pm on Monday, without fail, to the offices of RTÉ in Dublin.

Today was Sunday.

The words 'without fail' were at the forefront of Fergal's thoughts as he inspected his men. It wasn't much of an active service unit, he thought. He had received some bad news earlier that morning which meant that half his squad was missing but, even so, he felt particularly uninspired by the two men standing in front of him.

Morris 'The Cat' Donnelly and Gerry Cleary were decent enough men, Fergal knew, but he had always had his doubts about their unwavering commitment to the cause. Fergal himself was entirely focused on the goals of the IRA – Irish reunification following a British withdrawal from the north-eastern corner of the country – and he expected similar dedication from all of the volunteers in the organisation.

Morris, he felt, was a little too soft-headed to be a truly hardened guerrilla fighter, and his penchant for having frequent daytime naps did little to conjure up the image of the tireless and vigilant soldier of the revolution that Fergal liked to nourish.

Gerry, on the other hand, was sharp and clever, but Fergal reckoned that the armed struggle against British oppression did not feature quite high enough among his list of priorities.

Gerry Cleary made his living from producing video tapes of people's special occasions – weddings, birthdays, etc. – and his skill and his natural instinct for film-making gave his work a quality that was in high demand. He enjoyed his work so much that he harboured dreams of becoming a true professional and had made tentative enquiries at the BBC offices in Belfast. This had earned him a reprimand from Fergal and a stern lecture on the true spirit of resistance to British intransigence and brutality in Ireland. Gerry had replied that it was important to keep one's options open.

Fergal shook his head and turned away to pace around the courtyard of the farmhouse where they had met up earlier that morning. Gerry and Morris had arrived together in Gerry's car, which was now parked up against the gable wall of the house.

"We'll need to get that car into the barn," said Fergal. "All the equipment is in the Land Cruiser, so we'll be taking that."

"Righty-ho," chirped Gerry. "I'll just get my gear out first." He was happy at the thought of a day's filming and he had brought along some new filters that he was keen to try out. He was already composing the shots in his head; a heavy brooding sky with the stark silhouette of an assault rifle held aloft in defiance, a lone volunteer, wearied by the struggle, a wistful breeze gently stroking a desolate hilltop, a...

"Wait a minute," he said suddenly, looking around him. "I thought Tommy and Rab were meant to be here."

"They're not coming," said Fergal testily. "It's just the three of us."

"Not coming? Why the fuck not?"

"Because they..." Fergal rubbed the back of his neck as he turned away from Gerry. "They phoned in sick," he said.

"They fucking what?" cried Gerry. "Phoned in sick? In other words they were out on the tear up in Drogheda all night and they're still fucking blootered, that's what you mean, isn't it?"

"Look, it doesn't matter," Fergal insisted. "Like I said, it's just the three of us, so just hurry the fuck up."

Morris, who up until that point had been reminiscing about the particularly fine sausages he had had for breakfast that morning, spoke up. "Weren't they meant to be keeping dick though?"

Fergal spun around to face Morris. "I fucking told you before," he snapped, "it is not *keeping dick*, it is providing surveillance and assistance to volunteers operating in the field."

"Yeah okay, but they were still meant to be keeping-"

"Aye, that's right, Mo," said Gerry. "So, it's just going to be the three of us wandering around like a bunch of dickheads, not knowing what the fuck we-"

"Oh, for fuck's sake!" cried Fergal. "It won't be a problem, okay? Who the fuck is going to be out at this time on a Sunday? We'll just shoot on up to that wee spot by the bridge, get the filming done, and we'll be back here in no time."

"You know, you can't rush these things," Gerry was about to protest about the need for artistic integrity, but a savage glance from Fergal forced him to reconsider. "Right, I'll just get my gear," he said, "and we'll head on."

As Gerry went to retrieve his equipment, Morris opened the back of the Land Cruiser and pulled an assault rifle from under a tarpaulin.

"I'll hold onto this," he said. "Just in case like."

Fergal nodded impatiently. "Fine, fine, just get a move on."

Gerry approached with his camera bag and placed it carefully on the back seat. Morris climbed in beside the bag while Gerry got into the front passenger seat. Fergal jumped up into the driver's seat.

"Right!" Gerry said happily. "Here we go then. The media wing of the IRA. The Irish Republican Broadcast-"

"Don't say it!" Fergal growled. He turned to stare at Gerry as he turned the ignition key. "Just don't fucking say it!"

Gerry grinned and gave Fergal a wink as the Land Cruiser lumbered out of the courtyard and into the quiet country lanes.

The Irish Republican Broadcasting Corporation was off to make an outside broadcast.

Forty Nine

Wee Paulie gripped the edge of the sink in the kitchen. He was half-hoping that the next wave of nausea would result in a burst of vomiting that might herald the beginning of his recovery. The thought that maybe he should force the issue by sticking a finger down his throat briefly occurred to him but he didn't feel up to it. An empty vodka bottle mocked him from the kitchen worktop as the room revolved around his quivering form. He put his face to the water tap and let the cold water trickle over his lips and into his mouth. It felt good, but the respite was temporary, serving only to increase his sense of disorientation.

The doorbell rang and Wee Paulie squeezed his eyes closed in desperation. The doorbell rang more insistently and he forced himself to stagger to the intercom, accompanied by the sound of Gemma's snores coming from the bedroom.

"Come on to fuck!" Big Dennis' voice over the intercom helped Wee Paulie to sharpen his focus. Today was the big day. Today was the day when he needed to have his wits about him. He looked stupidly around the floor by his feet, as if searching for his scattered wits, before replying into the intercom.

"Hold on," he said, "I'm on my way down."

"Don't know why they have to use my fucking car," Big Dennis grumbled as Wee Paulie strapped himself into the front seat of the silver Ford Sierra. "You know what the bloody roads are like down south, don't you?" he continued. He started up and set off towards the Lisburn Road. "Might as well take a fucking hammer to the suspension. This car's not even a year old, you know. There's not even five thousand miles on the clock, and here's me taking it into the fucking wilderness."

"Mmm," Wee Paulie was trying to control the shivering and the queasiness that gripped his insides while he attempted to keep up the conversation. "Hopefully it won't take too long."

"Nah," Big Dennis agreed, "it won't take long at all. Here, are you okay? You look like shit."

"Yeah, I'm dead on," Wee Paulie assured him. "It's just a bit early in the morning, that's all."

"Aye, for fuck's sake. Still, at least there's no traffic about at this time. We've got the roads to ourselves."

Wee Paulie let Big Dennis ramble on while he concentrated on not throwing up. He felt quite sure that Big Dennis would not appreciate the inside of his new car being covered in foul-smelling sick. Eventually they pulled up at Mr Jippsen-Phillips' apartment. He was already waiting outside.

"Good morning boys," he said cheerfully. He climbed into the back seat and buckled his seatbelt. "How are you both today? Good God, Paulie, you look terrible, are you feeling okay?"

"Oh yeah, no problem, I'm dead on." Wee Paulie forced a smile. "Thanks for asking though."

"Right then," said Simon uncertainly. "So you're both still up for this, I take it?"

"Yes, yes," Wee Paulie assured him. "Absolutely!" Big Dennis nodded.

"Very well then. Let's go pick up the Boss Man!"

Michael stepped out through the front door when he saw the car approach and then walked down the drive to the gate. He looked tired, thought Simon. Deflated almost. He got into the back seat beside Simon and nodded to Big Dennis and Wee Paulie.

"Right, lads," he said.

"You carrying?" Simon asked him.

Michael shook his head. "If it's all the same to you lads, I'm happy to just stay in the car and watch. I'm not feeling up to it today."

Big Dennis caught Simon's eye in his rear view mirror, but Simon looked away, turning back to Michael.

"Of course," he said cheerfully. "It's fine by me. But it's going to take a while to get there and you might have perked up by then. We'll see how it goes."

"Yes, fine," said Michael. "Whatever."

Big Dennis pulled out onto the empty main road and headed south.

Fifty

It hadn't been a pleasant flight for Joker. The plan had been for everyone to get some sleep on the overnight train up from Valencia, but Joker, with his injuries, had found it impossible to be both pain-free and comfortable for more than a few moments at a time and so had slept little by the time he boarded the plane.

"Did you get any sleep at all," Jamesy asked him as they went through the arrivals hall at Dublin Airport.

"I think I might have dozed off for a couple of minutes here and there," Joker replied, "but nothing to write home about."

"Well, it won't be long now till you can crash out in your own bed."

"Can't wait."

Harry was already waiting when they cleared customs, so they went straight out to the car park.

"Here, Harry," said Gary. "I was talking to Rosie on the phone the other night and she said she had a big surprise waiting for me. I was just wondering if I should be worried or not. Do you know anything about it?"

"I've been told not to say anything," said Harry as he helped load the luggage into the van.

"Right..." Gary prompted, then waited expectantly. Harry gave him a look and Gary realised the matter was now closed.

'Shit!' he thought, and he began to worry.

"Maybe she's found out the baby isn't hers," Bobby suggested.

"Yeah, very funny, Bobby," said Gary, "but I could be in the soup here."

"Why, what have you been up to?"

"Well, that's the thing," Gary moaned, "it could be anything."

If Harry thought it was odd that Joker was limping and had a bandage around the top of his head, he didn't say, but when Joker struggled to sit down while trying to keep his right leg straight, he decided to make a comment.

"You all right there, Joseph?"

"Yeah, Harry, I'm great, thanks."

"You sure? Do you not want to sit in the front?"

"Nah, the back is better," said Joker, "in case I have to stand up."

"Why? What's wrong?"

"Let's just say," Tone interjected, "that Joker's coming back with more holes than he went away with."

"What?"

"It's a long story, Harry. We'll tell you all about it over a couple of pints. It's worth hearing."

At this point, Harry seemed to lose interest. He climbed into the driver's seat and, once everyone had settled, they headed for home.

Fifty One

The old fence had long been left to rot, and just a few uprights with some warped horizontal bars in between could still be seen. It had once run alongside the track that led to an ancient stone bridge just up ahead.

The ground behind the fence rose steeply to form a ridge that looked across the track to another, less steep, rise in the terrain, giving the impression of the road threading along the floor of a small valley as it made its way to the bridge and the woodland beyond.

On one of the decrepit old bars that ran between the fenceposts sat a pair of blackbirds. The male blackbird was nuzzling the female – his mate of many years – in an attempt to arouse a little friskiness within her. Mrs Blackbird was by no means averse to some spontaneous canoodling but she felt it was only right for her partner to make a bit more of an effort.

She was not the type of bird to just give it away – not like those sluts, the sparrows – so she was acting aloof as she worked out a strategy, wondering if maybe she could persuade him to stand on one leg and puff out his chest like she'd seen the male pigeons do.

Not that she would be impressed by such behaviour, she thought, but it would give her a laugh at least. She was about to make her proposal when a sudden noise drew her attention. She turned to see a silver car slowly appear along the track and pull up in the little clearing across from thc fence. She frowned with disapproval at this unwelcome interruption to the peace of the morning. She frowned even more when all four doors opened.

"I still don't see what we're doing here," Michael grumbled as he got out and walked a little way towards the bridge. "We're nowhere near the main road."

"Yes, I know," Simon explained, "but we're still early and we would look a tad conspicuous if we just sat waiting by the roadside. Besides, this gives us a chance to stretch our legs a bit, don't you think?"

Michael stopped and gazed ahead at the distant woods. He would be happy to get this whole business over and done with, he thought. He had other, more important, matters that had been keeping him distracted just lately, and there were some things on his mind that he…

"Oh, and Michael?" Simon went on. "Consider this a hostile takeover."

"What?" Michael turned to see Big Dennis and Wee Paulie both produce handguns and raise them towards his head. At that moment, the Irish Republican Broadcasting Corporation appeared on top of the ridge just behind and to Michael's left.

Wee Paulie had walked around the car to stand beside Big Dennis. His head was spinning as he stood quivering and nauseous when, all of a sudden, he caught sight of the unmistakeable outline of a Kalashnikov assault rifle. Panicking, he squeezed the trigger of his 9mm several times, making himself jump at the sudden noise.

On the ridge, Morris reacted instinctively and, swinging the AK onto his hip, fired a short burst towards the enemy before ducking behind the skyline. His bullets all sailed harmlessly into the scenery, apart from one which took a brief but eventful detour through Big Dennis.

"Hold your fire!" Simon yelled. "Hold your fucking fire!"

The clipped south of England accent carried across the valley and convinced Fergal that the British forces had finally caught up with him. He crouched alongside Gerry and Morris below the ridge, hidden from the roadway, while his mind raced.

"Fucking SAS bastards!" he cried. "Fucking sneaky bastards!"

"SAS?" asked Gerry.

"Who the fuck else would it be?" Fergal demanded. "Bastards have been after me for years."

Gerry considered this for a second and decided it was highly unlikely that the Brits would send a crack unit into the Irish Republic, just to take out Fergal. *Fergal,* for fuck's sake! He was about to share this opinion with the others when Morris spoke.

"I think I got one of the bastards!"

"Good man!" said Fergal. "Good man yourself! Don't worry, lads," he went on, "I'll get us out of this."

Gerry thought that this was only fair, considering it was Fergal who had got them into it in the first place, but he couldn't say that he had any great confidence in Fergal's abilities in a crisis. Then again, he thought, he had never witnessed Fergal reacting to any real pressure before and there was always the possibility that Fergal would surprise him.

"I'll tell you one thing, lads," Fergal shouted maniacally, "they won't fucking take us alive!"

"*Us?*" Gerry yelled in alarm. "What the fuck do you mean *us*? I'm more than happy to be taken a-"

A fresh volley of shots from the valley floor caused them all to duck instinctively.

"Jesus Christ!" shouted Gerry.

"Fuck this!" cried Fergal, and he reached for the suspiciously long canvas holdall that Morris had been carrying, and which was now lying at their feet. "Death or glory, lads," Fergal yelled. "Death or glory!"

When the first shots had been fired, Michael, believing he had just been executed, had dropped to the ground and had adopted what he felt was the correct position for the recently murdered. It soon became apparent, however, that he was unharmed and so, confused but relieved, he jumped to his feet and took off in the direction of the old bridge, hoping to find refuge in the woods on the far side.

Simon, panicked by the automatic gunfire, had run back behind the car, glancing momentarily at the bulk of Big Dennis, crumpled in the roadway, and had clambered over the high ground on that side of the road. As he settled into the cover provided by the shape of the land, he struggled to make sense of what was happening.

It was unlikely, he decided, that some local farmers would be out hunting rabbits with an AK-47, so the chances were that they had inadvertently stumbled upon an IRA unit out on manoeuvres, or whatever the hell an IRA unit did on a Sunday morning. He was just about to curse his own rotten luck when he remembered why he was there. He slowly raised his head above the natural parapet and was horrified to see Michael making his escape.

Simon had been planning this for weeks, and all of his machinations, all of his plots and dealings and schemes, and all the little details of the complex manoeuvrings he had been involved in, were entirely dependent on one simple fact: Michael McClelland needed to be dead.

He fumbled in his pocket for the pistol he hadn't planned on using and, taking aim at the fleeing figure, he emptied the clip just as Michael disappeared below the bank of the stream that flowed under the bridge. Simon swore helplessly and then turned to see Wee Paulie twist one way and then another as he vacillated in the road, paralysed by panic and sheer terror. He seemed to be especially confused by the car which barred his way to the relative safety of the hill where Simon lay.

Simon thought he could hear someone shout *Death or glory* as he waved to Wee Paulie and gestured for him to go around the car. "Around the side!" he shouted. "Go around the side!"

"Bastards are trying to outflank us!" Fergal shouted through a wild and crazy grin. He hadn't expected it to be like this, he thought. He hadn't expected the adrenalin surge, the feeling of exhilaration, the undeniable joy of battle.

Through Fergal's veins coursed the blood of an ancient warrior race and in his head he could hear the old rebel songs. Songs of resistance and defiance. Songs of freedom. He pulled from the canvas holdall something that Gerry initially mistook for a large rifle, but the bulbous, diamond shape on the end betrayed it to be a shiny, new, Soviet-made rocket propelled grenade – designed, primarily, for punching through armour plate.

"What the fuck?" Gerry was becoming increasingly concerned about the way the morning was panning out. "What the fuck do you think you're going to do with that?" he yelled.

"Cover me, lads!" cried Fergal with a mad gleam in his eye. They would remember this day, he was certain. Poems would be written, and tales would be told of his actions on this day. A great ballad, no doubt, would be composed. *The Battle of the Old Stone Bridge* would be sung, Fergal was sure, for as long as men remembered heroes. He hoisted the RPG onto his shoulder.

"*Tiocfaidh ár lá!*" shouted Morris as he sent another burst from his AK down onto the road.

"Don't *you* fucking start!" Gerry cried. "I'm going to tell Molly on you!"

Fergal rose above the ridgeline and, making some slight adjustments, sent the armour-piercing warhead straight at the unarmoured and completely defenceless Ford Sierra. The grenade entered the car with ease and then proceeded to spray the interior with molten metal, causing a significant reaction when it reached the petrol tank.

Mrs Blackbird, flapping around the sky in fury at all the commotion, was considering a particularly loud chirp of outrage when the sudden and unexpected appearance of a gearstick from a 1989 Ford Sierra caused to her to veer away and to swoop back down towards the ground.

Wee Paulie's anal sphincter had had enough. It had been having a fairly torrid time of it already today – trying to keep a lid on things, so to speak – but the latest explosion had convinced it to take the unilateral course of jettisoning all extraneous material in preparation for imminent flight.

Wee Paulie, his eyebrows and fringe now smouldering and crispy, was in two minds about this latest turn of events. On the one hand, the noxious swill that had lately been infesting his lower intestines had now gone. But on the other hand, as Daffy Duck could testify, it hadn't gone far. He stood beside the corpse of Big Dennis as the quickly cooling effluent trickled down the backs of his legs and, as the car settled down into a cosy blaze, he reflected upon the fact that, as far as life decisions went, he may have recently made some poor ones.

Michael was feeling exuberant. He pounded across the meadow towards the tree line, now well out of the bullet range of that treacherous bastard, Jippo, and his goons. Surviving the attempt on his life had made him feel more alive than ever, and he made a vow that he would do right by his boy. He would do whatever it took to divest himself of all criminal ties, and he would do all that he could to make Peter feel proud. He felt good. He felt better than good. With his legs pumping away beneath him, he felt free. He felt more free than he had done in years, and it was glorious.

As soon as he reached the woods, he tripped on a tree root and smashed his face into the trunk of a stately old elm.

In Fergal's mind, it was a tactical withdrawal of the highest order. It was a textbook retreat in the face of overwhelming enemy odds. Covering all directions with a variety of weapons, they backed steadily across the field towards the Land Cruiser with a calm and ordered discipline that gave Fergal a feeling of intense pride in his men.

They made it to the car in good time and, with everyone on board, Fergal gunned the engine and set off, exulting in the fact that the imperial might of Britain had been thwarted by the plucky little rebel force of the Irish Republican Broadcasting Corporation.

Fifty Two

"That's all well and good," said Gary, "but what if I need to leave the country sooner rather than later? I think you're being a wee bit selfish there, Joker, with all this *hospital treatment* business. You should try thinking of others for a change."

"Jesus, Gary," Seamus said, exasperated, "you don't know for sure that it's something bad. How did she actually sound on the phone?"

"Hard to say really," Gary answered thoughtfully. "Bit weird, to be honest."

"In what way?"

"I don't know. It was like…it was like she was *happy*."

"Happy? Rosie sounded happy? Really?"

"Yeah."

"Shit," said Seamus, "maybe you *are* fucked!"

"Hey, Joseph," Harry called out, as he peered at the road ahead. "Isn't that your man there?"

"Who?" Joker asked as he pulled himself up to stand between the two front seats. He stared through the windscreen for a moment and then nodded. "Yeah, it is," he said. "Yeah, it's Sticky Micky."

Michael had managed to stumble, dazed and bleeding, into the woods for a little way before realising he would have to double back if he wanted to reach the main road. He knew he would have to be cautious as it was likely that Jippo would still be out to get him.

He had watched, bewildered, as the car had exploded, and he had a vague notion of seeing Big Dennis lying on the ground, so he reckoned that Jippo would be on foot with just Wee Paulie for support. The odds were still in Jippo's favour, he knew, but they were better now than they had been earlier.

He still couldn't figure out what had happened. What should have been a treacherous but perfectly straightforward assassination had gone completely haywire. Jippo had obviously planned it all down to the last detail – Michael could only admire how cleverly he had been manipulated – but then at the very last minute it had all gone chaotically wrong. At least it had for Jippo.

For Michael, it had given him a new lease of life. Despite the fact that he had probably just fractured his skull, he was thinking more clearly now than he had done in years. He now knew what he wanted to do, what he wanted to have. He wanted the tedium of normality. He wanted the security, the banal routine, the family life. He wanted legitimacy, transparency and acceptance. He wanted the parents' evenings, the camping trips, the chilly Saturdays standing on touchlines, and whatever it took to achieve this, he decided, he would do.

But first things first. He had to get back to Belfast. He turned left and walked for a bit through the trees and then turned left again. After a while, he came upon an open field surrounded by overgrown hedgerows. By crouching down and skulking gingerly along the hedges, he eventually emerged onto the main road. It was quiet, but then he had known it would be at this time on a Sunday, so all he had to do was wait for someone to come along.

He knew he wasn't looking his best, but he reckoned that he was in such a state that some kind soul would see him as someone in urgent need of help, so he sat himself down by the roadside and waited.

A while later, he spotted a vehicle cresting a hill in the distance and he groaned with relief. He got to his feet, held out his hand, and tried to look as needy as possible. As the van got closer, he could only gape in horror.

The van pulled up beside Michael and the passenger window was wound down. A familiar face appeared from the back.

"All right there, Micky Boy?" said Joker. "Need a lift?"

Michael shrugged. "Nah, it's okay," he said. "I'll just wait for the next one."

Joker laughed. "Wise up, you stupid fucker, and just get in the back!"

Michael understood he had little choice. The longer he waited around here, the more chance Jippo would have to catch up with him. As he dithered, the back doors of the van were flung open and he made up his mind. He climbed in the back.

"Been in the wars there, mate?" said Tone as he moved to let Michael sit down. "You can sit beside Joker there, and the two of you can compare brain damage."

Michael sheepishly took a seat.

"Nasty cut that," Joker pointed out. "What happened?"

"Um, nothing really. I just bumped into a tree."

"Bumped into a tree? You must have been going at a fair old clip."

"Yeah well, I sort of tripped."

"This here?" Joker pointed to his own head wound. "A cow threw me at a pole."

Michael took this to be gay slang. He deduced that Anderson and his homosexual lover – his "cow" – had got into some sort of altercation with a Polish lad – a love triangle that had gone wrong, perhaps – and Michael decided, as they plunged northwards, that today could hardly get any more surreal.

Fifty Three

"Hello, Joseph. You're looking well." The voice came from behind Joker and was apparently addressing his exposed buttocks. He was lying face down on the treatment room bed and wasn't able to turn his head far enough to see the speaker. It didn't matter though. He recognised the voice.

"Carol?"

"Been through the mill a bit, haven't you, Joseph?" said Carol, before turning to the nurse who was cleaning Joker's wound. "Hi, Jenny," she said. "How's it looking?"

"It looks a lot worse than it is," Jenny replied. "They did a good job over in Spain."

Carol leaned forward to get a better look. "Mm, there's quite a bit of tissue damage, but you're right, there's nothing too serious there."

"Well, it's bloody painful," said Joker, feeling that he ought to contribute something to a conversation that revolved entirely around the condition of his rear end.

"Oh, I'm sure it is," Carol sympathised, "but we'll get you fixed up with some painkillers. What are you taking at the minute?"

"Just paracetamol," said Joker.

"*Just* paracetamol?"

Joker's shoulders seemed to slump in resignation. "Paracetamol and whiskey," he admitted.

"Yes well," Carol said primly, "I'm sure we can do better than that."

"Is this going to take much longer?" asked Joker. He couldn't help thinking that under different circumstances he would be flattered by two attractive women discussing the various merits of his backside which, in his opinion, was one of his best features. But this was too clinical, the scrutiny too intense, and besides, his backside, he had to admit, wasn't looking its best at the moment. He wanted it over with.

"Not long now," Jenny assured him. "Just finishing up."

Carol moved forward a little, and Joker could take a look at her by turning his head to one side. She was absorbed in his notes, frowning slightly with concentration, and Joker made a mental note to have a stern word with his memory for being so hopelessly inadequate.

He furtively devoured every tiny detail of Carol's face, while reflecting on his own stupidity for having lost her. Just what the hell was he thinking, he wondered. Just what exactly…?

"Bullfighting?" Carol asked suddenly as she looked up from the notes.

"What?"

"You were in a bullring? What were you doing in a bullring? Was alcohol involved?"

"Alcohol had nothing to do with it," Joker said defensively. "Why do you have to blame the alcohol?"

"Well, generally speaking, people don't normally run around bullrings getting gored by bulls."

"Well that's where you're wrong," Joker declared, triumphant in his small victory. "It wasn't a bull, it was a cow!"

During the brief silence that followed, Joker felt that maybe he should have kept his mouth shut.

"I'm sorry?" said Carol. "What was that? A cow? Did you just say you were gored by a cow?"

"That's right," said Joker, deciding to brazen it out, "it was a cow. And for your information, the cows in Spain are more dangerous than the bulls. They're faster and more agile, you know."

"What? Um, yeah." Carol looked serious as she nodded her head. "Of course," she said. "I see what you mean." She handed Joker's notes to Jenny who had started to clear away the used swabs and empty wrappings from the bedside cabinet.

"Could you just excuse me for a second?" said Carol as she slipped quickly from the room.

Joker had to admire Jenny's professionalism as she carried out her duties with a quiet and impassive efficiency, apparently oblivious to the howls of laughter coming from the corridor.

Sullen and tight-lipped, Joker lay on the bed and stared at the wall.

Carol came back into the room as Joker was getting dressed behind a curtain. When he was ready, he pulled back the curtain and stood by the bed as the nurse gave him a prescription for his medication along with some details of the outpatients' clinic.

"There you go, Mr Anderson," said Jenny cheerfully. "All done."

"Thank you," he said, then glanced sulkily at Carol. "Right, I suppose I'll see you about then," he said as he headed for the door.

Carol laughed. "Oh, don't be like that," she said. "Come on, I'll buy you a coffee."

"Why?" he demanded. "So you can have a good laugh at me?"

"Well yes, obviously."

"Fine then," he conceded. They set off for the cafeteria with Joker limping slightly at Carol's side. "I thought you'd gone to live in Africa," he told her.

"What? Really? Why did you think that?"

"Just something I heard, that's all."

"No, I just went over for a couple of weeks," said Carol. "I went to see my Nana Ijemma, but I wasn't planning on staying. I think you just got the wrong end of the stick." She looked up at him and laughed. "As usual."

"Yeah, well..." he said gruffly.

"Funny though," Carol went on, "I met this woman when I was over there, when I went to Lagos. I was staying at a hotel she was working in, and she noticed my surname. Well, it turns out she knew mummy and daddy way back, like before I was born. When I got back to Belfast, I asked daddy if he remembered a woman called Zara, and he just got really teary."

Joker looked at Carol. "Really?" he asked.

"Yeah. And then he went straight out and booked a flight to Lagos."

"Jesus!"

"I know! Mad, right?"

Joker limped on thoughtfully. He felt embarrassed and humiliated. His pride and his dignity had been shredded by the woman he...he tried not to think about it. He felt mentally drained. He was battered, bruised and weary, and his arse was killing him.

But his heart was squeezed by the music of Chiaza's giggles.

And Joker's brain was singing.

Epilogue

She thought of a forest. No, she decided, that wasn't enough. She thought of two forests, but still that wasn't enough. She wasn't particularly good at coming up with analogies, she realised, but she was determined to persevere, believing it to be a worthwhile exercise.

She thought of *every* forest. She pictured the vast coniferous forests of Scandinavia, the sweeping rainforests circling the equator, the majestic sequoias of North America and the dark, deciduous woodlands of central Europe and Asia.

She could see every palm grove, every orchard, every copse, every jungle, every dappled glade. She imagined the evergreen timberlands of the Arctic tundra, stretching silently from horizon to horizon, and the tree-lined avenues and manicured parklands of the world's great cities.

Oaks and elms, willows, elders, sycamores and silver birches. The exotic baobabs of Africa and the gingkoes of China. The great green blanket of life that was draped around the Earth.

And all of it, she imagined, for the sole and solitary benefit of one tiny insect, spending its entire existence on the underside of a single leaf that hung from a lowly twig on an unremarkable shrub that pushed through the broken concrete of some desolate and long-abandoned waste ground, and suddenly God – *her* God, the tyrant of her childhood – the God of Scripture, squabbling with His creation in the dust of an ancient desert seemed somehow…*small*.

She exhaled slowly as she stared at the far wall.

And then, pushing her chair back from the desk, Hannah started to rise.

Printed in Great Britain
by Amazon

65676851R00220